YOU EXIST TOO MUCH

YOU EXIST TOO

 *A Novel*

ZAINA ARAFAT

dialogue
books

DIALOGUE BOOKS

First published in the United States in 2020 by Catapult
First published in Great Britain in 2020 by Dialogue Books

1 3 5 7 9 10 8 6 4 2

A CIP catalogue record for this book is available from the British Library.

Hardback ISBN 978-0-349-70178-3
Trade paperback ISBN 978-0-349-70179-0

Printed and bound in Great Britain by Clays Ltd, Elcograf S.p.A.

Papers used by Dialogue Books are from well-managed forests
and other responsible sources.

MIX
Paper from
responsible sources
FSC® C104740

Dialogue Books
An imprint of
Little, Brown Book Group
Carmelite House
50 Victoria Embankment
London EC4Y 0DZ

An Hachette UK Company
www.hachette.co.uk

www.littlebrown.co.uk

For my mother, Randa

Pleasure disappoints, possibility never.

SØREN KIERKEGAARD
Either/Or

YOU EXIST TOO MUCH

In Bethlehem when I was twelve, men in airy white gowns sat at a three-legged table outside the Church of the Nativity. They ran prayer beads through their fingers and sipped mint tea in gold-rimmed cups shaped like hourglasses, steam floating off the surface and up into the bright blue sky. I walked past them with my mother and my uncle as we wandered through the holy city. One of the men called out, "*Haram!*"

Forbidden. For the especially devout among us, it's *haram* to eat meat unless the animal has been killed in a specific way. *Haram* to drink alcohol. *Haram* for a pubescent girl to expose her legs in a biblical city. It occurred to me then that I wasn't a flat-chested kid anymore, that curves had begun to appear along the length of me. I was no longer indistinguishable from a boy child. Somehow, I had stopped noticing my body long enough for it to change.

"What should we do?" I asked my mother. I felt a pulsing lump take shape in my throat as I noticed her teeth gritting, her jaw extended and temples shimmering. My great-grandparents' house was where we were staying and where all of my clothes were, thirty-six miles and three checkpoints away. I felt myself go cold as I closed my eyes and prepared to receive her reaction—I knew better than to try and preempt it with an apology. All I could do was strategically try to calm myself, to remember that the anticipation was heavier than the thing itself.

I should've had more sense than to dress in such a way when we were visiting the birthplace of a prophet, albeit not our own. My mother had, and still has, a native's knowledge. She knows the rules instinctively, in that part of the world, and I only ever learn them by accident.

But then, why did she let me leave the house that way? Was this all part of some plan to teach me a lesson? To my uncle, I was *ajnabi*, a foreigner, which essentially gave me permission to dress however I pleased. But not to my mother. I'd grown used to maneuvering within the lanes of her behaviors, looking to them as guidance, her innate instincts precluding me from finding my own.

"*Baseeta*," said my uncle. It's okay.

My mother looked me up and down. We approached the main door of the church and the men hissed again. My uncle ran the tips of his fingers across his mustache, then looked to my mother and me. "Come," he said. "I have an idea."

We followed him into a gift shop just off Manger Square. He dropped a few coins on the counter, then asked the shopkeeper if we could use his bathroom. My mother grabbed a Kit Kat off the shelf and tore it open, breaking apart two sticks without a second thought. My uncle dropped three more coins on the counter. The man pointed toward the back. My uncle thanked him and led the way.

His master plan was that he would trade me his trousers for my Roxy surfer shorts. He went into the bathroom first, and I could hear sounds of fumbling, his belt buckle jangling as it hit the floor. He opened the door slightly and handed his pants to my mother, so she could administer the swap. She then stood in front of me while I took off my shorts. "*Yalla*," she said, her most frequently used word. Hurry.

I pulled on the pair of pants. They sagged on me. I had to tighten the belt buckle all the way up to the last hole and then roll the waist so that they wouldn't fall off, leaving me even more exposed than I had been before.

I stepped out of the bathroom and looked at my uncle. I examined my new curves against his ridiculous pasty legs, gangly and covered in sporadic patches of hair, my shorts tight against his thighs like boxer briefs. It occurred to me in that moment to question why, as a man, his bare legs were somehow less troubling than mine. It was a double standard, a shame I had simply accepted until then. In acquiring my gender, I had become offensive.

But as I stood in front of him, an unexpected pride began to swell inside me. I liked the way his trousers made me feel. I felt, for once, seen. Like I could get attention from boys, from girls.

"*Inti walad, willa binit?*"—Are you a boy or a girl?

A security guard at the InterContinental hotel in Amman had once asked my cousin Nour this question when deciding whether to lead her into the curtain-shrouded "women's check" for an intimate pat-down before she could enter the lobby.

"*Binit!*" Nour had responded. "Girl!" She'd been insulted by the question, the uncertainty it revealed. But not me. Not that day. Wearing my uncle's baggy trousers, I enjoyed occupying blurred lines. Ambiguity was an unsettling yet exhilarating space.

As we walked back toward the Church of the Nativity I looked at my mother and smiled, desperate for her to smile back. But she withheld. She offered only a freshly disconcerting look, scrunching up her forehead so that lines appeared, her cheekbones protruding, her mouth forming a terrifying expression of indifference. At the time, I couldn't quite place the source of it. Had she noticed my contentment? Did it scare her?

Only now, years later, do I think I understand. It was in that moment that she first realized: I wasn't like her. The trousers were a demarcation line, one that separated me from my mother and her lineage.

I wonder sometimes if that day was the start of something. Whether it's when I began this habit of constant seeking, of endlessly striving to earn my way back, a pattern that would send me on a misguided and self-destructive quest for love. I communicated something to my mother as I stood there smiling in a pair of men's pants, a message I didn't know I was sending her. She has always known first what I have yet to discover, has always seen it before I could.

Look at me, I wanted to say to her then. Please don't look away.

1

I WOKE UP ALONE ONE MORNING WHEN I WAS TWENTY-six. Anna had left for the day. Her side was already made, to the extent that half a bed can be: the comforter pulled up over her pillow, sheets crumpled underneath. She'd opened the curtains before leaving, knowing I liked to be woken by sunlight. Though it was finally bright out, I felt the usual pang of dread. "Your death hour," my best friend, Renata, liked to call it. "Seems normal."

I looked at the cat clock that Anna had brought with her when she moved in, the calico tail twitching: it was nine fifteen. Early, given that I'd spun a double set the night before and taken a lot of tequila shots to stay fueled. Anna had an afternoon class on Tuesdays and Thursdays, meaning she'd still be at the café beneath our building. I then reached to the surface of the night-stand for my grad school acceptance letter. I'd gotten into an MFA program for writing in the Midwest. It was the deadline to send in my decision.

I lay there for a few moments willing myself to get up before finally tossing off the sheets and swinging my legs off the bed in one swift motion. I pressed my feet to the cold hardwood and walked to the kitchen, which was an extension of the same room, only the flooring different, linoleum instead of wood. I touched my hand to the silver coffeepot—still relatively warm. Anna must've just left; I had only just missed her. Lately I'd been trying to make a point of waking up earlier. Renata had suggested it a few weeks ago: "Maybe your girlfriend would like to see you in daylight, from time to time? Wouldn't that help things?"

I dropped a piece of bread into the toaster, then sat down at the kitchen table and opened my laptop. It purred to life, the cursor unfreezing. I typed *g* in the address field and the rest of the url filled in. The screen turned to white as an hourglass twirled. When my inbox appeared, my eyes descended to the chain I wanted, mine and the professor's. I had written to her the day before; we were arranging to see each other one last time before I left New York. Her name wasn't illuminated—no response yet.

I clicked refresh, as though an email would appear in that split second. I refreshed my inbox a few more times before emptying my spam. I was about to close my laptop when a text from my mother flashed across the top of the screen:

On train to NYC. Staying two nights.

Stress washed over me, the familiar lump forming in my throat. I ran my fingers through my hair until a few strands came away into the palm of my hand. I heard the spring of the toaster, but no longer felt hungry. My mother lived in D.C. and regularly came to the city without warning. "You don't own New York," she'd say whenever I requested advance notice or logistical details, which I'd since learned not to do. Any attempt to get a firm date from her, some degree of commitment, made her uncomfortable and irritable, as did any reaction to her arrival that fell short of sheer delight. "And no one's asking you to even see me," she'd say. True, but the onslaught of her presence was impossible to resist, the promise of days spent shopping, the alluring sound of *r*'s rolling off her tongue, the smell of her perfume lingering long after she would leave.

I began to type a series of questions—*Where will you be staying? For how long?*—then deleted them. I took a deep breath and responded, *Can't wait to see you.*

Downstairs, the café beneath our building was full, the window seat taken. I glanced around and spotted Anna hunched over a tiny round table near the back. She wore a red plaid shirt buttoned all the way to the top and a black Patagonia fleece vest unzipped, her knuckles pressed against her cheek and her bangs combed back, making her look a little like Luke Perry or the lead singer of a boy band. Handsome pretty, I would call her, and she liked that, each time beaming with pride. She looked up and saw me, her eyes brightening as I ordered a coffee from the barista. I smiled back, but as I walked toward her carefully, trying not to spill, I felt guilt, which almost instantly morphed into shame. "Hey," I said, taking the chair across from her, my attention caught by a community bulletin board with tabulated flyers, the middle teeth all ripped off. "I see Brokeback's at our spot again."

A woman wearing cowhide chaps and cowboy boots sat with a mug steaming in front of her. The sight of her always made me uncomfortable, and my discomfort usually disappointed Anna. "Yep," she said, forcing a laugh. Then she leaned forward and kissed me. The experience was new enough that I still felt a wave of exhilaration at the ability to kiss a woman in public, as though what we were doing was illicit, two high schoolers smoking pot on the football field. I kissed back and pulled her closer for a second kiss when the first had ended, overcompensating. Anna reached across and pressed her thumb to the side of my mouth. "You've got a little . . ."

"Oops," I said, wiping away a dried bit of drool. "I meant to wash my face." I realized that I hadn't combed my hair, either, and was still wearing the T-shirt I'd slept in. "You look pretty rough yourself," I said, grinning with contentment. "Tired?"

After climbing into bed the night before, I'd woken her up the way I knew she liked, pressing my nose against her neck and breathing deeply until the vibration roused her. I then switched up our usual roles, pulling myself on top of her while at the same time scooting her beneath me. I could tell she'd been wanting me to initiate sex more often; she'd made several underhanded, Mrs. Roper–like comments about how rarely I did so. With our drastically different schedules, sex had gone from being an every-other-night thing to a weekend thing to a never thing.

"I am," she said. "Worth it, though."

She touched my leg with the toe of her shoe. I felt tenderness for her in that moment. I could tell that she was getting tired of our asymmetry. We'd been together on and off for four years, and by now she was beginning to resent the way I treated her, the decreasingly little effort I made, the fewer gestures of affection, the amount of time I spent elsewhere. I resented her for offering no resistance, for refusing to say something directly and choosing instead to let passive aggression seep through. She knew me better than anyone—we'd met in eating-disorder treatment; she had seen me at my most vulnerable. But it sometimes seemed like she still couldn't see through me, still chose to believe in a version of who I was that we both knew no longer existed. And yet, as each other's first relationship post-recovery, we were desperately clinging, terrified to let go.

I reached into my bag and pulled out an envelope, my acceptance letter folded up inside. "Well," I said, tapping its short side on the table. "I signed it." I felt a surge of fresh anxiety.

"Yay," she said, halfheartedly. She sucked the straw in her drink; the last of the liquid rumbled as it gave way to emptiness. "Need me to mail it?" she asked. She had access to stamps on campus.

"Would you mind?" I said, sliding the envelope across the table. "By the way," I said, shifting in my seat. "Guess who's on her way to town?"

Anna hesitated for a moment. Then: "She is? Right now?"

I nodded. We both knew it was impossible to predict her visits. My mother was a consultant of sorts, a "cultural liaison," which meant she was never tied to an office or location. "I bet she works for the CIA," Anna would jokingly suggest.

"Where's she staying?"

"I don't think she knows yet," I said. "But I'll probably stay with her, at least the first night."

This always annoyed Anna. "Isn't that a little weird," she'd asked several times before, "to share a bed with your mom when you're in your twenties?" And I would assure her it was normal in our culture. But by now, she knew better than to address it.

As a consolation I offered, "Want to have dinner with her tomorrow night?"

Anna perked up. She'd been waiting for this invite for quite some time, and I was just as surprised as she was to find myself extending it. My mother had met Anna only once before; I'd introduced her as my "roommate," and tried not to think about what I'd do if things got serious between us, never letting myself visualize our future, a family, anything beyond the present moment. Ever since then, anytime my mother came to town I tried to hide her visit, which wasn't easy to do. And if I failed, then I'd have to explain to Anna why she couldn't join us. "I don't get it," she would say. "I've introduced you to mine." This was true; I'd met her parents and entire extended family on numerous occasions. She'd introduced me as her live-in girlfriend and they seemed completely fine with it, which had always seemed very strange to me

Anna looked at me dubiously now. "Wouldn't she rather meet your boyfriend?"

I rolled my eyes. "Stop," I said. "You know I hate having to lie."

I'd invented Andrew, an imaginary boyfriend, to tell my mother about whenever the topic of relationships came up, which seemed to happen more and more often. I'd transposed Anna's background and statistics onto him, in male form. "Are we ever going to get to meet this famous boyfriend of yours?" my mother would ask.

"Someday," I would say. "He travels a lot for work."

Anna now seemed faintly excited. "Are you—" She hesitated. "Are you planning to tell her about us?"

I thought about this. Was I? And why now?

Why not now?

I told myself it was Anna who'd been pressuring me to tell her, though really it was me who probably wanted to. Guilt, for one thing, in both directions. I was tired of the weight that filled the air when the topic of my family came up. I was tired of deceiving my mother. Maybe telling her would precipitate something, some change, though I wasn't quite sure what I felt was in need of changing.

"Yes," I heard myself say. "I'm planning to."

Anna touched my shoulder. "Then I'll come," she said.

My stomach dropped, air rising and then escaping from inside me. At the table beside us, a couple was discussing their daughter's after-school pick-up plan. Anna checked her watch. "I'm going to be late," she said. As she stood up to leave I found myself noticing her as if for the first time, her lanky figure, her pale freckled skin and short auburn hair. "See you tonight?" she asked. And then, before I could interject: "Oh, sorry, I mean tomorrow?"

We kissed once more and she rushed out. Alone again, I looked around the café and expected to see people staring, but no one was. "We're not in Saudi Arabia," Anna would say whenever I drew back if she tried to take my hand in public. "No one here cares." I pulled the bowl of whatever she'd been eating closer to me—granola—and finished the last few spoonfuls. Then I looked past Brokeback and out the café window. I watched Anna wait dutifully for the walk sign to flash before jutting across the circle, underneath the Pavilion Theater's marquee, and into the mouth of the subway.

2

THE NEXT DAY ANNA AND I MET UP AT OUR APARTMENT before dinner. She was wearing a V-neck sweater and a corduroy skirt, an awkward effort to look feminine in spite of her boyishness. Maybe she thought it would better ingratiate her to my mother. But her efforts were in vain—I knew my mother wouldn't be all right with this situation, especially if she looked even *more* like a woman.

We took the Q train into Manhattan, and as it hurtled across the bridge over the East River, I had a brief image of it derailing. Wouldn't that make things easier? I felt nauseated with worry at the thought of the three of us sitting there, attempting to have a normal dinner, my mother potentially piecing things together. Before that night I'd tried coming out to her once; after things ended with Kate, my college roommate and secret girlfriend, and I was desperate for comfort. "I like both," I'd confessed into the phone. I could practically hear my mother weakening down the line; all the strength she seemed to normally possess had disintegrated. "Is it official?" she'd asked.

I was unsure of what "official" meant, in the context of

sexuality. I imagined it to mean "are you sure" or "is there no way you could just *not* be that way?"

She hung up before I could respond. In the weeks after, she would complain to me about her life, as though I were an objective observer. "I should've had better," she'd say. "I deserved so much more than this."

I supposed my phone confession counted as *official*, but still I couldn't imagine how my mother would handle it, face-to-face.

"What are you thinking about?" Anna asked.

"Nothing," I said.

It was dark by the time we ascended the subway steps onto Canal Street. We passed vendors folding up their makeshift shops selling fake designer bags and sunglasses. We turned the corner onto the narrow street where the restaurant was. We walked in and I looked around for my mother. She wasn't there yet, a temporary relief. I checked my phone and saw a text from her: *Still shopping. Will b there in 15.*

We put our name down at the hostess desk. It was still relatively early; we wouldn't have to wait too long for a table. We sat down at the bar and ordered drinks: me prosecco, Anna a beer. "You seem nervous," she said.

"I am," I said.

"I wouldn't be upset if you wanted me to leave," she said. "I would understand."

I considered taking her up on it, but I knew it would make me feel terrible. I touched her arm gently. "Of course not."

We didn't speak much, and soon the hostess called out Anna's name. "Are you all here?" she asked.

"Almost," I said. "The third person's a few blocks away."

She led us to our table. I sat down, giving Anna the booth side. My eyes glazed over the menu without processing anything. Moments later, I could feel my mother's presence as she entered the restaurant. "Hello!" I heard her call out to no one in particular, in her thick Arabic accent, which hadn't subsided in the twenty-seven years she'd been in the States. As she made her way toward me, I watched her reflection in the mirror above the booth: her almond-shaped eyes flanked by Palestine-reputed cheekbones, her thick brown hair reaching the small of her back and framing her face. We caught eyes in the mirror just as she approached. We greeted each other with a kiss on each cheek. Anna stood up to introduce herself, but my mother preempted her. "Hi, I'm Laila Abu Sa'ab," she said in one breath. I had already told her that Andrew couldn't make it, and that Anna would be joining us instead. "Why can't he?" she'd asked over the phone, suspicious that something was off.

"Another business trip," I'd said, then quickly changed the subject.

"So, ladies!" she draped her coat over the back of the chair beside me before scooting into the booth. "What shall we order?" She assumed we would want to share, which Anna and I usually didn't. Part of eating-disorder recovery meant controlling your portions, which was easier to do with individual meals. "I'm open to anything!" Anna said, trying to be flexible. We chose two salads and two pizzas—arugula and beet, margherita and prosciutto. Until the food arrived, my mother talked about her work. Anna pretended like it was all new to her. Our waitress brought everything all out at once, overwhelming the table. We piled salad onto our plates while the pizza cooled. As we were taking our first bites, my mother mentioned a friend whose daughter was getting married. I felt a burn of jealousy. Anytime I heard of another Arab girl's engagement, it immediately snapped me out of my gayness. "How'd she meet him?" I asked.

"Through the community," she said. Years ago I'd drifted away from *the community*, which consisted of Syrians, Lebanese, and Palestinians living in the D.C. area. When I moved back to D.C. after a year in Italy post-college, I'd taken part in week-ends of pregaming at posh lounges followed by bass-pumping, douchebag-frequented clubs, an activity I would've gladly traded for, say, cleaning toilets. "He's from a very good family."

Anna silently observed this interaction. I could tell she felt left out; my mother had taken no interest in her, hadn't asked her a single question. She was selectively observant—a female room-mate's background was of no consequence. In a misguided at-tempt to ease the tension and make Anna feel included, I decided to broach the topic of our relationship. I started with a hypothet-ical. It was a risky one, but at the restaurant that night, I felt safe with my mother. "How would you feel if I married a woman?" I asked. It was too much—I could've started with "dated"—but for some reason I chose to go extreme.

My mother dragged a slice from the plate in the center of the table and placed it onto her own. "I would be very upset," she said, avoiding eye contact. She took a bite and chewed it slowly, her breaths getting louder and deeper, her eyes blinking faster. Her instincts were onto us. I was becoming increasingly nervous—I knew all the signs. "Why?" she asked. She looked directly at Anna before turning back to me. "Are you planning on it?"

I panicked. "I was just wondering—"

"Because if you are, then stay away," she threatened. "Stay away from me and the rest of my family." In her mind, her lineage didn't trickle down to me.

Her breaths now sounded like crashing waves. She began to twitch. I tried to backtrack. "I'm not saying I'm going to."

"You know what . . ." She stood up, pushing the table forward, knocking over a glass and soaking the kitschy checkered tablecloth with red wine. "Do whatever you want."

Anna immediately grabbed napkins and started mopping up the wine. The people seated beside us looked over, then scooted in the opposite direction before turning back to their conversation. I gave them an apologetic look.

My mother ran out of the restaurant, forgetting her coat. I grabbed it before pulling on my own. "Can you get the bill?" I asked Anna. "I'll pay you back."

She nodded. "Just go."

I burst out the door and spotted her in the distance ahead. I tried to catch up. "*Mama*, please," I cried. "I'm sorry. I won't. I'm not!" By the time I caught up to her, I could see a tear streaming down her cheek. I could think of nothing more shameful—why was I doing this to her? At the time I thought the same thing: she should've had better. She didn't deserve this at all.

I REMEMBER FALLING DOWN THE STAIRS WHEN I WAS two and looking up to see my parents laughing at the top. They claim to have laughed so that I wouldn't cry. But I rarely cried. "You were a happy baby," Teta used to tell me, back when she could still remember my infancy. "You used to wake up singing in your crib. And you had such a healthy appetite." Once, when I was still in diapers, a friend of my mother's came over with a falafel sandwich. At the sight of it I crawled off the changing table and scurried over to the friend. I poised myself at her feet like a puppy and waited for scraps to fall.

I also remember when my mother asked me to tell my father she was in labor. I was three years old. He was in the living room of our house in the D.C. suburbs, watching the news; the Iran-Contra scandal was covered on every channel that year. Back then my father wore a black suit to work each day, with a white button-down shirt and a shockingly bright tie. "You need to find a way to distinguish yourself, to stand out," he'd say to my mother whenever she suggested a more demure color. He would spray a heavy cologne every morning that mixed with the scent of my mother's perfume, delicious and thick. I would monkey around as they got dressed, collecting pennies off the bureau and trying on my mother's heels, stabbing the carpeted floor with the spikes. My father wore only tighty-whiteys as he shaved, craning his neck with pursed lips as he dragged the razor through shaving cream like a plow through fresh powdery snow. I would pump Gillette into the open palm of my outstretched hand and watch it poof before patting it onto my cheeks. Having heard from my mother that shaving could cause hair to grow where it hadn't before, I resisted the temptation to drag the razor across my smooth face. Instead, I would derive satisfaction from dipping an index finger into the shaving cream cloud and holding it to the end of my nose, dotting the tip before smearing it onto my chin and upper lip. I'd watch myself in the mirror, unsmiling.

At my mother's request I ran down the stairs to tell my father it was time to go to the hospital, gripping the wooden banister and slowing down when I arrived at the knob that marked its end. "*Baba!*" I screamed.

"What! What!" The coffee table squeaked as he jumped up from the couch. Within seconds he was in the hallway.

"The baby's coming!" I felt both important and scared.

Hours later I was staring at newborn Karim through the glass partition, thinking him superfluous and knowing things would now be different, my mother no longer mine entirely.

3

A WEEK HAD PASSED SINCE THE RESTAURANT INCIDENT. Anna and I had been trying to act as though nothing had happened, but the memory of that night was still thick between us. That evening we were both at home, reading on opposite ends of the couch—me a novel, and she leather-bound law books—when my phone buzzed. My heart leaped when I saw who the message was from: the professor.

"I'm tired," I said to Anna, lying. "I'm going to bed early tonight." I looked up from my book and we made eye contact. She held my gaze for a few moments, as if she knew something was amiss and wanted me to crack. "Cool," she finally said. "I'll join you once I'm done."

I got up, cradling my laptop in my arms, then kissed her good night, shut the door to our bedroom and immediately opened the professor's email. It was just one line: "Where do you live?"

We'd met the previous summer, almost a year earlier. She taught French literature at the Alliance Française in Midtown East, in between semesters at Columbia. The class was on Thursday evenings, before my shift began. I was taking it to practice my French, a language I'd been learning since fifth grade and that seemed worth keeping up for the intellectual stimulation DJing failed to provide. On the first day, she'd announced that past students had told her she didn't smile enough. "So . . ." She placed her palms on the edge of the desk and leaned forward smiling, as if to say, "Here you go."

I'd loved her since the day she kept me after class and suggested I was too harsh on Emma Bovary for her childish fantasies and for cheating on Charles. "Emma's pathetic, sure," she said, pressing a polished fingernail to the word *méprisable* on my paper. From the dinosaur Band-Aid on that same finger I surmised a husband and kids. "But this is melodramatic." She looked at me, paused, then offered an effortful smile.

For the first time I noticed the dimple that appeared above her lip when she smiled, like a second, smaller smile. While we stood there, I began to fall into its span. As I gathered up my things and walked toward the classroom door, she asked, "Is it so bad?"

I stopped and turned toward her. "Is what so bad?"

"To have an affair?"

Her question seared—it felt both suggestive and forgiving. At the time, a photo of Eliot Spitzer and his scorned wife, Silda, adorned the front page of the *New York Post*. I felt myself blush. "I don't know," I said. "But it is in this country."

She laughed. Her laugh was deep and started in the back of her throat, getting increasingly lighter as it worked its way forward. "True."

My body surged with heat. When I got home after my set that night, I googled her. I discovered that she wrote fiction. A short story with her byline came up, a simple piece about a woman struggling to keep her marriage intact as the other couples in their circle divorced. I wondered if it was based on truth, and I searched for details that matched her reality as I knew it. During class the following week, I made a point to mention it.

"I read your story," I said, nervous to admit it and tingling with excitement, as though I'd accessed some part of her that was now laid bare between us.

"Oh," she said. She nodded once, then offered the smile. "Thank you."

She appeared not to care whether I liked it, confident that it was good without my approval. Still, I felt encouraged to say, "It would be nice to meet up sometime. Maybe after the class is over."

She nodded in return. "It would."

We met in early September, at the Nespresso store in Midtown East, three blocks from our classroom. I showed up in a pencil skirt and a silk sleeveless shirt. We sat down and ordered cappuccinos, and I resisted asking for skim milk so I wouldn't seem too weight-conscious or too American. The conversation flowed. She talked about walking her daughter to school, her husband's startup, their vacation home in Saint-Paul-de-Vence, on the Cote d'Azur. I tried to match her level of privilege and exposure. "I've been to Nice once," I said. "For a week." I didn't mention that I'd gone with Kate, toward the end of our relationship. Nor did I mention Anna, worried that, as a straight French woman, the entire concept of queerness would make her uncomfortable. I felt slightly tipsy as we left, though we hadn't had anything to drink. When the bill came I hesitantly asked if she would send me some of her unpublished writing to read.

She placed her credit card on the table as I reached for my

wallet, waving my hand away. "You want to read more from me?" she asked, sounding almost suspicious.

I panicked—until then I'd felt emboldened, but her response made me embarrassed. "I thought I'd ask," I said. "If that's okay."

"Sure," she said. She smiled again; it was starting to feel more natural anytime she did so. "I'm just surprised, is all."

We stepped outside the café, and I felt overwhelmed as we walked off in different directions. I wanted her, I wanted her life, I wanted to live inside her life while still living inside my own. I wanted, above all, for her to like me.

Two days later, when she still hadn't sent any of her work, I followed up. Three essays arrived in my inbox that night. She seemed to be a guarded person, so reading her unpublished writing was like cutting to the front of a long line. She wrote about her French Colonialist guilt, which as a Palestinian I felt uniquely qualified to absolve. She wrote about reading La Fontaine fables to her daughter. She wrote about middle-of-the-night despair, about wanting more. I couldn't believe how much her inner world resembled mine.

The problem, as always, was asymmetry. Not only was she straight, but she had a husband to share her inner world with. I presumably had Anna's world, yet somehow hers was never nearly as captivating.

I read each of the essays several times. "They're nice," I wrote in response, still afraid to shatter a veneer of detachment.

A month later we went to lunch, but I couldn't eat. I wore a dress that once belonged to my mother, her gold hoop earrings, her Michele watch. Anything beautiful that's mine was once hers. Now that I'd read the professor's writing, now that her sapphire wedding ring was refracting light from every surface, I was too conscious of my motions to land the fork in my mouth, so I stopped trying. "Sorry," I said, laughing dumbly. "I can't eat and talk at the same time."

She had chosen a place on the Upper West Side known for its burgers, but I ordered a salad. I imagined she was judging me in that moment. I'm familiar with that judgment, after years of anorexia. I was past it by then, but still, how could I eat something so unsexy as a cheeseburger in front of the sexiest woman in the universe? She continued to look attractive and in control as she ate her burger, chewing with unapologetic authority. I had the ridiculous salad packed up though I knew I'd never eat it. When the check came I offered to pay. I'd looked up the place beforehand—cash only—and I fumbled self-consciously through bills fresh from the ATM. My eyes began to blur, I put down too much for the tip. We got up and left, and the minute she turned the corner from the restaurant tears spilled down my cheeks. I was certain that I'd given myself away, though I admit: by then, a part of me wanted her to suspect.

I assumed that would be our last encounter. But in the spring, I heard from her again. We exchanged a few emails, mostly about writing, and eventually developed a frequent correspondence, delving into what I perceived to be intimate and pointed subject matter, including love. Though usually we discussed it theoretically, rather than applying it to either of our specific relationships—I continued to keep Anna out of our conversations. When she needed a reader for an essay she was planning to send out, about Laclos's *Les Liaisons Dangereuses*, she came to me. I immediately bought a copy, bypassing a second viewing of

Cruel Intentions. The central theme of the piece danced around the question of marital infidelity and its moral implications versus its permissibility. "Maybe you should come out and say what you think," I suggested in my feedback. "As of now, it's hard to tell where you stand on the issue. I'm sure readers are curious to know!"

Where do you live? As I sat in our bedroom, Anna on the other side of the closed door, I repeatedly read the professor's question, which I interpreted as an imperative. I imagined her sitting in front of her computer, staring at me from behind her Prada glasses. It was a direct challenge—was I ready to pluck her from possibility and encounter her reality? Sometimes I closed my eyes and pictured her while kissing Anna. It was always somewhat awkward and not as exciting as when I pictured it in the abstract, devoid of hideous circumstance. What if our sex was clumsy? I was in between post-anorexia plump and all-night double sets, with no snack breaks—what if she didn't like my body? My mother had recently impersonated me, puffing up her cheeks and holding out her arms beyond her stomach like an ape. Maybe I could love her from a distance and keep myself intact. Maybe I needed to protect myself against debilitating and devastating heartbreak. Maybe I thought that was possible.

Three weeks earlier, the professor had written to tell me she was four and a half months pregnant with her second child. After reading her note, I put my head on my desk and cried. I continued to cry for two weeks: on the subway into the city, at the taco truck outside the club, inside the DJ booth. I was used to feeling envy when it came to pregnancy. It's something I've looked forward to since I was seven, after a day spent with a pregnant friend of my mother's who I thought was the most beautiful woman in the world. I cried tears of jealousy the whole car ride home, and my mother promised me I'd have a turn one day. "You're just too young right now," she'd said as I buried my face in stuffed animals. But I wasn't prepared for the unbearable pain I would feel when it was a woman I fancied myself in love with. Nothing highlighted the one-sidedness of our relationship more than having no idea she was midway through her second trimester, thinking instead that she was falling for me. How stupid was I to believe she could've cared about me in some way, in any way at all, that I was anything more than just a fleeting thought, an email in her inbox, an occasional lunch date. Every time I pictured her with her husband, whom I'd only seen in a thumbnail-size photo I'd found online, my stomach turned metallic and I felt I was choking. Maybe it was the subtext, the one my shattered ego invented, that taunted, *I have what you don't have. You pathetic thing, don't you see I'm so much more than you?*

I'd heard those words before. But I knew the professor would never think such mean-spirited thoughts, even if I chose to hear them. It was shameful to expect her to care about me enough to condescend.

I called Renata, my go-to support for this sort of thing, forgetting that she was in an especially self-righteous, not-taking-any-shit mood, as her own relationship was faltering. She and Thomas, her boyfriend of five years, were on break, his choice, which meant all of her frustration with him got transposed onto me. We were planning a trip to Joshua Tree at the end of May to celebrate her graduation from med school, a trip that was also partly intended to get her mind off Thomas while he "mulled things over" and decided if he wanted to commit. Though everyone else advised her to move on—it was their second break, the first time came after he'd slept with someone else—I'd told her he was worth waiting for. Maybe I was overcompensating for how our friendship had begun: with an unwanted advance and subsequent rejection. But in truth, I'd been hearing about Thomas since college, his Sigma Chi days. I knew that she had stuck with him through much worse.

Fed up with the professor and her precursors, Renata sighed into the phone when I gave her the update. "Unbelievable," she said. "How dare she get pregnant by her husband without asking you!"

I hung up immediately—it wasn't the time for sarcasm. I was experiencing the same pain I'd felt at the end of three years with Kate. As I lay in bed feeling shattered, my phone buzzed with a call from Anna. "Oh good," she said, "you're awake."

It was two in the afternoon. Her passive aggression seethed. She was growing tired of my "profession." Being a DJ entailed sleeping until some disconcerting hour of the day, drinking my first coffee while everyone else was enjoying happy hour cocktails, and then leaving for work as Anna returned home for the evening. It also entailed an unexpected loneliness, one that tugged at me like a dog that needed to be fed. On the early-morning F train from the Lower East Side back to South Slope, I'd scroll through pictures of friends clustered together in both familiar and exotic locations, announcements of new relationships and engagements. I craved a normal social life, a normal *life*, or at least a job that didn't completely preclude me from having one.

But the sting of alienation was outweighed by the ecstasy of performance, its unrelenting command of attention. What I enjoyed most about spinning records was the feeling of being in control, of being responsible for everyone's good time. Me, and alcohol. I loved keeping the crowd on the verge: fading the bass in and out, speeding up the rhythm and then slowing down just before the crescendo, saving the explosive tracks until the very end. Sometimes, I would catch eyes with someone—woman, man, I was open to either—and we would chat after the set, before heading to the back room for a hurried and furtive encounter that was at once empowering and exhilarating. In the time that each lasted, which varied in proportion to the amount of liquor consumed, my mind would have respite from both Anna and from the professor, or whomever it was that particular season. I'd emerge afterward and return to the booth feeling pleased with myself, prideful if not actually confident, and at the very least soothed, the obsessive thoughts momentarily suppressed, with a sneaking suspicion that there was more to me than this.

I tried to keep these sessions minimally invasive, so that I could emerge from them unruffled and return home undetected. But there were occasional slips. "You smell like sex," Anna said one night when I crept into bed at four a.m., too tired to shower. My stomach flipped. I laughed off her comment and blamed it on an especially packed and sweaty night at the club. She appeared convinced at the time, or at least temporarily placated.

"Want to meet for lunch?" Anna asked.

We met at a diner near our apartment, a well-lit place that was always empty yet managed to stay in business. We sat across from each other in sea-foam vinyl seats. "You seem off," she said. Melted cheese dripped from her panini. "Is something going on?"

I looked up at the ceiling lamp suspended above us. I wanted to tell her the truth, so she would know what I was feeling, in the hope that she would comfort me, or berate me, or leave me. That way I could at least transfer my pain onto something that made sense, something real. After all, the professor did seem fabricated. Perhaps, to the extent that I'd cobbled together the pieces I had, she was. Though like the "Orient," I chose to believe she was an idea with some corresponding reality; she was more than simulacra.

I rushed to think of a response that wouldn't betray my heartache. "I looked up flights," I said. "Visiting next year is going to get pricey."

We hadn't yet discussed how our relationship would survive my move to the Midwest. When my acceptance letter arrived, Anna had panicked and offered to transfer out of Columbia Law to come along. I couldn't let her uproot her entire life, I'd told her, and give up such a great opportunity. But more than that, I knew: grad school offered a natural and guided transition out, less traumatic than a breakup, smoothly delivering me into a new life.

"Yes, I'm aware that flying costs money," she said. My once-endearing naiveté had become annoying. "I'm surprised you've only now realized this."

"I'm just worried," I said. "I'm thinking of not going. I'm not sure we can afford a long-distance relationship."

"Is this a nutritionist situation?" she asked.

"What? I haven't thought about her since—"

"Not her specifically," Anna clarified. "I mean, are you obsessed with someone new?"

"Are you being serious?"

"Really, I'm asking. You sound completely irrational right now, so it would make sense."

"No," I said. "I'm not."

"Because if you are, I hope you've learned by now that those people aren't real? And that they'll never love you back?"

I closed my eyes and waited for the surge of anger to subside. She had no idea what the professor and I shared, how intense our connection was, that she could never compete. I took a deep breath before responding. "I obviously know that," I said. "I'm not delusional. I wouldn't jeopardize what we have for someone I hardly know."

And yet there I was, less than a month later, ready to do just that for a married woman approaching her third trimester.

"Well, then I'm sure we would find a way to work around the distance," she said, sounding at once sad and hopeful. "I could borrow mileage from my parents or something. Maybe I'll find a job out there." She smiled, touching her fingers to mine. "We could live in a little farmhouse."

Where do you live? I was typing out directions when it dawned on me. The professor was just being practical. Considerate, at best. Where do you live? as in, "How can we choose a coffee shop that's convenient for both of us?" I nearly laughed out loud; she had no idea the distance I would've traveled for her. That I would risk an actual relationship for just the idea of her.

"Next to the Pavilion Theater," I responded, adding, "the corner of Thirteenth and Eighth," just in case. Even though I was ambivalent—my conscience was finally kicking in this time—I was still hopeful.

•

A week later, I went by the club to pick up my final paycheck. The owner was sitting at the bar with a notebook and calculator, drinking coffee and filling out the ledger with numbers from the night before. "So you're on to better things," he said. "Probably for the best. Stay in this job too long and it'll kill you."

"It already has," I called out as the door swung shut behind me, the check clenched between my fingers.

The next morning, a day after her med school graduation, Renata and I flew to California for our Joshua Tree trip. We would stay with her parents for a night in Santa Monica before trekking into the desert. The timing of the trip couldn't have been worse; the tension with Anna had felt like clouds waiting to burst open. On the few evenings when we were both at home we barely spoke. Instead we watched television or read in separate rooms. When I'd ask what she felt like having for dinner she'd tell me she'd already ordered takeout for herself. "Did it occur to you that I might want something, too?" I once asked.

"Not really." She shrugged. "You rarely seem to want what I want."

Leaving when things were that bad felt irresponsible and unsettling. But at the same time, I was happy to escape, if only for a week. Anna was still asleep when I left for the airport, and I decided not to wake her. I wanted to avoid any guilting remarks about me flitting off for a week when I was moving away for good in just a few months, and why did it always seem like I was pushing her away?

I felt increasingly uncomfortable as the plane hurtled down the runway, the unresolved tension coating my stomach. The moment we landed at LAX, I switched my phone back on and called her. She didn't answer, so I left a voice mail, then hung up and sent her a text: *You okay?* An hour went by and still no response. Later that evening, I realized that I still hadn't heard from her. I texted again. I called a second time. I kept calling, again and again. Nothing.

"Weird," I said to Renata. "Anna's not answering."

"Maybe she's busy," Renata responded. "She does exist outside of your relationship, you know."

I forgave Renata her misplaced annoyance. She had put up with me panicking about nearly everything for years. "Your worries are like water," she often said. "The moment one flows out, another floods in to fill the space."

By the next day, an amorphous ball of anxiety had formed in my stomach, made up of concern for Anna's well-being and fear that something else was wrong. For the sake of the trip I tried not to let my worry show. Plus, I didn't want to exhaust Renata's patience this early on. I had other anxieties that would need to be addressed, mostly pertaining to the professor. I was still critiquing her academic analysis of *Les Liaisons Dangereuses*. Renata kept pronouncing the title in an exaggerated French accent anytime it came up, followed by a dramatic flip of her hair. "Do you think she's trying to tell you something? Maybe she wants you to be her Marquise de Merteuil?"

We were packing snacks for the desert when my phone finally pinged. I jumped to check it: an email from Anna.

As I read, relief quickly gave way to fear. "It's a good thing I don't trust you," she had written. "Because if I did, I wouldn't have had a reason to search for confirmation."

My stomach dropped. Her letter continued, "What I saw was worse than I expected. I feel like I've been living in a fantasy for years."

My laptop. I'd left it at home. And my password was saved. In my emails, Anna had found the proof she'd been looking for: throughout the four years we'd been together, I had actively longed for others. I'd formed relationships that resembled courtship more than friendship, some that lingered in the realm of inappropriate emotional connection, others that led to sex with strangers as a means of distraction. "Now you'll no longer have to deal with any reality that comes with us, and you can live happily ever after with your obsessions. Though I'm amazed to see how unrealistic they've become. A married pregnant straight woman—you've really outdone yourself with this one!"

My first concern was that Anna had written the professor from my account and said something crazy or revealing, as a means of revenge. I had enough sense to know that she wouldn't do such a thing, and that I was incredibly selfish for worrying about myself right then. I tried desperately to recall each illicit correspondence that existed among my emails. I was almost certain there was no trace of the club encounters—they had all cropped up spontaneously, and I'd kept in touch with none of them. Still, what Anna had found was bad enough.

"I'm devastated that you could be so careless with my heart," she wrote, and I shuddered. It was exactly how I felt my own heart had been treated throughout my life—carelessly, *callously*. "I want you to really sift through your issues and face them, and feel a fraction of the torture I feel as a result of this."

The last line was the hardest to read, the one that made my throat burn: "Maybe one day you'll learn you can't treat people with such disregard. Even yourself."

Finally, Anna had mustered the resistance I'd been craving.

It was at once frightening and attractive: never had I wanted her more. I felt my body go cold, and for a moment I thought I was going to be sick. "What's the matter?" Renata asked.

I handed her the phone and watched her deflate while reading the email. "Well, there you go," she said. "Again."

For a moment I was pissed. She was *my* friend, after all, not Anna's. Then I remembered what she'd been through with Thomas. How he'd lied to her, how she'd found out in the most humiliating way, walking in on him with his high school girlfriend. I knew I had managed to let her down, too.

She handed back my phone. I stared at Anna's email. I had never felt so exposed—I wanted to take back every vulnerability I'd ever shown her, every moment that I had asked for comfort. "What do I do?" I asked Renata. The question was genuine; I truly had no idea.

"I mean, what *can* you do? We're here, she's there. And she's seen everything."

I got up from the table and called Anna. It rang and rang, and still no answer. Fear soaked up every other emotion. I told Renata I needed to change my return flight and leave the next day. I had to get home and deal with this.

"I will seriously kill you if you do that."

"But what if there's still a chance to fix things?"

"You do need to fix things," she said. "But it's not the relationship that's broken."

I looked down at my phone and reread the email. I began typing a response. "Please," I wrote. I didn't know what else to say, any attempt to defend myself felt shameful and useless. "I have no idea what I've been doing." I really didn't: it was as though

35

I'd been sleepwalking, going through the motions without any control.

For the rest of the trip I checked my email compulsively. "I wanna throw your phone in a dune," Renata said. In the times when we were out of range, we talked. Renata suggested that I'd set myself up to get caught. "Isn't that essentially what you've been asking for, by being so reckless?"

She had a point. Why, after all, would I leave my laptop out in the open, as though inviting Anna in? Hadn't I wanted for things to end? I must've known what I was doing was wrong, that I was hurting her, and yet I couldn't stop myself. I needed something to stop me, Renata said as we hiked, if only for a chance to redeem myself.

But I knew that my reasons for sabotage went beyond that.

•

All of Anna's stuff was gone from our apartment by the time I got back to New York. The cabinets were half empty, her closet shelves bare, the stark ceramic of the bathroom sink visible for the first time in months. I was simultaneously shocked and impressed that she'd had the strength and resolve to actually move out. I stood in the doorframe feeling alone and afraid, and dreading the days until the lease ended in August, too far away—it was only the beginning of June.

My laptop sat inconspicuously on the kitchen table. I lifted the screen and it brightened. Anna had left it on; the browser was still open to my inbox. Now that I was alone, without Renata's input, I reread Anna's email. It felt even worse reading it in our

Old Windsor Library

Customer ID: ******5315

Items that you have borrowed

Title: The monsters we deserve
ID: 9580000118386
Due: 12 August 2023

Title: You exist too much : a novel
ID: 9580000164910
Due: 12 August 2023

Total items borrowed today: 2
Account balance: £0.80
Items currently on loan: 2
Overdue: 0
Reservation requests: 0
Ready for collection: 0
22/07/2023 11:08

To renew items go online at www.rbwm.gov.uk/libraries
Automated renewal line 0303 123 0035 or phone us on 01628 796969

apartment, imagining her sitting at the same kitchen table, the humiliation she must've felt. The walls were practically radiating with her hurt. I searched for the professor's last note. I began to describe what happened, hoping that communicating my pain would somehow alleviate it. I then remembered that I'd never mentioned Anna to her, and I didn't have the energy to do so now, to recount the entire story, especially since much of it actually involved *her*, though of course she had no idea. I stopped midsentence, an emptiness swelling inside me. For the first time in a while, the thought of the professor didn't send me reeling into fantasies. Without the security of a relationship, longing felt less safe. It felt lonely.

As I sat alone in my apartment, I thought back to that night at the restaurant in SoHo, the last time I'd seen or spoken to my mother, by then nearly a month earlier. I'd trailed behind her all the way to the entrance to the Brooklyn Bridge. Once I caught up to her, she stuck out her hand to hail a taxi. One pulled over immediately. She opened the door, and before stepping in she turned to me, her top lip resting on her lower lip in that furious non-smile. "I don't care what you choose to do anymore," she said, and I crumbled. I *needed* her to care. Worse than anger was indifference: her approval was my compass, even when that meant resisting it. She then shot me a piercing look before shutting the cab door. "Good luck finding someone to love you like I did."

I WAS FOUR WHEN THE FIRST INTIFADA BEGAN. AS A FAMily, we would gather around the box-shaped TV in our woodpaneled basement in the D.C. suburbs and watch the seven o'clock news. I would spread out on the floor, taking in scenes of distant carnage while laying my Barbies atop one another in unintentional 69 positions. Karim would spring up and down in his bouncy chair. My father would pour some of the newly introduced Cool Ranch Doritos into one ceramic bowl and medium-spicy Old El Paso salsa into another. He'd then empty an already-cold Heineken bottle into a frosted pilsner glass from the freezer. Often I'd go searching for chocolate chip ice cream and instead find *mulukhiya*, a vegetable you could only ever find in Middle Eastern supermarkets, along with the frosted glasses on the freezer shelves. My mother was the only one who kept her eyes glued to the television, the distance from her homeland enhancing her longing and attachment as she felt it slip away.

On the television screen, scenes appeared from Nablus of coffins shrouded in Palestinian flags. Young men in stonewashed jeans and bandanas peeking out from behind graffitied walls and stacks of flaming tires, throwing a seemingly endless supply of stones. Israeli soldiers in tan uniforms and laced-up combat boots pacing around checkpoints with machine guns, chewing gum and looking both vigilant and bored. These were my first images of the conflict that shattered our homeland and scattered my family. Terms like *civilian casualties* and *Molotov cocktails* and *cease-fire*, later replaced by *negotiations* and *peace talks* and *Camp David*, resounded in the Peter Jennings voiceovers as the footage of violence played on screen. We watched at a cool remove while enjoying the comforts of our American suburb, seemingly untouched, oblivious of the underlying trauma.

4

"YOUR LAST STOP BEFORE HEALING." THE WORDS WERE displayed in bubbly cursive across the Ledge's homepage. I'd stumbled upon the website after a semi-targeted search with the words *destructive, relationships, help.*

I was mildly put off by the fatalistic tagline, but I was also desperate. The past week alone in the apartment had felt like a year. The days I'd tried to spend writing dragged on with no productivity. I was constantly aware of Anna's absence, each time I sat down on the couch and she wasn't on the other end, or ate takeout for one at the kitchen table, or when I crawled into bed at night, now at a reasonable hour, since I no longer DJed. I could never fall asleep, so instead I'd watch reruns of shows I'd already seen dozens of times. Anything that entailed minimal thinking. I couldn't resist reading through the emails she had found, cowering in embarrassment, imagining her reading them. Soon I began taking pills to numb the pain—I'd gotten the number for a notoriously irresponsible psychiatrist whose contact info had made the rounds among my coworkers at the club. He put me on a cycle of amphetamines during the day and Xanax at night, to come down and get a bit of sleep. The uppers had the added benefit of stripping away the need to nourish myself, my appetite for food entirely diminished. Soon I was stick-thin, almost back to my pre-recovery weight, which provided a comfort akin to an old friend and a semblance of control. Each day I woke to an excruciating crash, the pain-numbing meds no longer in my system, and thus the cycle began again. I wanted nothing more than to escape my life.

In an attempt to do so, I went out every night, sometimes with friends, often alone, situating myself on a bar stool, pushing my chest forth as I scanned the room in the hope that I might meet someone, anyone—for love or for sex, either would do. I revived every flirtatious email chain, but no one wrote back—not one bite. I needed a distraction. I regretted quitting my DJ gig so early in the summer, and I tried to undo the mistake. But when I went to the club to ask for my job back, or at least a few shifts, the owner told me that he'd already hired someone else. Apparently I was easy to replace. By the time I got home I felt suffocated by depression. Desperate, I turned to the internet.

I clicked through the various pages on the Ledge's website. The place was in Bowling Green, Kentucky, a two-hour drive from Louisville. That was one of the few concrete things I came away with; the site was rather cryptic—what exactly was this place? Healing, how? I clicked to the "Contact Us" tab, where an email address and a phone number were listed. I began to draft an email, then decided it was easier to just call. It rang four times before someone picked up. "This is Nancy," said a strikingly upbeat voice on the other end.

"Oh," I said, startled. "Hi!" I hadn't expected an actual human to answer, more like a somber recording. "I think I called the wrong number."

"Are you looking for the Ledge?"

"Yes."

"Well, then you've got the right number! What brings you to us?" She sounded breezy, too casual, as though she were taking my order at a drive-through.

"I don't know exactly," I said. I looked at the wall in front of me, where Anna's cat clock eyed me accusingly. "I guess I just know I need help."

Nancy proceeded to ask me a series of questions about my childhood—"happy until it wasn't"—my family—"if you can still call it that"—my relationships. I told her about the professor, about Anna, our breakup. "I'm not sure what's wrong with me," I said.

"Let me ask you," said Nancy, "have you ever heard of something called love addiction?"

"No," I said. "Is that a real thing?"

"Do me a favor," she said. "Look it up. And feel free to call us back afterward."

At the Strand bookstore that evening, I slinked into the personal growth section. Google had informed me that a woman named Pia Mellody, who ran a treatment center in Arizona that was far more expensive than the Ledge, was the foremost expert on love addiction. She sounded like a character out of a self-help fairy tale; I pictured her with a tiara and a wand. I picked *Facing Love Addiction* off the shelf and opened it to the beginning: "Love addicts have an uncontrollable appetite for the object of their affection."

Her Barthesian language was slightly off-putting, but I felt soothed by the sentiment. "When love addicts reach a certain level of closeness with their actual partner, they often panic and do something to create distance. Frightened by healthy intimacy, they devote an obsessive amount of time, attention, and value to someone who cannot or will not love them back." I ran through the list in my head: The nutritionist. The editorial assistant. The ambassador's wife. The sacrifice. The professor. And in a way, Kate. I kept reading: "Unable to be present in their own relation-ships, they find an escape hatch to numb the pain."

I felt myself light up—this was a real, diagnosable condition! One that seemed to perfectly circumscribe my behavior. It was a designation that abstracted my obsessions from all context and almost sanctified them, while obscuring their actual source.

I bought the book and tucked it deep in my bag.

I called the Ledge again at nine a.m. the next day. Nancy picked up. "Morning!" she said, chipper as an Egg McMuffin.

"I read about love addiction," I said. "Do you treat it?"

"Oh, honey," she said. "We treat all kinds. Alcoholics, drug addicts, sex and love addicts—you name it, we got it covered."

I asked about the daily schedule. "Well, you're in group all day, then dinner, then meetings. On Tuesdays and Thursdays you'll do an hour of yoga, and equine therapy on Wednesdays."

"Will I be able to drink coffee there?"

"You'll be able to drink decaf anytime. Caffeinated is only served from seven thirty to seven fifty a.m."

"Does that mean that if I'm not done at seven fifty, they'll take it away?"

Nancy paused. I imagined she'd hadn't encountered many people who anticipated every hypothetical. For a moment I felt slight shame. "I doubt it," she said.

I then asked about food.

"I think you'll be quite pleased on that front," she said. "We're proud to offer a range of gourmet options. Our chef's from the big city, Louisville."

Her reference to Louisville as the "big city" inspired skepticism. "Can we eat whenever we want?" I asked.

"Breakfast is at eight, lunch is at noon, and dinner is at five."

"What if I'm not hungry at those times?"

"You still have to eat."

"Will they force me to finish my plate?"

"No, it's cafeteria style, you can eat as much or as little as you want."

"What if I get hungry late at night?"

"They usually keep yogurt and fresh fruit in the fridge at the women's house." Not true, I later discovered, when I snuck into the kitchen for a nighttime snack and found just a rotten apple and some Smucker's jelly packets pilfered from the cafeteria.

Still disgruntled about the early-bird suppers, I asked, "Dinner's really at five? What if where I'm from we never eat before nine?"

"Doesn't matter, sweetheart," Nancy said. "Here, we're all Americans."

•

The first thing I noticed when I walked into the main office at the Ledge was that Nancy was wearing short shorts. She stood by the photocopy machine and smiled a tight smile, and her shorts were at least eight inches above her leathery knee. The rules I'd received before arriving, along with a credit card authorization form, explicitly stated that tank tops and short shorts were forbidden at the Ledge. So I went to the Gap and bought knee-length shorts. I then scoured my closet for T-shirts and came up with three. They hung on me like curtains. I showed up looking like either a cabana boy or a seventh grader. And there, standing in front of me, was Nancy, tanned and glowing with an aura of recently laid contentment, wearing freshly cut Daisy Dukes. She extended a manicured hand and said, "Nice to meet you in person!"

Nancy offered to show me around the main lodge. As she led me down a long corridor I was both surprised and annoyed by how unclinical the place felt. The carpeted floor was covered in redundant shaggy rugs. There were houseplants and skylights overhead that brought in lots of sunlight. There were paintings of dull-colored landscapes alongside motivational posters with random nouns like *Persistence* and *Teamwork* scrawled beneath droplets of water. I could've easily been at a friend's summer cottage or a bed-and-breakfast. The warm home-style feel seemed suspicious—white walls and the smell of ammonia inspire trust. I followed Nancy to her personal office, which appeared to double as a bookstore, the shelves lined with books by authors whose names I recognized from the website, price tags dangling off of their spines. She directed me to a wooden desk at the front of the room, pulled out a file, and proceeded to read off the medications that I'd listed in my pre-screening questionnaire. "I'll need the Adderall and Xanax from you now," she said, the smile never disappearing from her face. I rummaged through my bag and handed her two green-tinted rows, both with seven separate compartments marked by letters, four pills in every slot, enough of each med to last a month. "You'll need to give me your cell phone, too," she said, and then looked down at my pocket, where white wires poked out. "And your mp3 player."

I asked where she planned to put them, how she would remember that they were mine. "What if someone else checks out before me and pretends they're theirs?"

•

One summer a few years earlier, I'd stood against a fence outside the Israeli customs office at the Allenby Bridge, on the way to Nablus, my parents' hometown. Depending on the political climate, some of our summer trips were worse than others when it came to crossing the Allenby, the main entry point into the West Bank for Palestinians living in the diaspora. In the late 1980s, during the intifada, it had been a consistently hellish process; the holding room a swarm of families all kept waiting for hours with no water or air-conditioning in desert heat.

Though the intifada had long since ended, that particular summer had been an especially bad one for crossing, even for American citizens, which is how I would usually enter the West Bank. As an American. I'd tuck my Jordanian passport away, along with any visual sign of my Palestinian heritage. I would sport my Asics Tigers, flaunt my Hanes V-neck. I'd flash my American passport. Nationality is partly a matter of convenience.

Still, a guard called me over that day and instructed me to hand my luggage to another guard on the opposite side of the fence, who took it and tossed it into a tube that looked like an MRI machine. He placed no tag on the bag, no receipt was printed, and no record existed to show that it belonged to me.

The look on my face must have signaled worry. "Calm down," he said. "You'll find it once you get through security."

I was the last person to get through that day, likely because of my twentysomething, volatile, and presumably rebellious age. The Lebanese stamps that decorated every other page of my passport didn't help, either. When I finally got to the luggage area my suitcase was gone.

•

"They'll go in a safe," Nancy assured me, "in a plastic bag with your name on it." She handed me a roll of masking tape and a thick red marker. I ripped off a piece and wrote my name in all caps, and then pressed it onto the Ziploc. I was about to ask if I could at least keep my iPod when a man with a soft brown beard, bulbous red nose, and topaz-colored eyes walked into the room. He wore khaki pants with a hunter-green polo and Merrell shoes. He looked like one of those doctors you see in the movies, the kind from the 1950s, like he could administer shock therapy on you and make it home in time for a TV dinner and the six o'clock news. He knelt down beside me and spoke quietly, smiling. "Hi, I'm Richard. I'm the psychiatrist here."

I looked into his eyes and saw it, that familiar thing. Rage. I could tell he'd acted on it before, a number of times, but had since built his career on repressing it. I smiled back at him. He stood and patted me on the back. "Glad you're here," he said.

"Well," Nancy interjected. "It's four thirty now, so dinner's in half an hour. Why don't you go out into the living room until then and meet some of the other clients?"

I looked over my shoulder and into the other room. "Just go out there?"

•

On my first day in treatment for anorexia, nearly five years earlier, I walked in with my hoodie pulled over my face. The center was just a few blocks from my summer sublet in Porter Square, and I was afraid I might see someone who recognized me. It didn't matter that I'd only been in Cambridge a few weeks and knew practically no one. During dinner a counselor tapped me on the shoulder and told me I'd put too much food on my plate, a move that propelled me to enact an independent seventy-two-hour hunger strike. Across the table a woman started crying onto her burrito. "Will I ever escape this?" she wailed.

I turned and faced the wall to hide my laughter. We were all so perfectly absurd, so perfectly pathetic.

•

"Yup!" Nancy nodded. "Just right through there."

Suddenly I didn't want to leave her. I wanted Nancy to take my hand, lead me into the living room, and introduce me. But she was rearranging plastic baggies in the safe to make space for mine. Why wouldn't she stop smiling? Her permanent grin made me afraid I would say something I'd regret, so I turned toward the living room. And I closed my eyes.

The notion that everyone will eventually cease to exist brings me great comfort and temporary courage. Often I try to visualize the coming apocalypse: barren tree branches, scrap metal, tumbleweed. As the images appear in my head, a wave begins to curl in my stomach. Together they propel me forward, and I act.

Right then, it wasn't working. I kept trying, but all I could picture was Nancy. When I opened my eyes, I focused my gaze on the floor. It was as if by not looking at anyone, they couldn't see me either.

Toys were scattered all over. Nerf guns, bouncy balls, teddy bears. I noticed a bongo drum in the corner. I sat down on a denim-duveted love seat while two guys arm-wrestled on the opposite couch. One of them had sun-bleached hair that was almost white, thick muscles, and a strong jaw. I watched him pin down the other guy's forearm. "*Booyeah!*" he called out, claiming victory. He then looked up at me. "Hey, little lady," he said. "I'm Greg. What're you in for?"

I was surprised by the bluntness of his question. "What're *you* in for?" I asked in return.

"Heroin."

My stomach twitched, and for a moment I wondered if I wasn't supposed to be there.

"*I want you to really sift through your baggage and face it.*" That line from Anna's last email played in my mind like a chorus. I'd held on to her words, as if they justified coming to such a place. Anna and I hadn't spoken for weeks until right before treatment. She'd ignored all my attempts to communicate—every call, text, and email—until the night before my twenty-eight days. She picked up, as though she could sense my desperation. "I'm scared," I confessed. "I don't want to do this."

Anna said nothing, just breathed heavily into the phone as I continued. "But I know I need to, even if it won't fix things with us." She kept breathing in a way that I recognized, a way that used to betray hesitancy. "Right?"

"Yes," she finally responded. "That's exactly right."

I asked Greg where he was from. South Carolina. His voice was deep and his mouth barely moved when he spoke. "I've been to Charleston once," I told him, not mentioning that I'd felt completely strange there, like the only Arab for hundreds of miles, maybe thousands. I asked him about the toys.

"They're for when we do inner child work," he said, picking up a stuffed turtle from beside him. It was awkward, the sight of the furry innocent thing in his rough, cracked hands. "Don't worry, you'll get your own soon," he continued, "and they'll make you bring it *everywhere*." He rolled his eyes and jutted his elbow in my direction. "I know it seems silly. But trust me, you'll grow to love it."

He looked down at his turtle and gave it a tender squeeze. Just as I was wondering if I could leave and still get my money back, the doors leading from upstairs opened and about twenty or so people streamed into the living room. I looked to Greg, who called out, "Dinnertime! Sloppy Joes tonight."

I thought back to my pre-treatment phone call with Nancy; apparently this counted as gourmet dining. I reluctantly followed the stream to the cafeteria, where I scooped fluorescent orange meat onto my plate. I added a little salad and then sat down at a table with Greg and a few others. "Sloppys taste a lot better with buns, you know," he said.

I lied and told him there were none left. I was too uncomfortable to eat, especially bread that looked like the cotton stuffing inside of furniture. Instead I stabbed at a browning piece of iceberg lettuce, zigzagging it across my plate. After dinner, Richard came over and knelt beside me with a clipboard. "You'll be going in the blue van to the Al-Anon meeting in Bowling Green," he said. "Sex and Love Addicts Anonymous only meets in Louisville."

In addition to having no idea that Twelve Step meetings would be a part of this, I was surprised that they didn't have their own Ledge members-only meetings on site, that we'd be mingling with locals. Apparently, that was the point: to humble us, so we'd avoid feeling special and distinguishing ourselves from other addicts. I wondered why Nancy hadn't bothered to mention any of this to me before I'd signed up.

"What's Al-Anon?" I asked Richard.

"That seems right," he said, ignoring my question as he scribbled something on his clipboard, beside my name. He then directed me to the van that was going to the community center, where the Alcoholics Anonymous and Al-Anon meetings took place. Greg was already buckled up in the back row, and I was glad for it. He was the only person I'd spoken to so far, which made me feel disproportionately close to him. On the way to the meeting, I learned that he was a surgeon at one of South Carolina's top hospitals. He was married to Vivian but sleeping with his intern, Jill. "The thing is," I heard him saying in the row behind me, "I love Vivian, but she treats me like shit."

"Could it be because you're fucking someone else?" I asked without turning around.

As the van pulled up to the community center, I realized that I had goose bumps and was frantically tapping my foot. Half of us spilled out of the van and into the center, which was one big sparse room containing a gray folding table surrounded by ten folding metal chairs. A coffeemaker with a brown-streaked carafe and powdered creamer sat on an aluminum-rimmed table in the corner. When we arrived, it was mostly women, only a few men, including Greg. Once we were all seated, a woman with an authentic beehive hairdo opened the meeting, introducing herself as Bonnie. "Hi, Bonnie," everyone echoed.

•

"I'm Anna," Anna said, though I already knew her name, we'd been in treatment together for a month by then, learning why food and fullness weren't our enemies. When I confessed to the group that I had developed feelings for the center's nutritionist, after an all-night G-chat correspondence precipitated by her filling in the second half of a Shins lyric that I'd posted as my status, Anna approached me. "It was brave of you to admit that to everyone," she said. She had wolf-blue eyes and golden retriever warmth. She then handed me a scrap of paper. "Here's my number, if you ever want to talk."

I felt seen, in that moment. I also felt curious. I called her that weekend. "Want to meet for coffee?"

•

The topic at the Al-Anon meeting that night was detachment. How to detach from your alcoholic with love. From your drug addict, with love. From your personality-disordered relative,

YOU EXIST TOO MUCH

with love. As people around the room shared stories of sons' arrests and daughters' relapses, husband anger, parental neglect, panic crept up inside me. Those weren't the kinds of stories I'd expected to hear, and they were resonating a little too well. I felt embarrassed by the similarities of our experiences, the way they overlapped, the banality of what had been so painful to me. I also felt an unsettling disgust with the presumption that I could relate to these people in some way, in any way at all, really. When Bonnie asked if I wanted to share, I chose to pass. "I'm just listening tonight," I said, and a round of "glad you're here" sounded throughout the room. The woman sitting beside me reached out and pressed her palm against the back of my hand.

We waited in the parking lot after the meeting. Some people wandered off and smoked, others ran to the Walgreens across the street. Greg ranted to no one in particular. "I'm sorry," he said, "but that meeting was just a bunch of horny housewives who probably drove their husbands to drink."

He was still going on about the meeting when the van pulled up, everyone piling in with contraband sodas and a lingering smell of smoke. "They should change their statement," Greg said. "Al-Anon: friends and family of alcoholics who wouldn't need to drink so much if their friends and family weren't so goddamned whiny!" He chuckled and snorted a little. I turned around and glared at him. He shut up. I then looked straight ahead, through the windshield, and smiled. He didn't need to know that I thought he was kind of funny.

EVERY JUNE THROUGHOUT OUR CHILDHOOD, KARIM AND I were loaded onto a plane, our mother seated between us, our suitcases stowed in the plane's underbelly, and hauled across the Atlantic Ocean to Jordan, not to return to the States until Labor Day weekend. We'd arrive exhausted at Queen Alia Airport, named after King Hussein's third wife, who was, ironically, killed in a helicopter crash. We'd hire a taxi and ride along the airport road, past Bedouin tents and the occasional herd of goats, to Teta's home in the Shmeisani neighborhood of Amman. Just like Karim and me, my cousin Reema and her sisters were hauled to Amman at the end of every school year. Reema had light brown hair and green eyes, and was five years older than me. She lived in Paris during the year and spoke with a French accent, which I and Karim both deemed to be exaggerated. One particular summer, her parents got two suites at the InterContinental, one for themselves and the other for Reema and her sisters. We spent all of June at the hotel pool; me, Reema, and our other cousin, Nour, occasionally allowing Karim to hang out with us. Everything I did was designed to win Reema's approval. I drove the bumper car out of the ring and around the lobby at the hotel's fun fair, until the manager dragged me back in by my ear. I knocked on room doors on every floor and ran away. When one door that I kept knocking on opened and a woman's hand emerged, promptly smacking me across the face, the game ended. I tortured the pool staff; Reema bought itching powder and I was tasked with slipping it down the lifeguard's shirt, which angered him so much that he beat me with a flip-flop. That time I cried and threatened to call child services, to which Nour, who lived in Amman year-round and was my main competitor for Reema's attention, smirked and said, "Do you really think we have such things here?"

Every summer I was forced to see my father's side of the family—his sisters, brothers and their kids. I'd pout all morning as I packed my bag and during the car ride to their neighborhood, which was far busier, noisier, and dirtier than Teta's. They'd take me to the community pool, and I usually enjoyed it, but not that year—not compared to the hotel pool. I hesitated to get in the water, which was full of undiapered street kids, something that had never bothered me before. My paternal cousins and I weren't allowed to order poolside entrees and Pepsis like at the InterContinental. Instead, we had to wait until we got back home to eat. As we scarfed down hummus and pita sandwiches, I sat there wondering what my mother's cousins were doing. How much fun were they having that I was missing out on?

Finally, one of my dad's bearded brothers drove me back to my grandmother's apartment. I leaped from the car, entirely forgetting to say thank you or even goodbye, and rang the bell. The *haris* let me in. I rushed upstairs to the apartment, where the red and yellow lights above the hot water switches were both lit. My grandmother told me to hurry up and get in the tub: my mother had requested to see me at the hotel. I quickly peeled off my swimsuit and bathed, washing off the filth of the day. Afterward, Teta combed my hair as I chose an outfit. The sun was setting just as we arrived at the hotel's terrace, where my mother and her aunts sat sipping rosé, a tray of sliced mangoes and melons in front of them, a waiter refreshing the coals in their shisha, which sent off little flecks of red embers. "Hi, *mama!*" my mother called out to me in the traditional, self-referential way Arab parents refer to their children: as *mama* and *baba*. My walk became a run as I dived toward the table and attempted to kiss her. But she wouldn't stop talking long enough to let me, everyone laughing at the story she was telling, which I couldn't understand: she was speaking too fast in Arabic, a language I was still struggling to grasp. For the majority of my childhood, I only ever understood a third of what anyone was saying. "Come," one of my great-aunts said, waving me over after noting my disappointment. I wandered to her and received conciliatory affection before I was patted on the behind and sent off to play by myself.

At the time I didn't realize what it was that separated the two sides of my family: that my paternal cousins did not live in the noisy neighborhood, go to the community pool, and wait to eat hummus sandwiches at home by choice.

5

IN ELEMENTARY SCHOOL ONE MORNING, AFTER MY ALARM had been ringing for twenty-seven minutes, my father blasted into my bedroom, grabbed the clock off the nightstand, opened the window, and hurled it into our front yard. This occurred after numerous attempts to wake me up by song; he'd float into my room in his flannel pajamas, singing "*Ya madrassa, ya madrassa*," which means, "School, O school" in Arabic, or, depending on which dictionary you consult, "terrorist training camp."

Though as an adult waking up hasn't gotten much easier, on my first morning at the Ledge I was wide awake and at the main lodge in time for coffee. I wanted to get as much caffeine as I could. At seven thirty exactly the kitchen door opened and a bald man with bright eyes and a warm smile emerged, carrying three carafes. He put them down and then checked to make sure the sugar tray was full. I pawed through the pile of mismatched mugs, chose the tallest, and pumped the carafe until my cup was full to the brim, sitting down carefully so I wouldn't spill.

The night before, I had stayed up late chatting with my roommate, Molly. "I'm not sure I belong here," she'd said.

Molly was a love addict, too. Tucked into bed, her makeup

still thick on her face, she told me about the meth lab she and her boyfriend ran out of their kitchen in Chattanooga. Her instincts were screaming at her to get out of the marriage and the meth, but she couldn't bear to leave him. The thought of disappointing him was just too much. He couldn't bear it either, and when she once attempted to leave, he threw himself in front of her moving car, breaking both of his legs and relegating her to be his caretaker. "It's how I was raised," she told me. "To please others. You know?"

I did know. "I think you're in the right place," I'd said before drifting off to sleep.

As I sat in the lodge lapping up coffee, I looked around at the posters on the walls. There was one with a gnome walking down a long fairy-tale trail. Beneath him was a quote by Proust: "The real voyage of discovery consists not in seeking new landscapes, but in having new eyes."

Something about it unsettled me. I figured it was supposed to make us feel better about being in Bowling Green, Kentucky, rather than elsewhere. I was thinking of the other places I could be when Greg walked into the living room carrying *Why Men Love Bitches*, a contraband item, as we were only supposed to be reading self-help literature that Nancy had sanctioned. His blond hair was slicked back, making it hard to tell where his forehead ended and his hairline began. He was wearing white patent-leather loafers and a T-shirt that said, "Your Village Called, They Want Their Idiot Back!" After he poured himself a cup of coffee, he sat down beside me and snapped his book against my thigh. "Hey, baby girl!" he said. "How you doin' this morning, you sleep well?"

He smiled a big game-show-host grin. Was this an attempt

to flirt? I raised an eyebrow and sneered in return. "Yo, Miami Vice," said a guy with a lip ring, tapping his foot against Greg's, "are those your dancin' shoes?"

"These bad boys?" Greg said, pointing down. "They better do more than that, I paid three hundred bucks for 'em!"

The guy with the lip ring shook his head and laughed. Greg laughed along earnestly, unaware that he was being mocked. I gazed at the pine trees outside, and as the sun rose, streams of light poured in through the windows and illuminated the dust in the room. Greg looked at me and smiled again. "It's your Higher Power saying 'good morning,'" he said.

"Yeah, right." I smirked. He seemed momentarily deflated. I realized I had mistaken his earnestness for sarcasm, and I immediately regretted mine.

I had breakfast; a glass of water and half a grapefruit. Afterward, I was about to step outside when I heard a cowbell ringing. Then someone called out, "Phase Two in the big room, Phase One in the small!"

Phase One. The newbies, lumped together in one group with our various addictions and afflictions. There were four of us: Greg; my roommate, Molly; another guy, named Alex; and me. I appeared to be the youngest. Following the three of them, I made my way upstairs to the small room. Richard stood in the doorway, waving us in. I chose a seat against the back wall. As Richard shut the door and walked toward the whiteboard at the front, I felt as if the room were shrinking, the walls zeroing in on me. I was terrified by the prospect of sharing anything vulnerable with these people, of being in such a confined, intimate space with them, every day for a month! I raised my hand and Richard nodded at me. I looked at Molly, then squinted at Greg. "Will the four of us be doing all of this together?" I asked. "As a group?"

•

My resistance to groups is likely a response to my culture's fervent embrace of them, which locates value not as much in the individual as in the cohort they belong to. "Why don't you be friends with her?" my mother would suggest, speaking of a friend's daughter. "She has a nice crowd," by which she meant "she has *a* crowd," the distinct identities of its members less of a concern. Indeed, cliques are the norm among Arabs, but they are never easy to break into. I know—I tried, and failed. Even my cousins wouldn't have me. After each day at the InterContinental hotel pool that summer, Reema invited Nour to sleep over, but never me. They acted as if I didn't notice, but of course I did. Though I usually wouldn't find out until the next morning, when I'd interrogate my mother about whether she'd seen Reema and Nour together at the hotel the night before while she dined with their mothers on the terrace. Yes, she'd respond, she'd seen them. And I would cry, because I desperately wanted to be closer to them, to stay up until dawn playing cards and watching rom-coms. But I was the American cousin, which inspired a resentment that my mother, depending on her mood, promised me was rooted in jealousy or lambasted me for, as though I had chosen to grow up in the States. Being regularly excluded, I developed a preference for solitude, one that I wasn't so ready to exchange for the incessant company of complete strangers. I chose careers accordingly. DJing was one that worked well with my need to be alone, and also with love addiction: it limited my time with Anna and introduced me to a swathe of people who adored me, or some version of me, without expectations. With gigs on prime socializing nights I got used to skipping nights out with her. Besides, I didn't need a partner to feel loved: I was a DJ! I was loved from a distance, the safest way to be loved.

•

"I'm afraid you don't get much alone time here," Richard said. "We're modeled on a group system. So the four of you better get comfortable—you'll be getting to know each other pretty well."

Before I could respond, he walked over to the whiteboard and picked up a marker. He drew a rudimentary tree, and at the tips of its various branches he wrote *Alcohol, Drugs, Food, Sex, Love.* At the tree's roots, designated by hyperextended squiggly lines, he wrote in big block letters: CODEPENDENCY.

"Can anyone tell me what that word means?" he asked.

I raised my hand but didn't wait for him to call on me. "It's an inability to be in a healthy relationship with the self."

"Right," he said. "How'd you know that?"

In her book, Pia Mellody had made a significant effort to distinguish codependency from love addiction: While love addicts turn to a person as a drug of choice for soothing the pain of their difficult relationships with themselves, the absence of healthy self-love is itself codependency.

"I read it somewhere." I shrugged. "I remember things."

"That's one definition of it," he conceded. "Here we like to think of it as the pain from childhood that manifests in adulthood."

"So unless you grew up in a 1950s sitcom," I said, "you're codependent?"

Richard forced a laugh. "It's true that most people have unresolved pain from childhood. But not everyone ends up self-medicating with one of these." He ran the capped marker back over the words at the ends of the branches. "The goal is figuring out how we got from the root of the tree to the branches. From codependency to addiction."

We began by telling our life stories. "There's no time limit on how long you have, just however long you need to take," Richard said as I clenched the edges of my chair. Having known these people for less than twenty-four hours, I wasn't too enthused about hearing their entire personal histories. I assumed everyone else must've felt the same way, but to my surprise, they seemed engaged, leaning forward attentively to listen to one another. Though I mostly scribbled in my notebook and did equations, calculating the cost per hour of being there, I picked up bits and pieces.

Alex, who I kept wanting to call Eugene because he looked like one, was an engineer with a perpetually exasperated expression on his face. I noticed him for the first time on the way to the Al-Anon meeting the night before. He'd sat beside Greg in the back row of the van with his brows raised and eyes popped, wiping sweat off his forehead with a handkerchief. At the end of the meeting he furiously gripped my hand and chanted, "Let go and let God. Keep coming back, it works if you work it!" Alex was from New Hampshire, and his wife was an alcoholic. He'd been a member of Al-Anon for twenty-seven years. "I just keep trying to fix her," he told us, honking into a Kleenex and then throwing the wet balled-up tissues across the floor. "I mean, I've sent her to rehab twice, I've written her letters describing how it's tearing our family apart, I've laid out charts for how she can gradually stop drinking," he said. "But the more I try, the more she wants nothing to do with me."

"Maybe you should stop trying," Greg suggested, "and see what happens."

"I can't just *stop*," he snapped. "We have kids. There's too much at stake."

When Molly started speaking, I started panicking, afraid I'd have to hear everything about her twice. I learned a couple of new things; she ran her own day spa, she'd been married three times. Her mother had been hooked on painkillers for most of Molly's life, and after burning through several husbands and their bank accounts, she began relying on her only daughter for cash. Molly had been supporting her for over ten years. She told us about times when her mom was able to hold down a job, and how proud Molly was of her when she did. I felt a sharp tinge of empathy, the guilt and resentment both exceedingly familiar.

By four o'clock that afternoon, Greg had already spent three hours telling his story, about how his biological father had given full custody of Greg to his mother and her new husband when Greg was twelve, how the pain of feeling unwanted had led him to binge drinking and reckless sex with "cheerleader sluts" in high school, how being berated by his "bitch wife" led to opioids as a way to ease the sting of her insults, how heroin became a way to drown her out entirely. I stared at the clock as the minute hand eclipsed the hour hand for the third time and decided that only a white man would feel comfortable taking up so much space. I glanced around the room. No one else appeared to be bothered by it. In fact, they were asking follow-up questions and for clarification! I had to interject. "You've been talking for two hours longer than everyone else."

He hunched forward, appearing to shrink. "Calm down, I'm almost done."

I sensed I should've stopped there but something twitched inside me and I kept going. "And can you stop being so derogatory about women," I felt heat rising up my neck, "and villainizing us?"

"I'm not talking about women, I'm talking about my wife."

"Right, well, that distinction is irrelevant to me."

"Jesus!" he muttered. "Thanks for your support!"

"I don't support you."

"I know," he said, "I was being sarcastic." By then his voice was quivering. For a second I was afraid he was going to cry. "What is the matter with you, anyway?"

Finally Richard jumped in. "All right, that's enough for today." As everyone got up to leave, Richard insisted Greg and I stay behind to talk about what happened. "So what was going on just now?" he asked me.

I told him I didn't like the way Greg spoke about his wife.

"You're offended by his use of profanity?"

"No, she isn't offended by it," Greg answered on my behalf. "She's been running around calling me a 'fucking pussy'!"

I had called him that, during lunch, but I hadn't expected it to get back to him. I was quite pleased that it had. Richard shot me a look and I lowered my head. Then he asked, "So what is it?"

•

If my mother was Hamas—unpredictable, impulsive, and frustrated at being stifled—my father was Israel. He'd refuse to meet her most basic needs until she exploded. Then he would point at her and cry, "Look at what a monster she is, what a terror!" But never once did he consider *why* she had resorted to such extreme tactics, or his role in the matter.

Some of my strongest memories of my father involve him weeding the garden or watching television. He did not want to be bothered, especially not by his immediate family. Activities that allowed him to completely shut out our needs and emotions seemed to resonate with him. There were moments of genuine attendance, and even concern for our betterment. He would tutor me in Arabic, he'd show up to Karim's soccer games, he'd sing me awake. But the things that we craved most, like fatherly guidance or affection, he would not, *could not*, provide. He was almost robotic in his affection—an arm around the shoulders, strained and unnatural, or a pat on the back the most he could muster. Kisses or hugs were out of the question. As a child I would ask my mother what was wrong with him. "Why can't he look me in the eye?" To which she would answer, "Because he's afraid of women. In fact, he hates them."

One of the few things he did actively and passionately was complain about my mother. Didn't I remember how she slapped him in line for the ski lift in Pennsylvania? How she tried to jump out the window of our hotel room in Orlando? How she drew blood from his face and then ran naked through our neighborhood screaming?

During my sophomore year of high school, he moved out. He didn't tell me or Karim that he was planning to, nor did our mother.

65

One night he just didn't come home, and we were left to make our own assumptions. He ended up renting a place, in a gerontic apartment complex with a permanent EMT squad in the parking lot. It was twenty minutes away, close enough that we had no excuse not to surrender our weekends to visit him. "I'm all alone," he'd whine to us over the phone. "Don't you guys want to come see me?"

And so we would. I had just passed my driving test and was already regretting it, as there was no structure to the aftermath of my parents' chaos, our visits to our dad's apartment determined by guilt level rather than any set schedule. We'd sit there for hours, Karim and I, on his new plastic-covered couch and stare at the television together. When we'd leave, after an undesignated number of hours on undesignated days, he would stand in the doorway of the apartment, his eyes burning into our backs as we walked to the elevators. I'd turn to look at him one last time before stepping in and catch his half smile, his half wave that sent us off to the house he once lived in. Then the elevator doors would shut, and guilt would flood in.

Guilt gnawed away at me through the rest of high school, even after my father got a girlfriend my junior year. Ash, who my mother affectionately nicknamed Trash, was only eight years older than me, which is probably why my father chose to keep her a secret. I met her by accident at TGI Fridays in the mall. I walked into the restaurant after choir practice with the rest of the ensemble and spotted my father in a booth with a woman, both of them sitting on the same side, sharing a milkshake. I was stung by the sight of my father with a woman who wasn't my mother. As I walked toward him, I felt both anger for having been lied to and unnecessarily guilted. He introduced me to Ash, and I tried to smile as she burrowed her head into my father's shoulder like a shy toddler. The next morning he called me at my mother's house and said, "You were so aggressive last night. You were *so* incredibly cold."

But I had been too shocked to be either. I hung up, threw the portable phone against the wall, and watched the batteries fly out as a black smudge appeared on the white paint.

Along with the twelve-year-old girlfriend came a Mercedes convertible and two motorcycles. "Men like their toys," he responded when I asked why he needed so many vehicles, especially when he spent most his time parked in front of the TV.

Now that Trash was in the picture, it seemed like he was building a new family. And yet he still complained, still spited my mother. When guilt morphed into resentment and grew so big that I was blinded by it, it seeped out of my pores and left me feeling powerless. And so I raged, sometimes just to get him to turn away from the television and feign interest in my life, to acknowledge my existence. I would act out in the hopes that he would notice, that he would tend to me. Instead, my outburst would only provide further evidence for what he already believed. "You don't see yourself," he'd say, sneering in my direction before turning back to the TV. "You don't see the way you act. You're just like her."

•

I rotated my ankle and it cracked a few times. "He's just always blaming her for everything, punishing her for having needs," I said to Richard. Greg looked up as though he was going to defend himself, but then stayed quiet. "Making her out to be some kind of monster."

My first sexual experience occurred midway through fifth grade. Upon learning about sex and its effects from my science teacher, Dr. Sabinne—she was the only teacher at our grade school with a PhD, and she insisted on being recognized for her credentials—I immediately became fascinated. At the time I couldn't wait to try it, likely because of Dr. Sabinne's description. "Ladies," she said to a roomful of twelve-year-olds, "it is so good. It is so great. Girls, it is worth it!" Worth what, I wasn't sure, but I was ready to give it a go. I had started feeling the tingle of desire a few months earlier, and during her presentation it grew into a full-fledged burn. The boys had been taken to a separate room by Mr. Nell, and I imagined they were given the same sales pitch. I figured all that was left was the pairing up. The tall girls could go off with the tall boys, the blonds with the blondes, and so on.

I chose my parents' friends' son, Tarek. We were about the same height and both Arabs. He came over one day after choir practice, and instead of bringing him to the kitchen for a snack I led him upstairs to my bedroom. He lay on top of me and gyrated, never quite achieving an erection. He rolled off and his blubber jiggled—he was a chubby boy—and I nuzzled my way into his arms, seeking affection. He kissed me repeatedly, closed-lipped. He smelled like Bazooka chewing gum. When he left, I wanted more.

It turned out the guys weren't given the same pep talk as the girls. A few days later, Tarek admitted that he enjoyed the kissing but not the "heavy petting," the term we used in class. He obviously preferred Nintendo to human contact. After our first encounter I did everything I could to get him onto his top bunk and under my shirt. He'd curiously fiddle around for a bit, then sit up, climb down the bunk bed ladder, press the TV/Video button on his television, and take out his controller. I lay frustrated underneath his *DuckTales* bedsheets, watching his on-screen avatar jump over brick castles and sink down tunnels.

Accepting that preteen boys didn't have as strong a sex drive as their female counterparts, I turned to the internet for fulfillment. AIM had just come out. My screen name was Juniper18, a combination of my favorite scent of Bath & Body Works lotion and my purported age. "What size are your tits?" BigCoq4U would ask.

My breasts were buddingly present but still quite nascent. Daily examinations in front of the bathroom mirror suggested glacial-speed growth. "36D," I'd lie. Sometimes I'd give my number to whoever I was chatting with—I had received my own private phone line that year for Eid al-Fitr, so I didn't need to worry about my parents listening in. I twirled the cord and spoke to whoever was on the other end as he touched himself. I liked the power of it, of exciting someone with my voice. I would sit on my windowsill with the phone pressed to my ear, my mother and father screaming at each other down the hall just as Andy or Joe or Matt would moan into the receiver, drowning out my parents. There was one male caller who happened to live just a few miles away, and of whom I became especially fond. He was different from the others. He seemed to genuinely care for me, and we discussed topics besides how big he was, like the weather, what I was majoring in, bands we liked. He broke the news to me that Jerry Garcia had died, and for that I will never forget him.

Once, we agreed to meet. I rode my bike to his house and hid behind a bush across the street. I watched him step outside onto his porch in an oversized Nike T-shirt and athletic shorts, scratch his head, then place his hand above his eyes like a visor and peer into the distance, presumably searching for me. He looked different than he did in the pictures he'd sent me: older, balder, fatter. The drastic difference between his actual appearance and his virtual persona would've been less of a shock had AOL and the entire online world not been such a novelty. I would've expected the contrast. I planted a foot on each side of my bike and remained in place, waiting for him to step back inside. The moment he did, I furiously pedaled home.

By the time I was in high school, I decided I liked older men. They felt safe to me, and oddly familiar. And they seemed to appreciate me so much more than the guys in my class, including my age-appropriate boyfriend at the time. It was as if they'd spent forty days in the desert or had just returned home from war and were ready to project all that pent-up desire onto me. I encountered quite a few of them in person; I spent my high school summers answering phones at a tech company. Periodically, coworkers would approach me at the café below the office. The first time I drew back in shock. "I'm fourteen!"

"Shit," the poor fellow answered, "I'm sorry!" Feeling guilt for shaming him, as along with curiosity, I scribbled my number on my lunch receipt and dropped it on his tray on my way out.

I came to worship them, these older men. I craved the wisdom and guidance they willingly offered and that my father withheld. I adored how sexy they made me feel, likely because of the discrepancy between our levels of attractiveness. They, in turn, approved of my young body, one that was still tight due to its relative newness rather than its purity. "I treat my body like a temple," said my childhood friend Eman, whose parents were Syrian and friends with mine. Eman was a few years older than me and esteemed herself worthy of doling out wisdom. She was always lecturing me about how important it was to wait until marriage, or at least until I was in love. I rolled my eyes, though not without slight envy. There was judgment beneath her assertion, one that cast my dalliances as acts of self-desecration and sacrilege rather than attempts at validation. *Get over yourself,* I wanted to respond. Besides, wasn't she just bitter she couldn't land a guy of her own?

6

"Secrets keep us sick," Richard said during group on Day 4. It sounded like the tagline for a horror movie, too melodramatic to have any impact. "They keep us from being our authentic, real selves. So we're each going to tell one."

Richard was working with us that afternoon. Or evaluating us. I could never tell which. He was always jotting things down in a notebook, nodding when we spoke or asking generic questions like "Can you say more about that?" or "How did that make you feel?" and consistently failing to offer any insights or useful advice. The counselors didn't seem entirely comfortable with him, either, and I was getting the sense that he didn't work there year-round, only in the summer, like he was the seasonal guest star in a long-running series. I wasn't particularly shocked by Molly's or Alex's secrets; Alex had slept with a man while his wife was away at rehab, Molly had stolen money from her parents to bail her boyfriend out of jail. After sharing, they were each required to ask the group for forgiveness. I was uncomfortable with the forced pardoning, though both of their secrets seemed pretty forgivable. But Greg's involved "possibly" taking advantage of a drunk Tri-Delt when he was a Kappa Sigma at Vanderbilt. His voice was solemn when he told the story. He looked up at Richard when he was done.

"Now, ask your group members if they think that makes you a bad person," Richard said.

Greg asked us each individually; Molly and Alex each pardoned his behavior. When he looked up at me with a pathetic but expectant look of hope, thinking I would absolve him of what I deemed to be rightful shame, I was tempted to respond, *Yes, that does make you a bad person. You should probably be castrated.* I imagined he would then attempt to defend himself, and I would quickly dispel his efforts. *Poor you,* I would say, *she's only been through a lifetime of therapy for what you did to her and here you are, a middle-aged man ten minutes into rehab thinking this can all go away!* He'd then break down into sobs and I would really lay into him, continuing to describe what this poor woman had likely gone through on account of the unfortunate coincidence that they'd attended the same frat party. I smiled, imagining this situation playing out, until my fantasy was interrupted by the sound of my name. "Helll-*ooo!*"

I looked up at Richard. "Huh?"

He chuckled along with the others; apparently he'd been trying to get my attention for some time. "I said, 'Do you want to share a secret?'"

"Do I have to?"

"You don't have to divulge anything if you don't want to," Richard assured me. "But I bet you'll feel better if you do."

•

Every time a woman was about to light a cigarette, one of Eman's lesser-known bridesmaids would swoop in to light it for her. Eman was always quick to point this out, that she'd barely known the girl, but that she'd managed to find her way into their social circle and had practically begged for a role in the wedding. Most everyone seemed uncomfortable by the gesture, scooting away as her hand approached, then reluctantly moving back toward the flame. I played along with their reactions, raising my brows, rolling my eyes as she put away her lighter.

It was the summer before college, and my mother and I had flown from Amman to Beirut for a week for Eman's wedding. In lieu of academics, Eman had devoted the majority of her energy at Lebanese American University to finding a husband, and by the time she was twenty-three she was engaged to a Lebanese chiropractor. In the days leading up to the event we speculated about the lesser-known bridesmaid's sexual orientation. "I think she's a lesbian," Eman said, and we joked about her hitting on me and the other female guests. I felt guilty laughing along. But I was afraid if I didn't, they would see through to my secret.

Sometimes I would try to communicate recognition to the bridesmaid, burning a deep stare into her eyes whenever she'd offer to light my cigarette. I wanted *her* to know, but never for anyone else to suspect.

Stereotypes exist for the inhabitants of different Arab cities. People from the Syrian town of Homs are reputed to be dim. Tulkarem in the West Bank is made up of hillbillies—*fellayin*, the Arabic word for peasants. Folks from the village of Isdud—now the city of Ashdod—are cheap. "They heat up their leftover salad and serve it for dinner," the expression goes. In Gaza, the girls are all lesbians. Maybe the stereotype stems from their geographical isolation from the rest of the country; women turn to each other for lack of more options. Regardless, it is implied that as a Palestinian, to be gay is unacceptable. "I'm homophobic," a cousin once proudly asserted before telling a story about visiting Mykonos. "I just feel sick when I see two guys together," he clarified, as though informing us that he was lactose intolerant.

To be a woman who desired other women seemed even worse, especially shameful and shocking in its lack of reverence for the male-centric culture. Why would you want to exclude men, the stronger, better gender, from the equation?

In high school, it didn't take long to realize that I coveted Eman, whose body was like a temple. It was a place where I wanted to worship. When my thespian boyfriend cheated on me with the prettiest madrigal, I was jealous of him, not her. Then there was Julia, captain of the soccer team, with puffy lips and cheeks red with rosacea. Adrienne, lead cheerleader, with massive green eyes and crescent-shaped lashes. And of course the Air France stewardesses on my transatlantic flights from the States to Amman, with their tinted nylons and hair pinned back in little buns. When I saw a cute girl, the feeling in my stomach, the wave that seemed to take shape there, excited and inspired me. But mostly, it terrified me.

In the days leading up to Eman's wedding, I would accompany my mother to the Vendôme hotel along the corniche in Raouché, where most of the out-of-town guests were staying. The two of us were staying with a friend of hers from Washington who summered in Lebanon, and who was also invited to the wedding. Each day we would meet up with everyone in the hotel's lounge area for tea. I would wander to the veranda and smoke. I'd often find Eman's bridesmaid at an outdoor table, in a T-shirt and black jeans, her foot resting on the opposite knee as she peered down at her BlackBerry. She was twenty-eight, ten years older than me, and already had her own startup—a successful one, I'd heard. She would look up and see me, then smile in a way that suggested I should come over. She'd light us each a cigarette, having just arrived at the end of the last one, its butt still smoldering in the glass ashtray. I'd ask her questions about life in Dubai. "It has the feel of an Arab country, the food and the language," she'd respond, "without the conservative mind-set."

"Are you seeing anyone there?" I once asked. I was careful not to specify a gender, simultaneously avoiding an assumption of queerness and implying it.

"I'm seeing people everywhere." She exhaled a billowing cloud and then smiled again, a bravado ruffling up in her demeanor. "I've got someone in almost every major city."

The wedding was a display of straightness. Everyone I encountered told me my turn was next, essentially instructing me to meet someone. I felt surface-level excitement at the fantasy of being with a man and feeling emotionally fulfilled by one, rather than just sexually satisfied, along with underlying despair, knowing it was precisely that: a fantasy.

The night of the wedding I sang on stage. I chose a Frank Sinatra song, "Fly Me to the Moon," which was exactly my range. I knew I had performed well, and I stepped off the stage to rounds of applause and a feeling of empowerment. Eman immediately ran to hug me, kissing both my cheeks. Emboldened by her kisses and tipsy, I sauntered over to the bridesmaid and said that I had something to tell her. I felt giddy at the prospect of my confession as I stepped toward her, only to then trip on my dress and fall to the floor. She helped me up, but I ran back to my table feeling mortified.

I sat there for a while sipping a glass of wine before noticing that the best man was staring at me. He was cute, *m'rateb*, and single—the married people had already notified all the single girls of his relationship status. When we caught eyes he waved, then came over and asked if I wanted to dance. He seemed like someone my mother and the community would be impressed by, a good candidate for marriage. As we danced he draped his tie around my neck, and tugged the end to pull me in closer. After a few songs he asked if I wanted to go smoke a cigarette. We took the elevator to the rooftop terrace, where we made out haphazardly, the wind blowing my hair into our faces. "Shall we go down to my room?" he suggested.

Back in the elevator, he pressed the button for his floor and continued to kiss me. When the doors opened, I spotted the bridesmaid down the hallway, typing into her BlackBerry. My stomach flipped. I watched her put her phone in her pocket and walk into her room. The tie guy put his arm around my shoulder, and I walked with him down the opposite side of the corridor. We stopped in front of a door and he fumbled for his room key.

He slid the key into the reader above the knob. A green light blinked. "Actually," I said, "maybe it's better if we don't."

"You don't want to?"

"You know how quickly gossip spreads here." I kissed him and tried to give back his tie.

"Keep it," he said. "It looks better on you."

We said good night. I walked toward the elevators and then continued past them. Nervous, I summoned the requisite apocalyptic imagery: *Scrap metal. Barren tree branches. Tumbleweed.* I knocked gently on her door.

"Hey there," she said when she opened it. "Nice cravat."

I looked down at the tie, its knot wide and loose, then looked back up at her. "Can I come in?"

She stepped aside and left a pathway for me to enter. She then walked to the wet bar and poured me a glass of water, though I hadn't asked for one. I sat down on the edge of the bed. I was wishing I hadn't come here, hadn't knocked. I felt myself shiver— was something actually going to happen? "Are you cold?" she asked.

I shook my head, taking off the tie and tossing it on the bed. I stood up. She was standing directly in front of me, inches away. I could feel heat emanating in the space between us. "I'm not."

She cupped my waist with her hands and I shivered again. My teeth chattered. She pressed her mouth against my neck, and I crumbled into her. We lay down on the bed and moved up toward the pillows. She slid her hand under my dress and pressed the base of her palm against me. I let out a slight, pained moan. She smiled before continuing and said, "You liked that."

The next morning, I thought I could sneak out of the hotel and back to my mother's friend's apartment without running into anyone I knew. I had messaged my mother the night before to tell her that I wouldn't be back until morning, and when she asked where I planned to stay, I responded that my phone was dying. When I stepped off the elevator and into the lobby, I saw that everyone was congregated by the front desk to say goodbye to Eman before she left for her honeymoon. As I attempted to slink away unnoticed, they called out to me.

"Shit," I mumbled, then shuffled over to where they were standing. "How was your first time?" I heard someone ask Eman as I approached.

"First time," she said, "yeah, right," and everyone laughed. When the concierge came over to us and announced that the car to the airport had arrived, I found myself taking Eman aside. "I have confirmation." My heart thumped so hard I could practically hear it. "That bridesmaid is definitely gay."

"No way," Eman said. "How do you know?"

"She came on to me last night," I said, keeping my eyes pinned to the floor. "She invited me to her room." The words practically burned as they left my mouth.

"That's disgusting," Eman said. "What did you say?"

"I told her she must've gotten the wrong idea." I felt the heat spread across my face. "And that I like men."

For a moment I worried that Eman would ask why I was still at the hotel and not with my mother, and where I'd slept the night before. Instead she said, "Well, you'd better be careful. I don't want to come back to a wedding announcement!"

•

I looked down and traced the stripes of my sneaker with my index finger. "My secret is that I slept with someone, then outed her while keeping myself in the closet."

79

The silence felt epic, and I wondered if mine was worse than everyone else's.

"Why did you do that?" Alex asked.

"I don't know," I said. Because I'm terrible? And a coward? "I guess I wanted to see what the reaction would be overseas to that sort of thing." I raised my shoulders. "I'm not really sure why I did it."

"Maybe you were scared," Richard suggested.

"Maybe," I said.

In New York several years after the wedding, I stood in the main quad of Columbia University's campus and watched a live feed from inside the auditorium, where President Ahmadinejad of Iran spouted incendiary statements about his country's superiority. When asked about Iran's horrific treatment of its gay citizens—half a dozen men had been publicly executed over the previous two years—Ahmadinejad proudly announced that there were no homosexuals in the entire country. His negation of their existence, uttered through a crazed smile, seemed simultaneously ridiculous and threatening.

I looked at Richard and continued, "But I know being scared doesn't excuse it."

"Do you want to ask your group members if they think you're a bad person?"

I looked up at my roommate just as she looked down and shook her head. "Molly," I said, my voice practically a whisper, "do you think I'm a bad person?"

Molly kept staring at the floor, refusing to look at me. She sighed. "I knew you were going to ask me," she said. "I just think you should've told me that you're a homosexual."

"Bisexual," I corrected, cringing at her use of that word and hearing the echoes of Ahmadinejad's voice. "The occasion didn't really present itself."

"I get it, but it seems like a pretty big thing not to mention."

I stared at the ceiling, my heart thumping. I wanted to point out that I hadn't actually lied, though she was right to imply that I hadn't been entirely honest, either. I'd deliberately sidestepped pronouns and specifics in our brief conversations about Anna. But did it count as deception if it was done in the name of self-protection? Withholding vulnerable information was a habit born of survival. I'd been lulled into letting my guard down before, only to later regret it, the admissions used against me as I bore her wrath.

"I would like to at least have had the option of switching roommates, not that I necessarily would've," Molly continued. "I just feel like I've been betrayed."

"Now, wait," Greg interjected. Later, he would tell me that in Molly's words he could hear his wife: *You could've at least told me you were a junkie before I married you.* She'd shriveled him down to a raisin of a man, so much that he couldn't look his own daughters in the eye when they told him they loved him. And for that he would always seek to hurt her back, cheating on her incessantly and injecting himself into oblivion.

"No one's under any obligation to announce their sexuality," he continued. "What do you want her to do, get a tattoo, wear a sign?"

He looked at me tentatively. I could tell he was scared of how I'd react, that I was going to be mad for some reason. But I just felt ashamed that he could still muster sympathy for me in spite of how cruel I'd been. He cleared his throat. "Richard, man, what's your secret?"

"Well," Richard said, "I can tell you how I landed here as a patient, fifteen years ago." I took a deep breath, slowly looking up as he continued. "I asked my son to rake the leaves one morning before I left for work. When I came home and saw that he hadn't done it, I went inside and unleashed hell on him. It was the last straw for me, the one that made me seek help."

When I realized I'd been right about him, I didn't feel vindicated, or smug, or pleased. I felt frightened, and disturbed by the familiarity. Worse than receiving rage was the ability to detect its remnants.

7

"YOU *BITCH*," SAID MY MOTHER WHEN I ANSWERED MY office phone one afternoon. I was twenty-three years old and had just started working at a magazine in New York after spending the past six months in Italy.

Fear took over. And confusion.

"Because of *you*, you bitch," she said, spitting out the last word, "I'm running around like an idiot in the fucking rain, looking for stamps."

It took me a moment to understand what she was talking about. That past Friday I had been visiting home and she'd asked if I could pick up a sheet of stamps. "Sure," I'd said. "Can I get them before I leave?"

"Okay, *mama*," she said. "No problem." By the time I left on Sunday evening I'd forgotten about the stamps, but she didn't seem to notice. Not until just then.

"I'm sorry," I said, cupping my hand over the receiver, "but I can't talk about this right now. I'll call you when I leave the office." The phone rang seconds after I hung up.

"Don't you *ever* hang up on me," she rasped.

"Mom, please. Please stop." Again I hung up. The magazine's

main line started ringing, her name flashing across the caller ID. I took the phone and placed it beside the cradle. She called my cell and left voice mails until the inbox was full. As the screen of my phone continued to light up, my boss poked her head out of her office. "Hey, can you send those honorarium checks? They need to go out ASAP."

"Sure!" I nodded so fast the room blurred.

"Why's the phone off the hook?"

"Oh. I don't know," I said, and I placed it back on the receiver. "Sorry."

At the Al-Anon meeting about a week into treatment, Bonnie had compared living with her husband to walking on eggshells. "I guess that's why I'm always so afraid," she said. Later, I found out that was the title of the seminal book on borderline personality disorder. It was a fitting analogy: the slightest misstep could unleash a force capable of shattering its recipient. Erratic, unpredictable cruelty usually coincides with the most vulnerable and tender moments. One must proceed cautiously and always be on the lookout, always withhold information and never reveal something that can later be used as ammunition. Never get too close because that's when she'll shoot. And if she does, always have an escape plan. It is essential to remember these rules. Yet this is the realm, the realm of my mother, in which I consistently forget how to survive.

"The thing is," I said to the group the day after that meeting, "she can't help it." I had just described my last encounter with her, at the restaurant in SoHo.

"Well, maybe she can't in fact help it," said Richard, "and she probably doesn't mean to be vicious—"

"She doesn't," I said.

"Right. But it still has an impact."

One morning during my second week at the Ledge, we did something called a H.I.T. list: Healing Internal Trauma. We were working with Richard and one of the other counselors, Charlotte, a Bowling Green native who also led our yoga sessions. A tattoo decorated each of her forearms as well as her ankles, all of them Sanskrit characters. Her hair was deep brown, almost black, her nose slightly upturned, and whenever she smiled, she pushed the tip of her tongue into the sliver between her two front teeth. She dressed somewhere in between sparkling femininity and early nineties grunge, dressed in capris and a loose-fitting T-shirt.

Charlotte suggested that I do a H.I.T. list on my mother. The activity seemed silly to me, but I decided I might as well try it. I looked straight ahead and attempted to visualize my mother as instructed. All I saw was an empty chair. "I can't picture her," I said to Charlotte, who was sitting beside me.

"That's okay," she said. "Just go ahead and start."

I looked down at the first statement on my list and felt myself blush. "When you tell me I don't deserve to be loved," I winced in embarrassment, "I feel sad?" I looked to Charlotte, worried I was doing it wrong.

"Good," she said. "Now can you try doing this without a smile?"

Getting me to stop smiling was a goal for all the counselors. According to them it was part of my armor. "We wear masks to protect ourselves, but they also keep us from being vulnerable," Richard announced the first week. "They keep us from achieving intimacy." During the Wednesday night Big Book meeting, a recovering alcoholic defined intimacy as "into-me-you-see." I'd written it down on the back page of my journal.

"Okay." I shook my head as if to shake off the smile and looked back down at my list. "When you told me you were from a better family than me, I felt bad."

"You're my mother," Charlotte said. "Tell her, 'you're my mother.'"

"You're my mother," I echoed.

"Tell her, 'I'm your blood. I'm your family.'"

"I'm your blood," I said to the chair. I realized that I was shivering. I looked at the list and couldn't distinguish the words. I looked at Charlotte. "Do I have to keep going?"

She nodded.

"When you told me you were beautiful, and I was average," I said, and then stopped. I couldn't speak through my chattering teeth.

Overseas, her looks, elegance, and status as an Abu Sa'ab all work together to ensure that she is loved. By the time I was in high school, our trips to Jordan had changed shape, contoured by summer jobs. One year, I got to Amman a few weeks before my mother. For days leading up to her visit I was questioned about when she'd be arriving. "I don't know exactly," I answered. Like a celebrity, my mother never told. When we found out she was on a connecting British Airways flight set to land at nine thirty, I watched as her friends and family changed out of their pajamas to meet her at the Four Seasons lounge once she arrived. I sat there with a glass of wine, exhausted by the anticipation of seeing her, hoping everyone would finish their drinks quickly so we could go home. I was fully aware that no one had forced me to join.

As a child I was lavished with attention for being Laila's daughter. In fact, that was the extent of who I was. *"Inti bint Laila?"* You're Laila's daughter? *"Yee! Habibti!"* For years I would freeload off of my mother's entitled adoration, reaping its benefits. I didn't have to do a thing to be loved, I just had to be. But as I got older the same people who'd kissed and pinched my cheeks would try to talk to me, assuming that I possessed her charming attributes only to discover that I didn't. My conversation was awkward, my gestures uncertain—a handshake or air kisses, and if the latter, two kisses or three? As an adult, my presence was off-putting.

I took a deep breath and tried again. "When you told me you were beautiful and I was average, I felt bad, because that's true, and I can't believe you would actually say it to me." My chest was heaving up and down, little bubbles rising like in water about to boil, rushing to the surface and popping in my throat. I couldn't see anything, not the faces of the others around the circle, not the list on my lap, not Charlotte beside me. I didn't want them to know these things. I didn't want anyone to know. I felt something on my knee—Charlotte's hand. "Tell her, 'that's not true.' Tell her!" she snapped.

"No."

"Say it!"

"I can't." And I really couldn't. "I want to go home!" Richard helped me up from the chair and onto my feet, but I collapsed into him, feeling exhausted and numb. He held me, kept holding me; he was so warm I didn't want him to let go. He walked with me in his arms to Greg and rolled me into him. Greg squeezed me hard. Richard instructed me to get a hug from everyone, and I obeyed, passed from one person to another. When I arrived at Charlotte, I was sobered by the sight of her. Before she could hug me I sat down and tried to collect myself, straightening my back and wiping the tears off my face.

In our room that night, Molly told me it was almost frightening, the way Charlotte seemed to be channeling me.

"It was like she could relate to what you've been through," Molly said. "She was genuinely upset when you were reading your list, which doesn't surprise me. It was really sad."

It's true: she had seemed upset. It was validating, in a way, but I didn't want Molly to know how much it meant to me. "Please," I said, folding my pillow in half and turning onto my side. Other Arab women have been mutilated by knives, shrapnel, acid, bombs, and I was shaken because my mother told me I was average? Is narcissism an inherited trait?

•

I'm not particularly fond of horses. I took a riding lesson once as a kid, and while walking the horse to the ring, it stepped on my foot and refused to move for a good five minutes. "Horses have a unique ability to heal," said the equine therapist, a stout woman with a thick straw-colored braid, once we'd all arrived in the stable. Several horses trotted by, raising their tails and kicking up dirt. The place felt more like an oversized playpen than an actual barn. "Today, you're going to work together to bridle Misty here." Misty snapped her tail and some flies scattered. A glob of drool fell from her mouth.

Alex took charge and started mapping out distances: the length between Misty's mouth and her back, the width between the bit pieces and the reins. Greg rubbed her snout and talked to her. Molly dusted off the saddle and wiped down her coat with a wet sponge she'd found in a bucket. I stood off to the side, wondering how petting a horse would benefit us in any way, and if the others were actually buying into it. It seemed so, given how pleased they were with their creative solutions, the herd of independent minds. Once Misty was all dolled up in her bridle, the therapist instructed us to sit on the log bench so we could discuss the activity. She paced back and forth like a drill sergeant. "Give yourselves a pat on the back," she said to us. "You all did an excellent job." Alex reached out for a high five, which she met with a heavy smack. Greg even tapped his own shoulder like an idiot. "Except for you," she said to me. "You just kind of checked out and wandered off."

I felt immediately compelled to defend myself. "I was still paying attention," I said, "but my group seemed to have it under control."

"Ah, so you're a freeloader?"

"I'm just saying they didn't need any more help, and I only like to do what's necessary."

"Uh-huh," she said. "Well, how do you know what's necessary, what you might be missing, unless you try it?"

But that was precisely my issue: wanting to try everything, and everyone. "I guess I don't," I said.

Next, she asked us to pick a horse and observe it. "What do you mean by *observe* it?" Molly asked.

"Whatever you want that to mean," she said, throwing her

hands up in the air, as if the thought of what we might come up with could be that exciting. "You can observe it up close, or from afar, or however you want."

After deciding to participate this time, I chose a mare in the distance and approached her slowly. When I reached out to touch her neck, she turned away. She snubbed the hay I tried to feed her as if I'd offered up a cow patty. "Fine, then." I sat down on a sunny patch of grass and watched the others. Greg's horse didn't appear interested in him, either, yet he was persistent. He tried smoothing out her mane, and every time she shook him away, he tried harder. "Figures," I muttered as I peeled apart a blade of grass. Molly made a garland out of dandelions and put it around her horse's neck. Alex stood scratching his head, his eyebrows in the upright position as his horse neighed at increasingly higher octaves. Soon the therapist instructed us to round up all the horses and bring them back to the barn. I tried to lure the mare along, holding an even bigger pile of hay a few feet in front of her. She stood there until another horse walked by, then trotted along beside it.

We piled back onto the log bench and waited for the therapist's diagnosis. "Looks like you're really starting to come together as a team," she said, "which is what it's all about here."

I was ready to accept the compliment when she darted a finger at me. "Yet again, you just sort of sat back and relaxed during that."

"I was respecting the horse's boundaries."

"Oh?"

"Clearly, she wanted to be alone, and I wasn't going to force myself on her. No one likes that. Not even horses."

She put her hands on her hips and nodded slowly. "Fair enough. But did you ever stop and think it might be your approach?"

I shrugged. "I tried giving her hay a few times but she didn't respond to it."

"Do you know what the definition of insanity is?"

I mumbled, "It's doing the same thing over and over and expecting different results."

"Right. And whatever that thing is, it's precisely what landed you here."

8

NINE DAYS DOWN. NINETEEN TO GO. BY THEN I WAS counting down with dread, rather than anticipation. At the end of group on Thursday, Charlotte told us that we'd be working with just Richard for the weekend, as she would be out until Monday. I was suddenly reminded of the artifice of the place. For them it was just a job; they left at the end of each day and stopped thinking about our problems. Instead they thought about their own: what they'd cook for dinner, their kids' homework, bills. Still, after Charlotte told us she'd be out, the noise in the room faded and all I could hear was my pulse. As everyone got up and headed outside to the vans, I stayed behind.

"Charlotte!" I called out without meaning to. "I'm not feeling well."

"What's the matter?" she asked.

I wasn't sure what to say to her. "I'm just very anxious." I started rubbing my thighs with my palms as though I was trying to start a fire.

"I'm going to lead you through some breathing exercises," she said. "Take my hands—"

"No," I said too emphatically as I pushed back in my chair.

"Okay, then just count to ten with me." We counted out loud in unison. I was painfully aware of the sound of my own voice. When we finally got to ten, she asked what was going on.

I tried to word it in treatment terms. "I feel myself acting out."

"Acting out, how?" she asked. "Is it your anorexia?"

"No." She'd read my file, of course. "I kicked that one. Well, sort of. I went to treatment for it a few years ago . . ."

"You're still recovering." She smiled. "I understand. I have an eating disorder, too."

I'd already suspected this, that we had this in common. I had watched her careful choices at the lunch buffet, noticing that she'd skip over mashed potatoes and pile on extra string beans or steamed carrots. I'd also pieced together a few random personal details based on things she'd mentioned in group, along with a few conversations I'd overheard between her and Richard: she was forty-five, married with two kids, and had been to treatment for meth addiction. "So what is it, then?" she asked.

"I feel myself acting out in my love addiction," I said, resisting the urge to roll my eyes. I couldn't use the term without wanting to mock it immediately afterward. The label was like something out of a teen movie, or some cheesy pick-up line—"Baby, I'm a love addict, and I need one more hit of you."

"Well, what does acting out look like for you?" she asked.

It usually started with the hollows of a particular collarbone—the professor's, the nutritionist's, the editorial assistant's, anyone's other than my actual partner's—growing into a full-fledged obsession with whomever they belonged to. In an attempt to escape my thoughts, I'd solicit and seduce others to the point of mental annihilation, only to wake up the next morning with my obsession fortified. Alcohol made it worse. So did drugs. Exercise, especially when combined with a playlist, was nearly lethal. And the factors that elevated the behavior from "bad crush" to addiction were time and intensity, as well as the compulsive behavior that accompanied it; namely, fucking to forget.

But at the Ledge, I was limited. "I guess it just means fantasizing," I said.

"Can you tell me who it is you're fantasizing about?"

"No. I'm sorry."

"Why not?"

"I just can't. I don't mean to be cryptic." I put my elbows on my knees and pressed my fingers to my temples. "I can't believe this is happening here."

"Well, sometimes, they say that when your addiction finds you in treatment, it's your higher power forcing you toward something you don't want to face." I tried not to remark on the mention of a higher power, which I'd regretted doing the first time. "Let me ask, do these people that you 'fall for'"—she made air quotes—"all have something in common?"

"What do you mean by 'in common'?" I asked.

"You know, like it's guys with dark hair, or guys with glasses, or something like that?"

•

When I got off the train in Florence from Paris via Turin, I realized I knew almost nothing in Italian. Not even *hello*. I knew "*ti amo*," as Kate had started signing off her emails with it when she returned from her semester abroad, the emails she sent asking if we could still be friends, a request she stopped making after a bar fight and a slap across my face. But that was the only expression I knew.

Why Italy? Kate, for one. I spent most of the semester Kate was abroad in my room, listening to *Kind of Blue* and feeling sorry for myself, wondering how many Italians she had slept with so far. Eventually I broke into her email and found out: all of them. I became enamored with the place, thinking that by experiencing it for myself and taking over a space that seemed to belong to her, I could conquer the pain and eliminate her from my memory. But by the time I graduated and boarded the plane, the pain of Kate had subsided, replaced by another relationship, another heartbreak. Still, I felt an urge to inhabit a new place, to detach myself from anything that felt familiar: the U.S., Jordan, Palestine. Those places all had notes in the margin that proved distracting. In order to think, I needed blank sheets.

It took me five years to finish college. After transferring to a new school, I took medical leave for a condition known informally as lollipop head syndrome, caused by acute anorexia. I finally graduated and returned to D.C. I spent that summer working at a coffee shop on Capitol Hill and living with my mother, money saved at a price much greater than rent. Our interactions were practically marital: I'd help her make decisions about travel, pick up dinner for us, deal with the bills. She seemed to think of me as a husband while still treating me like a child she could reprimand at any moment. By the end of August I could afford to buy a round-trip ticket to Europe. I left in early September and wouldn't be home for twelve months. By the time the trip arrived, I couldn't stand to stay at my mother's house for one more day.

"Via delle Carra," I said to the bus driver outside the Santa Maria Novella station in Florence. It was the name of my street, and the first Italian words I'd ever spoken. I had rented myself an apartment before getting to Florence. I got to the building and walked into the courtyard, where a group of young people sat playing cards and drinking. They offered me a glass of Chianti and I spent the evening drinking with them. There was a redhead from Copenhagen who worked in a local government office. There was a chef from Kerala who lived in Liverpool and had an effortful Cockney accent. There was a journalist from Madrid who wrote a weekly fashion column. And a designer from Prague, who spoke with a lisp and looked like she was post-lollipop, too. Everyone was referred to by their country of origin. They called me Palestina.

I couldn't sleep that night. Sleep would take away from my time there. Instead I stayed up with my *Let's Go Italy* guidebook, marking cities where I wanted to travel. Siena or Cinque Terre? Definitely Naples, which I'd heard was a lot like Nablus, pre-'48. Sicily, if I didn't run out of money by spring. I felt intoxicated by my levity. For the first time in years, I was bound to no one.

The following afternoon I enrolled in beginning Italian at the Dante Alighieri language school on Piazza della Repubblica. Every weekday I had lessons from nine to one with a mid-morning break at ten forty-five, which I would use to run across the street for an espresso. Sometimes I went to the deli next door for a pecorino sandwich or a Perugina chocolate. One morning a girl from class followed me there.

"Hey," a voice from behind me called. "Which is the flat kind?"

"What?" I turned around and looked where the girl's finger

was pointing, at the bottled water, two kinds, marked *frizzante* and *naturale*. "Oh," I said. "*Naturale.*"

"You're in my class," she said. She had blue eyes and blond hair, half a dozen friendship bracelets on each forearm, and the deepest voice I had ever heard out of a female. It was incongruous with her soft appearance, like a ballerina chewing tobacco. I chose a sandwich from the display and the man at the register rang me up. The girl grabbed a tray and asked, "Can I sit with you?"

We sat at a table outside with our sandwiches. Just as I was taking my first bite, she pulled out a pack of Lucky Strikes. "Want one?"

She was Dutch. Just finished high school, here for her gap year. Her older sister, who was twenty-three like me, did hers in Barcelona. She hoped she'd made the right decision by choosing Italy over Spain. She had one friend so far, a Salvadoran named Agos, also here for her gap year. They lived in a house with a bunch of American sorority girls. "They're loud as hell," she said, smooshing her cigarette onto the sidewalk and finally picking up her sandwich. "And it's fucking annoying."

"I live in a pretty cool building," I told her. "You should come hang out sometime."

"Can I come tonight?"

She showed up at seven, while my housemates were pregaming in the courtyard, the Keralan chef serving plates of penne with fresh marinara sauce. When she got up to use the bathroom, he asked, "Who's this blond bombshell you've brought to us? She's gorgeous!" The rest of the guys nodded along and chimed in with added praise.

All I saw was the blond hair, and after Kate I'd stopped

noticing blondes. "I didn't 'bring her' to you," I responded. "She's not some sort of sacrificial offering."

They nicknamed her the Sacrifice.

After that night the Sacrifice followed me everywhere. At first I found it irritating, a lost puppy trailing me wherever I went. She even showed me how to pedal my bike with her seated on the back. "It's how we do it in Holland," she said.

And so I pedaled through cobblestoned streets with the Sacrifice sitting behind me. We rode along the Arno River, over the Ponte Vecchio, all the way to Piazza de Michelangelo, way above the city, where a statue of the artist towers over Florence. In time I got used to the extra weight. And when it was absent, I found myself missing it.

•

Three months before Italy, I was living at my mother's apartment in Washington and learning how to call a coffee order. The various properties of a signature beverage—tall, grande, venti, skim, two percent, whole, extra shot, added flavor—had to be called to my "partner" at the espresso machine in the order that they were listed on the cup. After work I would return to the apartment, take off my apron, eat the free sandwich I'd received for working back-to-back shifts, and watch television.

I'd finally graduated, but had no idea what I wanted to do. So I accompanied my mother on her social outings. I would sit there smiling silently, my presence politely tolerated and largely ignored by my mother's friends. They all treated me like I was ten—"where's mama?" they'd ask if she left the table for a minute. But one friend of my mother's, a new friend who began coming to these outings more and more often, spoke to me like I was at least out of kindergarten. Each time I saw her she'd make a point to talk to me, a rarity among the others. I began to expect and look forward to it each time we went out. She'd asked what my plans were, did I want to stay in D.C., would I apply to grad school. She was attractive if not beautiful, her features dark and severe, except for her eyes, which were blue. It's rare for an Arab. She was Palestinian too, married to an ambassador, and from what I knew she played her role well.

One night I drove to a Persian restaurant in a rich D.C. suburb to pick up dinner. I walked in and spotted her at the counter. "I asked for three chicken-and-beef combos," she said to the man behind the register, raising her voice, "and *one* lamb. Very simple, I'm not sure how you managed to screw it up."

I started inching toward the door but she turned around before I could leave. "Oh, hello!" she said.

I waved awkwardly.

"It's just that," she fumbled for her wallet, "I have guests staying over." I nodded, unsure of what I was supposed to say. "Usually it's my husband who handles things like this," she continued.

My order was already waiting, and once hers was ready I helped carry it out to her car. I carefully placed the plastic bag of Styrofoam containers on the passenger seat and then buckled them in. I let her leave the parking lot first.

When I arrived back home, my mother was on the phone. After she hung up, she came into the kitchen, where I was pouring cucumber yogurt onto my rice. The ambassador's wife just called, she told me. I froze, the stream of yogurt slowing to a drip as she continued. "For some reason she wanted me to know that she's having a bad day today," my mother said. "And then she asked about you."

"Did she tell you I just ran into her?" I asked.

"You did?"

She leaned over and reached for a piece of chicken from my plate, her hair brushing against my arm. I could feel her eyes on me as she chewed, then swallowed. "Interesting."

•

The Sacrifice introduced me to Agos from El Salvador. Agos was boyish and still had baby fat, and she was warm like a grandmother. When she introduced herself to the guys in my building and told them where she was from, they nicknamed her the Savior.

The Sacrifice, the Savior, and I quickly established ourselves as a trio, going for long lunches after class, riding to bars and nightclubs on the back of each other's bike. We bought a pet hamster, Mr. Bandera. We got matching piercings through our upper ear cartilage, metal rods that all got infected within a month. We always knew where to find one another: at Caffè Giubbe Rosse, the coffee shop in Piazza della Repubblica where the Futurists used to congregate. Whenever I overslept I'd get there midway through class and attempt to read the paper in Italian, usually giving up in favor of the *International Herald Tribune*. I came to know the regulars, including an Iraqi playwright named Ahmed who'd fled his country after the war and was lucky enough to end up in Tuscany. We'd speak occasionally, sometimes in Italian, mine still rudimentary, and sometimes in Arabic. He asked me why I chose to live in Italy, and not Palestine or Jordan.

"I don't know," I said, feeling a pinch of guilt for being in Italy and not the West Bank, volunteering with refugees or resisting the occupation, or at least something related to my heritage. Every country outside of my own felt like a luxury, and at twenty-three, I wanted to indulge. In a way I felt I deserved to.

"I have no responsibilities here," I said. "And no ties to anyone."

He smiled, and his white beard spread like smoke. "You'll find that having someone who has a claim on you, and who you can claim, it's one of the greater things in life."

.

One night, after a double shift at the coffee shop, I met my mother and the ambassador's wife for dinner. I'd rushed to get there, mopping the floor in a hurry, forgetting to restock the condiments counter and toilet paper in the bathrooms. By the time I got to the restaurant, they were already eating dessert. I'd been starving when I left work, but when I sat down at their table I no longer felt hungry. Still, when the ambassador's wife offered me half of her chocolate ganache, I pretended as though I was.

Her driver had brought her to the restaurant, and as we were paying we decided that I would drop her off on my way home.

"My son's been having trouble in school," she said as we slowed to a stop at a traffic light. "He barely passed his classes this year."

I told her I wouldn't worry if I were her, that junior high's a tough time.

"I bet you were a good student."

I laughed as I put on my blinker. "I was kind of a troublemaker," I told her. "I didn't really have that many friends in school, so my main form of entertainment was driving my teachers crazy."

"I can't imagine that," she said. "You seem too sweet."

We inhabited a heavy silence for the rest of the ride. I attempted to make small talk, commenting on increased traffic and new housing developments, but she didn't respond to any of my remarks, just nodded in my peripheral vision. When we pulled up to the house, I turned to face her. I said good night.

"Do you want to come inside?"

I thanked her and said no, the expected response to the formality.

"Come. For a cup of tea."

I felt anxious as I put the car in park and turned off the engine. My heart beat faster—had I seen too many movies? I followed her past a security guard and giant blue hydrangeas. A Sri Lankan housekeeper opened the front door as we approached and took her purse as she walked through. In the foyer, a crystal chandelier lit the room from what felt like miles away. "Ampy, make Lipton," she said to the housekeeper. She looked at me. "Do you prefer something else?"

I shook my head. We sat down in the living room, me on the edge of the sofa and she in a leather armchair. I tried to think of something to say. Finally I asked how long she had lived in the house.

"A few years. Since my husband got the ambassador appointment. We were living in a smaller place before. Easier, I think." I gave a look that must've suggested confusion. "You need a lot of help in a place like this," she continued as Ampy walked in with a tray and placed it on the table. "And it's hard to find good workers in the States. They always want things—more money, time off to go back to their country. So we had to bring Ampy from overseas."

Ampy said nothing, just stirred sugar into the tea and handed her the cup and saucer. The ambassador's wife took them from Ampy's quivering hands, then blew the rising steam from the cup before taking a tiny sip. "Would you like to see the rest of the house?" she asked, putting the cup back on the tray and standing up. She brushed imaginary dust from her pants.

A shiver zipped through me. I stood and followed her to the kitchen. There was a granite-top island with half a dozen burners in the middle, pots and spatulas hanging above it. It looked like a restaurant kitchen. We barely stopped before she directed me through the next doorframe and into the dining room. She turned on the light. I stood in the doorway attempting to appear interested, though by then I was too anxious to notice anything. She flipped the switch off, and I followed her back through the living room to the foyer, to the bottom of the staircase that led upstairs, lined with framed family photos. She walked up a few stairs. I followed.

"This was in Courchevel," she said, pointing to a cluster of frames, "when my son was still a baby."

I tried to focus on the picture, on her son in his ski suit and goggles, but all I could think about was how close we were standing. Our upper arms touched and my teeth chattered. Unintentionally I dropped down a stair.

I told her I needed to go. She said nothing. I repeated it, that I needed to go home. I had no idea what was propelling me, but I was certain that I wasn't in control, that it wasn't me inching closer to her, and closer. I felt my spit dry up, abandoning me. She was still a step higher as I strained to reach her mouth. Before my lips touched hers, she pulled back. Her blue eyes seared through my brown ones. "I'm sorry," I said. What had I just done? "I'm so sorry."

She then took my hands, and again, and I let her lead. I stared up at her as we ascended the stairs, my stomach dancing. We got to the top and I peered down the hallway, which was punctuated by a series of doorways. She brought me to the last one, to a room with a canopy bed and a dresser on each side. One of them was covered with perfume bottles, makeup brushes, compacts. The other held just a box of tissues and a comb. "Our room," she said, reminding me that she was married, she had a husband. She kissed my cheek and I felt myself get excited. Ashamed, I looked away. She then took my chin and turned my face so that we were looking directly at each other. Again she kissed me. Her breath inside my mouth was hot, I could taste the chalkiness of her lipstick. She placed her palms on my shoulders and pushed me gently toward the bed. As the backs of my knees hit the frame, I instinctively scooted up along the side of the mattress. She climbed on top of me, her arms straight and her hair spilling onto my shirt. "I haven't done this in a while," I said, "but I'm not sure I should tell you that."

"It's okay," she said, "you don't have to say anything." She smiled, and gently touched the tips of her fingers to my face. "In fact, better if you don't."

•

Our trio took a train to Venice one weekend in early October. I had just started working as a production assistant at a Berlusconi-owned television station, getting paid under the table since I didn't have a work visa, so we could afford a hotel room over a hostel.

Agos slept on the couch, and the Sacrifice and I shared the bed. The Sacrifice fell asleep right away the first night. She breathed heavily and slowly while she slept, like an infant. I stared at the ceiling and thought about nights I'd spent sleeping in my mother's bed after my father moved out. I'd lie awake then too, listening to my mother's breathing, wondering if my father would ever live with us again, how long I would get to occupy his spot. For much longer than I'd expected, it turned out. I lay listening to the Sacrifice exhale until the rhythm of her breaths eventually lulled me to sleep.

•

After that first night, I only saw the ambassador's wife at her house, usually in her bedroom, after she had come home from whatever gala, whatever dinner, whatever event. Her husband was overseas for most of the summer, so she would accept the invitations on his behalf. By the time I arrived she had usually changed out of her evening wear. She'd be in her robe or her nightgown, sometimes in long-sleeved cotton pajamas, which were always disappointing. Didn't she want to impress me? I would spend hours getting dressed for her. I told my mother I was seeing someone new, which I was—a guy from the coffee shop, but just until ten or so. I needed him to counterbalance her. I'd make sure he got his orgasm before leaving his house and rushing to hers. Ampy would let me in without saying a word. I would climb the stairs to the master bedroom, and I'd stand in the doorway as she sat at her vanity mirror, removing makeup. "Why are you just standing there?" she asked once while blotting Lancôme Effacil onto a cotton ball.

I fidgeted and told her that I didn't want to impose.

She put down the cotton ball, glared into the mirror, and squinted. "All this, and you don't want to impose?"

What is *all this*, I wanted to ask, and why did I feel completely incidental to it? But I was afraid that asking for interpretation or definition would disrupt things. I was afraid that any verbal acknowledgment of what we were doing would somehow get back to my mother. So instead I stayed quiet, just as she'd instructed. I walked toward her. She was still staring at her reflection as I placed my hands on her shoulders, leaned over, and kissed her cheek.

•

After work I would pedal fast to the Sacrifice's house with vodka, ricotta cheese, little toasted squares, Nutella. Usually I'd find her sitting on the veranda, smoking cigarettes. "You're too young to be such a heavy smoker," I would say.

"Shut up," she'd respond, lighting one for me.

We spent weeks planning her nineteenth birthday; she'd requested a dinner at Il Tavolo, three-star Michelin ranked, followed by dancing. "Can you make the reservations?" she asked. Eventually I stopped learning Italian and started learning Dutch. "Hey," I called out while she was on the phone with her sister back in Holland. She looked over at me and I said, "*Badkamer!*" Bathroom.

We'd been playing a game for the past few weeks where I would call out inane Dutch vocabulary, and she would praise me. This time she burst out laughing, her laugh throaty, then she mouthed, "elephant shoe." I had taught her that trick, that when you mouth those words, it looks like *I love you*. I watched her practice it, her lips forming a pout each time she got to the word *shoe*.

In November, Karim came to visit with his friend Martin, who also happened to be Dutch. I brought the Sacrifice along almost everywhere we went, and if she wasn't there, then I was talking about her, telling stories about things she'd done, funny things she'd said. "Are you in love with her or something?" Karim asked.

"What?" I felt my cheeks redden. I had never told my brother about Kate, or that I was attracted to women. I couldn't imagine how he would react to it; the thought of him knowing was mortifying. "Of course not," I said. "Actually, I was thinking Martin might be interested, since they both live in Amsterdam." I turned to Martin.

"Um, no thanks," he said. "She seems like kind of a brat."

After their visit I got evicted. Apparently, guests weren't allowed in the apartment complex, and renter's rights seemed to hardly exist in Tuscany. I considered leaving the country. My entry visa had expired, and even with my job I was barely making enough to live on. Maybe it was time to go home.

The Sacrifice cried when I told her this. "You can't leave," she said.

"But I don't have an apartment anymore," I said. "And I could barely afford the one I had."

"Then you can live with me," she said. "You can share my room!" I felt my chest tighten, and immediately I thought of Kate. During an argument toward the end of our relationship she tried to break up with me, but I begged for another chance. "But I'm Catholic!" she said. I was able to muster a laugh through my tears. "And I'm Muslim! Isn't that worse?"

She then offered up a compromise: we could continue to live together, to share a room, a bed, even, but no sex. In desperation I accepted, and the torturous situation helped me slowly wither away.

I looked up at the Sacrifice. "Okay," I said.

That evening I got my stuff together and hauled it to her place.
I dragged my suitcase up the stairs to the bedroom and then lay
down on one of the two single beds. "Why don't we push them
together," she said, "and make one big bed?"

We stayed up most nights talking and watching movies on
a laptop in our makeshift full-size bed. I told her about Kate,
only I referred to her as "Jeremy," concerned that I might scare
her if I told her the truth. She told me about her last boyfriend,
how while she enjoyed the sex she didn't know if it was possible
to form an emotional connection with a man. "Sounds like you
had that with Jeremy, though," she said. And I nodded quickly,
unable to look her in the eye.

●

At the coffee shop I was delivering the wrong drinks, mixing up
orders, forgetting to froth the milk or add cinnamon. "I said iced,"
customers would complain. "Not extra hot." I'd smile as their
words bounced off my brain like flies off a window screen, refusing to allot even minimal mental space to anyone other than the
ambassador's wife. I pictured our future ahead: lots of traveling.
We'd swim in the Mediterranean, make love while tan and salty,
eat mussels and drink Sancerre. All of my fantasies were steeped in
simplicity and abstracted away her husband, her son. My mother.

"Tell me a secret," she demanded one afternoon.

I asked what kind of secret she wanted. At the time, *she* was my biggest secret. I struggled to think of something else. I started wetting the bed my freshman year of high school, I told her.

"What?"

"I had to go to a doctor about it," I continued, her interest shrinking my inhibitions. "And he sent me to a psychologist who told me I did it because I was afraid." I laughed, hoping that she would, too.

She didn't. "Afraid of what?"

I hadn't expected her to ask for details—she rarely did—and I hesitated before answering. "I used to hate going to bed because my parents would always wake me." My mind wandered to shattered glass on their bedroom floor, patches of water staining the white walls. I recalled my father's bloodied teeth as he elbowed his way in front of my screaming mother to tell me what she'd done. "He hit me first!" she would cry. "Call the police!"

I remembered Karim and me riding in the back of a cop car to the station at three a.m. We sat in a waiting room, not knowing where exactly they'd taken our parents. We held each other and wept until someone came and offered us blankets and candy that neither of us wanted. When we returned home the following morning, I went to our neighbor Heather's house instead of to school. I needed sleep but couldn't bear to be near my parents, so I napped in her bed while she went to class. The next day at school, an official-looking man pulled me out of homeroom and asked me questions about my mother. He kept telling me our conversation was private, that I didn't have to worry about him telling her. But I didn't say anything, because what if he *did* tell her? What would she do to me then?

I looked up and realized that the ambassador's wife still hadn't said anything. "Anyway," I said. "I guess I was afraid even while I slept."

A few days later, I was in the shower before work. My mother was standing at the bathroom sink, blow-drying her hair. As I stepped out and reached for a towel from the rack she asked, "What are those scratches on your back?"

I peered over my shoulder, examining my backside in the mirror as my heart pulsed. "Oh," I said, trying to sound relaxed, "I think it's just from work."

"How? You work at a coffee shop!"

"I don't know, maybe Lucy did it while I was sleeping." Our cat. I concentrated on drying off, squeezing my wet hair into the towel as my mother stared at me.

"You're *weird*, you know?" she said. "You scare me."

I reached for the hair dryer and turned to her. "Can you wait until I'm done with the bathroom?"

"I don't like you living here anymore," she said. "By the end of the summer I want you out."

"Don't worry," I assured her. I pictured myself with the ambassador's wife, on the Amalfi coast, my stomach surged with excitement. "I'm planning to get out as soon as possible."

•

We found the coat in a boutique near Piazza di Santa Croce. It was white, with fur around the hood that fluttered when she exhaled. And when she wore it she looked regal. I wanted her to have it, to think of me every time she slipped her arms into the sleeves, as if somehow that meant I could keep her. "I love it," the

Sacrifice said, trying it on and looking at herself in the mirror from various angles. "But it's so expensive."

"I'll buy it for you," I called out, like a last bid at an auction, surprising even myself. Even living rent-free, I was still spending more than I made at the television station. "As a present."

"Really? Are you sure?"

We rode home together, the Sacrifice on the back of my bike, in her new coat, her arms wrapped around my waist. I could smell her Gucci Rush as the cold air whisked it away. We locked up my bike and went to her bedroom, closed the door, and put on a movie. When she fell asleep I burrowed my nose in her blond hair, closed my eyes, and inhaled deeply.

I had never been more sure.

•

"So why did you marry your husband?" I asked as she lay next to me. It was six in the evening and I'd been there since ten a.m. I had called in sick to the coffee shop so that I could spend a full weekday with her, from start to finish, or at least until her son came home from a day at sports camp. When I arrived she was in the kitchen making toast. She led me upstairs and invited me into the shower. Afterward we had lunch and then sex that I didn't deserve—I was not attractive enough to be there, and I feared the moment she would realize it. Pink rays started to spill across the bed and I knew that I would have to leave soon.

"Were you in love?" I asked. She was far better-looking than her husband, she took better care of herself, so I assumed it was because he had status, power, money.

She pulled back. "Yes," she said, appearing insulted by the insinuation that she wasn't. "Very much so. I'm still in love with him."

I felt like I'd been pricked with a pin, the air escaping from inside me. "Oh," I said. I hesitated before deciding to press further. "Sorry, but what are we doing, then?"

"What do you mean?" she asked, as if she hadn't been there for any of it. The question crushed me in its honesty. Until then, I didn't know. I thought that the intensity of sex was correlated with love. That passion was specific and that adultery meant something was wrong.

"I don't know if you realize this," I said. I felt my face getting hot. "But you sometimes say 'I love you.'"

I'd been clinging to her I-love-yous like a refugee clings to a threatened nationality. They were the homeland that validated my existence.

She turned away from me. I watched her back muscles strain and flex as she got up and walked to the bathroom. She took her robe off a hook, covering herself before closing the door. I could tell I'd ruined things, I felt rejected, defeated, worthless. I felt myself shattered to pieces. I got up and pulled on my clothes. I knocked lightly on the bathroom door. She said nothing. I considered apologizing, though for what exactly, I wasn't sure. I was breathing heavily, anger welling up. I wanted to beg her to forget what I'd asked, to just keep going as we'd been. Instead I went downstairs, stopped in the kitchen for my bag, and left.

The next day I called her cell phone and got her voice mail. I called back, again and again. I left messages until her inbox was full, at which point I called her landline. Ampy told me she was out. "Where? When is she supposed to be back? Will you please tell her to call me? It's urgent."

As she had already made clear by not questioning my presence each night, Ampy was loyal to her boss's privacy. She didn't respond.

The following night, after it was dark, I drove by the house. The lights were on, and I peered into her bedroom window. For a moment, I thought I could see two silhouettes moving behind the curtains. Was her husband home? As I drove closer the guard stepped out of his booth. I rolled down my window. "I've been here before," I said, as if he didn't know.

He shook his head. "Sorry. No guests today."

I rolled the window back up and drove away, defeated.

In the morning I called in to work and told my boss I was still sick, that I probably had mono. I lay on my bed with Lucy at the foot of it and stared at the blank white ceiling. Our abrupt ending left me feeling abandoned, and the pain of it was unbearable. I needed an explanation. I needed to know that it wasn't my fault.

A few weeks later, my mother received an invitation for a gala benefiting Palestinian youth. Suspecting that the ambassador's wife would be there, I asked if she would bring me as her plus one, and she agreed. She even let me borrow a dress.

We arrived early, and from where we were seated I could see the entire room. I watched the main door as people entered, waiting for her to appear. Finally, I saw her. My stomach somersaulted. She wore a long dress decorated with traditional Palestinian embroidery, a black shawl wrapped around her shoulders. I observed her greeting people, tilting her head back mechanically and laughing, the tips of her fingers pressed to her clavicle.

Every so often she'd pop over to her own seat and take polite nibbles of whichever course had just been served.

After dessert, she floated over to our table. She seemed completely at ease, unfazed by my presence. I felt waves of euphoria tinged with fear. Anxiety rising and crashing inside me. She greeted each person individually with two kisses, sometimes a third, never actually touching her lips to their cheeks. She had perfectly crafted fifteen-second conversations with everyone she encountered, effusively complimenting dresses and offering remarks on weight loss, asking about kids and summer travel. As she was making her way around the table, closer to me, a man with a dark ponytail and thick mustache approached her from behind, sneaking up and wrapping his arms around her. She squealed with delight as she turned to see who it was, placing a deliberate hand on his chest and leaning in to hug him. Who was this guy—another lover? I'd never seen him before, not at any of our other events, and I immediately pictured them in bed together. I felt my chest swell, my throat quivering. He placed a hand on the small of her back and led her away to his table, shattering all my hopes for the two of us communicating.

I tried not to keep watching her but she was constantly present in my peripheral vision. When I noticed her walking toward the bathrooms I stood up, tossed my napkin onto my plate, and followed her. I turned the corner and called out, "What's going on?"

She swung around and her hair twirled like a whirling dervish. "Are you crazy?"

An electric current shot through my stomach. "What?"

"Honestly, what are you doing, following me?"

"Why are you acting like you don't even know me?"

She didn't answer. Instead she derailed, pushing past me and back out to the party. I stood there, fuming. "You *bitch!*" I yelled out loud to myself. I was sick of staying quiet, of keeping things secret. I am not an object—I'm not just Laila's daughter. I exist!

I went into the bathroom and stared at my reflection, trying to gather strength. I returned to the party but when I walked into the room my eyes blurred with tears. I ran to the coat check, which was empty since it was summer. My mother chased after me. "What's the matter?" she asked, and I turned around, collapsing into her. I couldn't help myself. But it wasn't safe to tell her what was wrong, and she never insisted on knowing.

•

By January I still hadn't gone anywhere besides Venice. I had made several attempts but each time I disappointed myself in my inability to pull away, even for a weekend. The Sacrifice was leaving soon, to go skiing with her family in Switzerland, then to Rome for the spring. One night I came home tipsy and found her in bed reading. Once I managed to get out of my clothes and into my pajamas, I started jumping on the bed. She laughed. "What are you doing?"

I kept jumping, spinning around in midair and tapping the ceiling with my palms, until I fell onto her. We lay there staring at each other, giggling and breathing heavily. When the room stopped spinning I looked down at her mouth. I had observed it intently over the past months, watched it suck the tips of cigarettes, lick gelato, sip wine, kiss cheeks, kiss *my* cheeks. I could feel her staccato heartbeats as I inched closer to her face, her breaths coming at me in short puffs. By now we were both quivering, goose bumps lining the surfaces of our bare arms.

For a brief moment, the ambassador's wife flashed through my mind. Within seconds, she was gone.

I pressed my cheek against the Sacrifice's. My eyelashes fluttered against her cheekbone. I then reached up and pushed her bangs back with my hand, and kissed her forehead, pressing my mouth against it fully. Finally I pulled back, rolled off her, and faced the wall. I didn't turn back around until I heard her breathing rhythmic sleep breaths.

A few days later, I accompanied her to the airport. We barely spoke during the bus ride or at the ticket counter. When it was time to go through security, she fumbled in her backpack and pulled out a neatly folded piece of paper.

"Bye," she said, handing it to me. She turned and walked away.

I waited until I could no longer see her to open up the note. It was just one line. *I'm tired of elephant shoe. I love you.*

I stared at it for a while before crumpling it up and putting it in my pocket. On the bus ride home, I sat against the window and watched cars whip by on the autostrada. When I got back I noticed that she'd forgotten to pack her Smurf pillowcase. I lay down and buried my face in it. Hours later I was still lying there when I heard, "Hey! Get up!"

Agos was standing in the doorway, though I didn't turn to look at her. "Come on," she said. "Let's go to Giubbe Rosse."

"I don't feel like it."

She sighed. "You're pathetic. You know that, right? It's draining."

I nodded, keeping my cheek pressed to the pillow. Agos then

lay beside me and tossed an arm across my back. "Completely pathetic, I swear."

I left Italy six months earlier than planned, at the end of March. I flew back to D.C., grabbed the rest of my stuff from my mother's apartment, and immediately moved to New York. I'd found a sublet in East Harlem that I could afford, and a job working as an administrative assistant for a magazine. It wasn't exactly the role I wanted—I would essentially be a secretary. But still, it was a start.

•

I looked past Charlotte as I answered her question. "I suppose it's usually unattainable women."

"Unattainable, how?" she asked.

"Like they're straight," I said. "Or married. Or there's a professional boundary." I looked off to the side, away from her. "Or all of the above." I was certain right then that she knew.

"Well, I encourage you to look at why this happens, and what's really going on."

She was starting to sound clinical and it made me nervous. "Do you think I'm completely fucked up?" I asked.

"No, I don't." Then she looked me in the eye. From that close I could see more wrinkles, like stars in a rural sky. I could smell her watermelon-flavored chapstick. She raised her shoulders and parted her lips, and said, "I really like you!"

My insides lit up like E.T. She didn't intend it the way I wanted her to—at least not yet—but still. It meant something.

By mid-July of my childhood summers in Jordan, I was homesick for America. I'd make a list in my journal of the things I missed most about the States: peanut butter, cow's milk, Nickelodeon, grass, Heather, my next-door neighbor and best friend. From a distance, the U.S. seemed so beautiful, so welcoming, so easy. How could I spend a minute unhappy there? I promised myself that when I returned I would appreciate every little thing.

This heightened fondness for the States lasted for the duration of the car ride from Dulles Airport to our house. The first night back in my bed always felt strange, like it was someone else's. By the time school started the next day I was desperately missing Jordan. I'd long for nights on Teta's veranda, watching her lay out Arabic newspapers and roll grape leaves, the combination of watermelon and halloumi cheese, fried falafel balls poking out of oil-soaked paper bags, roadside fruit tents with peaches spilling off the display and onto the earth, the sound of the three-stringed oud coming from the wedding at the nearby hotel, the sight of the green-lit minarets and the muezzin's lyric voice calling everyone to prayer. Above all, I longed for the smell

of the jasmine flowers that were outside every apartment building, though curiously I hardly noticed them while I was there.
It seemed I could only ever smell them from thousands of miles
away.

9

MIDWAY THROUGH THE TWENTY-EIGHT DAYS, WE WERE A given one free afternoon in "town," a strip composed of Plato's Closet, Pizza Hut, and a Christian bookstore. It was one of the perks advertised on the Ledge's website and that Nancy had touted, along with the "gourmet" food. During our outing, I picked up a few extra T-shirts and a pair of Umbro shorts at Plato's Closet. I then wandered into the Christian bookstore. "I would encourage you to look at why this happens," Charlotte had said, "and what's really going on." There was no psychology section, just philosophy, and I picked a book by Søren Kierkegaard off the shelf. I hadn't read him since an undergrad class on religious existentialism, but I recalled that angst was his specialty. I sat on the floor in back of the bookshop and started reading *Either/Or*. "Desire in our age is simultaneously sinful and boring, because it desires what belongs to the neighbor."

I tossed the book aside and took out my notebook. At the top of a blank page I wrote and underlined the word *Charlotte*. Underneath it, I wrote, *First sighting: Yoga class. No conversation. No attraction yet. 2nd sighting: Cafeteria. Skipped mashed potatoes, went straight to salad bar. Eating disorder suspected, later confirmed. Still no attraction. 3rd sighting: Group, Day 6.*

At the start of group each morning we did an emotional check-in. "I'm feeling frustrated," I'd announced on the first day that Charlotte was working with us, "by how much time we've wasted so far. A lot of the things we've done so far seem pretty unnecessary."

When it was Charlotte's turn to check in, she'd said she felt the same. "Time is money. It shouldn't be wasted." We made eye contact and she smiled, a thick curl falling onto her face. I smiled back.

Attraction detected.

In my notebook, I tried to identify that moment for others. "Let's say I was to write you a love letter," the nutritionist said to me during group three summers ago, and all the other lollipop heads turned to look at me as if something had actually transpired. "I would need to eat carbs to have the energy for that."

In my journal, I marked down, *Nutritionist: a hypothetical remark, misinterpreted as suggestive.* I had already scheduled a one-on-one session for the following day, and after our first appointment I started seeing her once a week. Before each meeting I would plan what issues I'd present and what references I'd casually toss into our conversation, ones specifically designed to impress her based on information I'd gleaned from her semi-public Myspace page. And it worked: a few weeks later we were deep in all-night online chats. "I would get in so much trouble right now if anyone knew I was doing this," she confessed, and I smiled at the illicitness of our correspondence.

"You're fun," the Palestinian social chair of the Arab Student Association wrote to me after an impromptu lunch my second junior year of college, during which we'd traded stories of our verbally abusive foreign mothers. "Luckily their English vocabulary is so limited," she quipped, "otherwise who knows how much worse it would be." A few nights later at an ASA barbecue, she asked if she could use my lip balm. I took it out of my pocket and tried to hand it to her. "My fingers are covered in chicken grease," she said, lifting them limply so I could see. "Can you put it on for me?" She puckered her lips and I traced her mouth with a moistened fingertip. I spent the next few months introducing her to different kinds of alcohol, which she hadn't been exposed to at her Islamic high school. "You've corrupted me," she said as she swayed through my living room before puking. We once spent a week sharing a single bed in Beirut, where her extended family lived—as '48ers rather than '67 Palestinians, their fate was to be exiled to camps in Lebanon rather than live under occupation—and where I had "coincidentally" planned to be that summer. The two of us slept side by side, her dark hair splayed across the pillow, indistinguishable from my own. I only stayed a few days—I'd driven from Jordan, something you could do back then, when Syria was still intact—and tried to keep my flirtations restrained so that her parents wouldn't suspect my intentions. She responded in kind, matching my restraint while remaining suggestive. During the day we'd wander through town shopping; I'd step into the dressing room with her and her mother as she tried on clothes. I tried to act natural, neither fixating on her body nor looking away entirely so that her mother wouldn't suspect something was off. At night we'd go to lengthy dinners with her cousins and pass around *argileh*; I'd watch her take long puffs from the decorated pipe, the water bubbling as she pressed her lips against the plastic mouthpiece. As hard as I tried, I couldn't get her to act on her flirtations. The closest I ever came to kissing her was at a pop-up nightclub in our college town that two Turkish grad students had started, and where I occasionally DJed. "Come get this ice cube from my mouth," she taunted. I didn't waste any time, abandoning the booth and capturing her lips with my own, the ice cube spilling onto my tongue. Somehow it was warm. I stepped back reluctantly, and she smiled. "You just kissed me," she said. "Gross."

But then, what to make of M.O'D., the editorial assistant at my magazine job in New York? "Can you bring me those author contracts by COB today?" she ordered, as if I were her personal secretary rather than everyone's. I did it anyway, eagerly. I felt compelled to impress her, as though her blanket disapproval made it necessary to dispel the assumption that I was an idiot. Every Friday, the staff would go out for happy hour, one of the few chances I had to speak with M.O'D. outside the office. But I was always stuck with a seat at the opposite end of a long picnic table, her back somehow always facing me. "Maybe she just feels threatened by you," offered the syndications coordinator, my only friend at the magazine. It was a generous interpretation, as M.O'D. clearly had no reason to be threatened. While she got to shape essays, my interactions with writers was limited to cutting their checks, then fielding passive-aggressive emails if someone hadn't received payment. The highlight of my time at the magazine was the month spent preparing to perform at the office holiday party, hoping my a cappella rendition of "Santa Baby" would win her over. When the evening finally arrived, my heart sank as I watched her get up from her table and leave the room just before I stepped on stage.

Editorial assistant: mild disregard, eventually morphing into a complete shunning.

I looked at the constellation of names scattered across the

page. I started randomly drawing a line connecting them until Molly bounded into the shop. "There you are!" she said. "We've all been sitting in the van waiting for you!"

Though she seemed uncomfortable after finding out I was a "homosexual," Molly now followed me wherever I went, never more than a few feet away, and chimed in on every conversation. When I'd wander off with someone else she'd trail along. "Groups of three at all times, guys!" she'd announce, as though she were a chaperone at a high school dance. During morning meditation I'd feel her staring at me as she anxiously peeled skin off her face, her feet, her nose. At night she'd sit on the edge of my bed and pick.

I tried to seem calm when I asked her to stop one day after group, while we were hanging out in the basement. "I'm just really OCD about germs," I said.

Molly paused, then said, "I think you're cool, but I get the feeling you don't like me."

My stomach churned a little, and a smidge of guilt tainted my conscience. "I do like you," I said, "but when you crowd me I feel irritated."

That's how we were supposed to express our emotions, with "When you . . . I feel" statements. Molly nodded, seemingly entranced. "Well, what I've learned," she said, "is that when someone bothers you in some way, like really gets under your skin, it's usually because they remind you of someone else in your life." She nodded vigorously as if convincing herself of her own theory, pleased to be in the counselor role. She looked to me for approval. I found myself wanting her to cite her sources—where had she learned this? From whom? It seemed somewhat ridiculous, almost too convenient. "So, me, for example, do I remind you of someone?"

"Yes."

"Who?"

"A person who crowds me and makes me feel irritated."

She laughed and pressed her palm against my shoulder. "Seriously! Like your mom, or maybe your dad?"

I shrugged and sat down on the couch. I tried to think of who in my life Molly reminded me of—my parents? my brother? Anna?—but my mind inevitably snapped back to Charlotte, like an excited puppy on a leash.

"What's wrong?" Molly prodded.

I looked around and then lowered my voice. "I like someone here."

"Is it Greg?" We both looked over at him; he was standing at the foosball table, dramatically twirling the rods. Earlier Molly had spotted us walking back from the woods, leaves stuck to our clothing and bits of dirt marring our bare legs. "Were you two doing what I think you were doing?" she'd asked.

"No!" we'd responded in unison. In fact, I had just given him a blow job, hoping that it would distract us both from the things we really wanted. Giving head was the easiest way to manufacture a sense of control, one that I'd been craving ever since I'd gotten to the Ledge. It didn't last long—we'd gone weeks without physical contact—and when he came, I realized I hadn't thought of Charlotte the entire time.

"Come on, you guys," Molly had whined while I'd removed pine needles from my shorts. "You're not supposed to be doing that!"

I looked over at Greg as he sent the players into a mad spin, the ball bouncing off the table and against the wall. "Someone else," I said.

"Well, why don't you say something to whoever it is?"

"It's not like that, with this person."

"Have you ever actually told anyone you've fallen for how you felt about them?"

Had I? I realized then that I had never confessed my feelings to any of the women. Not even to Kate. For a moment I considered saying something to Charlotte. But I was stuck there and would have to see her every day afterward. And yet, even if I never had to see her again, I wasn't sure that I'd want her to know. Because then what?

"I haven't, actually," I said.

"Well, maybe you should try it and see what happens," Molly said. "You know, the definition of *insanity*—"

"I know the definition of *insanity*, Molly, thanks." Again I felt the guilt smidge, so I softened my answer. "Look, don't worry," I assured her. "I've been rereading Pia Mellody." I took the book out of my purse to prove it to her. "I'm trying to figure out what's causing this, and how I can make it stop."

I'd just begun reading a section on the emotional cycles of love addiction, which Pia described with formulaic certainty. *As love addicts begin to develop a relationship with the object of their affection,* she wrote, *they stop seeing who that person actually is, but instead focus on a fantasy image, which they place like a beautiful mask over the head of the real human being.*

Molly shook her head and smiled. "Read all you want," she said with uncharacteristic authority. "But you'll just end up a more informed prisoner."

A chill passed through me. I thought about that for a moment before I opened the book to where I'd left off.

KATE AND I HAD BEEN SECRETLY SLEEPING TOGETHER for almost a month when I noticed a bruise on her upper thigh. "What's that?" As the question left my mouth I feared I wouldn't want to hear the answer.

"Oh. Blake," she said. "He does that when I'm on top of him."

Kate was a "best-looking" senior-superlatived, field-hockey-captained, Camel Light–smoking, Dead-bootleg-listening straight woman. She was also my freshman-year college room-mate. Blake was a golden-dreadlocked, sharp-nosed surfer. He was a townie, and older than both of us. Kate had been sleeping with him for two weeks. I pretended not to mind.

In the light of day, she and I had never spoken about our nights. The closest we came to talking about it was the morning after the first time we hooked up. We'd gone out for her birthday the night before, to the bar where I worked. She wore a Billa-bong hoodie that hugged her torso. Over drinks I'd given her a present: David Gray's *White Ladder*. After opening her gift, she leaned across the table and kissed me on the cheek. I could smell Blue Moon on her breath. We ordered stuffed oysters, a ques-tionable choice at a college dive. A pre-set eighties mix blared through the speakers; we got up to dance when "Take On Me" came on, moving our bodies closer and shimmying our way to the floor, then grabbing on to each other to pull ourselves back up. I could feel people watching, and I liked it. Once home we put on the CD—it was whiny, brooding, melodramatic—and we lay side by side to listen. Nothing out of the ordinary until she began caressing my face; tracing my eyebrows, my nose, my lips. Then she kissed me. Nervous, I stopped her. "I don't want to ruin our friendship," I said. It was a line from movies, what the girl always said when a guy friend made a move.

Kate tilted her head back a little too far and laughed. "Don't worry. We're just, you know, 'experimenting.'"

So I didn't worry. Besides, I wasn't attracted to Kate, so maybe it was safe to let her "experiment" with me. But when I woke up the next morning and glanced at her beside me, still asleep, the danger was apparent. She looked different than she had the day before. How had I never noticed her long brown lashes? Her strict, elegant nose? Her pink pastel lips? I slid out of bed and tip-toed to my side of the room. I had no desire to leave her, but was afraid that waking up beside each other would be too jarring.

It was the first day of spring break. We were spending the week road-tripping along the Florida coast with her friends. It was a thirteen-hour drive south to Fort Lauderdale, our first stop. After about thirty minutes I heard Kate shifting in her bed. "What time is it?" she called out from under the covers, her voice muffled by the comforter.

"Still early," I said. After that we said nothing to each other as we packed on opposite sides of the room. I filled the silence with paranoid speculation. Was she ashamed by what we'd done? Had it been awful for her? Or had she been too drunk to remember? For a moment I worried that I had somehow taken advantage of her, or worse, imagined it. But, no, she had made the first move. And it *had* happened. I could still smell her on my pajamas.

In the car on the way to pick up her friends we slowed to a stop at a traffic light. "So," she said, "does this mean we can't join the military?"

Over the next week, we made out in Fort Lauderdale, Boca Raton, Miami, Key West. She'd drop a quick kiss on my cheek when no one was looking, touch my thigh under tables, climb into my sleeping bag after everyone else had passed out. We returned home and continued, finally having sex.

Three weeks after Florida I watched her leave the bar with Blake in the middle of my set. I'd never seen him before, and I asked the bartender who he was. Apparently he was a local craftsman. He'd been in Costa Rica for the past few months on an extended surfing trip. He had honey-colored dreadlocks and a deep tan. I kept eyeing him, watching him order a succession of Red Stripes and greet the numerous women who came up to hug him. He seemed equally excited to talk to each of them, and I imagined that every last one of them walked away feeling wanted. I noticed him noticing Kate, which triggered deep panic. I kept looking over as he subtly inched his way closer to where she was sitting. I wanted to cry when I saw him tap her on the shoulder, then offer a little wave when she turned around to see who it was. A good move, I thought to myself. I overheard him ordering another beer, and asking if she wanted one as well, which she did. "Hey!" the chef called out to me. "Order up. Orders, in fact." I looked to the kitchen window and saw several steaming plates waiting to be carried out. I had no choice but to turn away from the horrific scene of Kate and Blake, just as they were laughing about something. Before heading to the kitchen I reached over the bar and poured myself a shot of Jägermeister, then another.

The place was packed, and I could only catch snippets of them talking. Why did they keep laughing? What was so funny? I thought I might die when she tapped his stomach, the lines of his six-pack visible through his shirt. But no, that came later, as I watched him drop a twenty on the bar, take her hand, and lead her out the front door.

After they left I drank three Rail Royales, the house specialty consisting of a shot of every liquor in the rail and a splash of Sprite. I clocked out, got in my car, and backed into a dumpster.

I'm not sure how long I'd been sitting there when a cop appeared and tapped on the plastic driver's-side window. Instead of unzipping it, I opened the door and spilled out of the car. "She's sleeping with someone else," I cried as I stumbled into the policeman. "And I'm falling in love with her." He collected me in his arms as I thrashed against his chest, tipsy passersby stopping to view the spectacle. I imagined that in fear, if not compassion, he dropped the charge from a DUI to underage possession. He called a cab and sent me home.

I didn't see Kate until the following night. I took the campus bus back to the dorms after my shift, and as it approached my stop I was dreading the sight of her, knowing she'd spent the entire night having sex with someone else, while also desperately hoping that she'd be home. When I got to our room she was sitting on the couch, eating a bowl of Easy Mac. "Hey," she said. "Where've you been?"

I told her about what happened after she left the bar. "I still have to pay a fine," I said. "For the dumpster."

Kate didn't respond. "Did you hear me?" I asked.

She stood up and threw the bowl at my head, something I'd only seen my mother do. Was I now my passive-aggressive father? It shattered against the wall as I dodged out of the way; orange elbow noodles splattered across the wall. "You think it's my fault!" she yelled. "Don't you? You think it's my fault this happened to you?"

At that moment I knew: her guilt, encouraged by my immediate surrender and lack of resistance, would eventually destroy us. At the same time, it would be my only weapon against her.

I apologized and assured her that of course it wasn't her fault that I'd crashed into that dumpster, it was mine. I cleaned up the mess and brought her a new bowl of pasta. I made sure to get a little smudge of orange sauce on my T-shirt, so she wouldn't forget what she'd done. We watched a movie and I held her while she dropped little kisses on my cheeks and said it made her sad to imagine me hurting. "I hate when we fight like that," she told me.

I pulled her closer and ran my fingers through her hair. "Let's never again."

When she smashed another dish the following year I slit my wrist with a piece of it. Blood dripped all over the linoleum. She took me to get stitches and didn't leave my side for a week.

Of course we both stayed in town for the summer, neither of us went anywhere. Kate was taking extra classes so she could double major, and because she'd failed astronomy that spring and needed three science credits to graduate. Blake was in San Sebastián until the fall, surfing. He had ended things with Kate before leaving, not wanting to be tied down and preferring to "preserve the time they'd spent together before it soured." She came home crying after he told her this, and I tried hard not to show how relieved I was.

I had spent most of the money I'd made in the spring on repairs to both my car and the dumpster, meaning I needed to keep my DJ gig and cast aside my tentative Summer at Sea plans. Instead, the only places I traveled existed along the length of Kate, beneath her clothes, inside her mouth, all on her white-sheeted bed that felt like a frothy ocean. An art and fashion major, she painted, drew, collaged, and dressed me. She drank and tasted me. She did everything but feed me, though not for lack of trying. I had lost control over my own volition, or maybe I'd chosen to wrap it up in her.

Once, as I sat naked in her bed, we both glanced at my reflection in the window and noticed the vertebrae of my spine through my skin. "You're getting really thin," she said. "I'm scared I might shatter you."

At work one evening I overheard my boss say to the bartender, "That girl who comes in here, the blonde?" he nodded in Kate's direction as she hovered over the pool table about to sink the eight ball. "I want to fuck her until her back shatters."

I fantasized about impaling him with the cue stick. But I said and did nothing. I was terrified that if I did, he'd know. And if anyone knew, if even Kate acknowledged our relationship, it might end. The less visible I was to her, the thinner I got and the less space I took up in her life, the more likely things were to continue.

I remember how we slept. I'd lie flat on my back and Kate would unzip my hoodie halfway down my chest, slide her hand onto my breast, and place her head on my clavicle. I'd burrow my nose into her hair. When she wanted sex she would gently caress my nipple; it would harden and she'd run her pierced tongue down my stomach, arriving underneath a pair of tattered boxers that I wore as pajamas. I'd pull her on top of me, aligning our bodies so that we practically snapped into place. I always came with such force that my back would shoot upward, propelling me forward and crashing into her.

"I want to marry you," she said one night as we lay wrapped in a sheet on the floor, having slid like salamanders off the bed.

I winced with fear and a fleeting disgust. A relationship with a woman meant failure: I had failed to get a man, failed to find something normal, failed to not be pathetic. "This is why you don't have a boyfriend!" my mother yelled each time I did anything she deemed wrong, even if it had no relation whatsoever to what I'd done or why I didn't have a boyfriend, even when I did have one. I'd spill juice on the kitchen floor and that was why no man would ever love me. I'd forget to get a pedicure on the first day of spring and it was the reason I would never get married.

"Marry me, then," I said to Kate.

"I love the scars on your feet," she said. She kissed the top of my foot—I had kissed the bottom of hers a number of times. "I love these scars." She placed her lips beneath my hipbone, tracing a thin scar that my mother had laid with a high heel's spike. "I want to protect you forever."

"Okay." I nodded. "I want you to."

Two years into our relationship, when I sensed that Kate was beginning to drift, I stopped eating. I'd try to initiate sex and she would swiftly turn it into a cuddling session. She'd come home later and later without explanation. If I asked, she'd say she was at her studio on campus. But what fashion student needed to pull all-nighters? The more she pulled away, the less food I consumed. Maybe starving myself was an act of passive resistance, a way of regaining the control I had surrendered to her and refused to take back, which would've been the healthier option. Instead, I chose to leverage her guilt.

Our relationship began its full descent over a winter break spent in the South of France. We had dinner at a seafood place in Antibes one evening. When my fish arrived, the garçon unveiled it, and Kate practically clapped with excitement. "Look!" she said. "It's so nutritious! Citrus fruits and julienned vegetables. And it's all grilled! Isn't that good? Something you can finally eat!"

I smiled as my eyes filled with tears. One escaped onto my tilapia. "I'm sorry," I said. "I don't know what's happening to me."

"Please don't cry." Her voice turned bitter as she shook her head. "Please don't fucking cry. Please stop fucking crying!" She slammed her palm on the table, wine leaped from her glass.

I sniffled and snorted and tried to suck back snot and tears, which only made me cry harder. I'm aware I can be exhausting—"you exist too much," my mother often told me.

"I'm sorry," I said to Kate, "I'll stop, I'm stopping." Deep breath, throat clear. Wobbling smile. "Okay. I'm better."

When we got back from France I took a medical leave of absence and applied to another university. By some devastating miracle—miracle because I'd dropped out twice in three years, devastating because I'd be leaving her—I got in. I would transfer right before what should've been my senior year, and I'd need to spend two more years in college to get my degree.

As for Kate, I filled out applications so she could study abroad, and waited until she'd committed to spending the coming fall in Florence before telling her that I was transferring schools. It was my way of saying sorry. Her apology came more directly. "I'm sorry I ruined your life," she said before leaving, her condescension excused only when imagining the guilt that must've spawned it.

"You didn't," I said. *You couldn't*, I thought, though I may've wanted it to seem that way at the time. I may've wanted to believe it was all her fault.

As Kate left for Florence, I headed to a new college town, one that was even more preppy, Greek, and white. A junior again with two years to go, I soon began obliterating my mind with rum and cocaine, and by Homecoming weekend I'd landed my first night in jail. At around four a.m. the warden tossed some brown bag lunches into the women's cell. Mine was stolen by a stringy-haired inmate who spent most of her time on the cell's toilet or yelling at me to stop crying and wipe the blood from my nose. I ended up confiding to the entire cell about Kate. "She sounds like a fucking bitch," the sandwich thief said, biting off a fingernail to chew. "You should find yourself a new broad." When I was released the next morning I begged them to keep me.

Eventually I got a job at a restaurant, in the hope that serving subpar pizza and watered-down beers might keep me from thinking of her. "Aren't you in my ethics class?" a customer asked as I refilled her fountain Dr Pepper.

"I am," I said, her acknowledgment of my existence a lifesaver.

"I'm Renata," she said. "A group of us are meeting at the library tonight, to study for that test. You should come."

When I got to the library after my shift, Renata waved me

over to a long wooden table where she sat with a few others from our ethics class, Swedish Fish and Hershey Kisses spilling out of plastic bags. When we left at around midnight, she offered me a ride home. On the drive she mentioned that a room was opening up in her apartment for the spring—one of her roommates was graduating early. "It's definitely the smallest room, and the loudest," she said, "but who knows, maybe you'll get a boyfriend with his own place and never have to be in it!"

I told her I'd come by the next day to look, though I already knew I would take it.

I moved in the following week. On our first night as roommates, after we'd unloaded the few bags I had from the car, we opened a bottle of prosecco to celebrate. Renata told me about Thomas, a Sigma Chi she'd just started hooking up with, who wasn't ready for a relationship. I observed her hazelnut skin, her green eyes dotted with black flecks. Though she was beautiful, I couldn't tell if I was attracted to her. Still, I listened for any sign of dissatisfaction, any note of curiosity, any hint of an invitation. It came just after we'd poured the last of the bubbly. "I swear," she said, "sometimes I think I'm done with men altogether."

She shut off the living room lights and we walked toward our catty-corner bedrooms. I lingered in her doorway. She stood in front of me, then reached forth to hug me. I held her close. Her nose grazed my neck and she pecked my cheek. As she pulled away I leaned forward and kissed her, pressing my mouth to hers. She jumped back. "What are you doing?"

"I, I'm sorry, I thought . . ." I didn't know what to say. I stood there, horrified. What the hell was I doing? Had I just messed everything up?

"It's okay." She shrugged. "We drank a lot."

Eventually I would come to recognize her refrains of absti-
nence, of swearing off men, of committing to her vibrator, as
wounded declarations of a boy-crazy woman with no plans to
give up on her boyfriend, who chose to value herself in proportion to his estimation of her. I would always envy that: her unambiguous craving for men.

As I turned toward my bedroom feeling like I had ruined my
one chance to escape isolation and loneliness, she called out, "I
usually brew a pot of coffee in the morning." I turned back toward her, keeping my eyes on the patch of floor between us. She
continued, "So if I'm gone before you're up, obviously have at it."

"Cool," I said, half smiling as I met her eyes. "Thanks a lot."

She nodded in a way that seemed forgiving, then turned toward her room and switched on the light. "And you should probably chug some water before you get in bed," she said, her back to
me. "That prosecco was like the cheapest shit ever."

I took her advice and went to the kitchen, where I searched
the cupboards for a glass. I reached for one, held it under the
faucet, and gulped it down. I took a deep breath, then exhaled.
Finally, I had a friend.

10

ON DAY 13, THE GROUP TURNED ON ME. THEY'D BEEN EX-
changing glances across our semicircle all morning. "Something
feels off," I said. "Is everything okay?"

Again the group exchanged looks; Greg nodded in Molly's
direction and she was silently deemed the spokeswoman. "We're
tired of your condescending attitude," she said, crossing her
arms with forced conviction.

"What condescending attitude?"

"You know, how you get all frustrated when we don't know
something, like about the Middle East."

The night before, the van driver had agreed to let us stop at
Pizza Hut on the way back to the Ledge after the meeting. We'd
all piled into a red vinyl booth and grabbed for slices when the
pie arrived. "Now," Greg said, folding a pepperoni slice in half,
"the Palestinians have no legitimate claim on Jerusalem, right?
Because that's what Alex says."

It turned out that after we went back to our rooms at night,
Alex had been giving Greg lectures in Arab-Israeli affairs. A
self-proclaimed Zionist, he came at the issue from a different
vantage point than I did, to say the least. A few days earlier he'd

asked if I was planning to do an H.I.T. list on Israel. "I thought about it," I told him, though really I hadn't. "But I've got too many people I'd like to do first."

"Alex says that you're so pissed off all the time because you think you're entitled to the land," Greg continued, "but that the Torah promised it to his people."

I could tell Greg was being extra incendiary just to get a re-action. And possibly because a day earlier I'd told him I wouldn't be offering any more blow jobs—I was going to start following the rules, I was paying enough to be here, after all. Either way, his effort to annoy me was working. Then Molly jumped in. "Wait, so where's Palestine, again? Is it next to Afghanistan?"

I admit that in the years since 2003, I've begun to expect significantly more when it comes to knowledge about the Middle East. I'm troubled by the number of people who lump all Arabs and Muslims into one large, threatening category, support U.S. intervention in the region under the guise of "spreading democracy," without any contextual understanding of the situation on the ground, and vote for xenophobic, uninformed candidates who also have limited knowledge of the region. My expectation is in some ways hypocritical, as I myself have displayed a great lack of political and cultural knowledge in the Middle East. In moments of fury my mother has suggested I write a book called *The Way It Should Be for Everybody but Me*. I've fumbled in Arab countries many times, and in Egypt I once inadvertently bought a one-humped camel.

I was visiting Cairo with my mother at the time. For all the summers that I'd spent in the Middle East, I hadn't really visited any of the landmarks that people travel specifically to see. Every year I said I would sightsee the next year, I would visit Petra, Wadi

Rum, Ba'albek, until it became clear that I would spend my summers in the same hotel visiting the same relatives. But that summer in Egypt I would finally be a tourist. Naturally, any Egyptian sightseeing expedition entailed a trip to the pyramids, and I went with my mother's friend's daughter, Farah. She seemed friendly enough and I didn't mind having company. Plus, Farah was from Cairo, so I assumed her native knowledge would come in handy.

The sky in Giza that morning was untainted; an interrupted expanse of blue. I climbed up a few rows of the Great Pyramid, dipping into the openings between the weathered limestones, as Farah stood at the base and snapped pictures with my camera. I inched my way back down and we waited in line to see the Sphinx, batting flies and taking in the cacophony of mostly Scandinavian languages around us, blond people in hiking boots carrying large backpacks and clutching guidebooks. We got up close to the mythical cat and walked along her perimeter without ever actually touching her. Once I'd had my fill, we headed back to the parking lot to find a taxi. As we approached a cluster of cabs I heard a voice call out behind me, in English, "Ride the camel?"

I turned around to see a very old man with burnt-rubber skin pointing to a camel draped in a red carpet and flanked by furry, multicolored puffballs, its lips moving methodically as though it were chewing gum. A little boy stood on the other side of the animal, holding a rope as its rein.

I'd ridden a camel once before, in Jerusalem, when I was a kid. As I dismounted, the camel began to pee with such vigor that the piss ricocheted off the earth and all over my jeans. I wasn't too enthused about climbing onto one again. But if this was going to be an "authentic" tourist experience, then surely I had to take the customary camel ride. "Okay, yeah," I said, attempting to sound spirited. "Why not."

The old man smiled, revealing several missing teeth. He nodded at the boy, who then tapped the camel's knuckled knee and pulled on the rein, bringing the camel toward the ground. Witnessing the process was like watching a marble zigzag through a maze. First the camel sloped backward, then forward, then backward again, until its legs were folded neatly beneath it. I grabbed the pommel and swung my right leg over the hump, placing my feet into the stirrups. I was afraid I might tumble forward as the camel began to stand up, jerking me back and forth until it was entirely upright.

At ten feet off the ground the air seemed cleaner, free from the smog enveloping Cairo. I straightened my back and indulged in a feeling of grandeur. The boy led the camel along and the three of us hobbled forward, a slow, steady dance, my hips rotating each time we took a step.

Four minutes later we were back at the point where we started. Farah and the old man were still standing there, both smoking. Once again the boy tugged the camel's rein and it began to descend. And again I felt myself falling forward, then backward, then forward again, until the camel was kneeling. I slid off and stood up, brushing pieces of carpet off my pants. I then turned to the old man and asked, "How much?"

He dropped his cigarette into the sand and buried it with his bare toe. "Normally the price is one hundred dollars. But for you"—he exhaled, and smoke he'd been holding in his throat came forth—"because you're special, it's fifty."

I stared at him for a few seconds, certain I'd misunderstood. "Fifty *U.S.* dollars?"

"Yes. Down from one hundred."

I looked at Farah, who simply shrugged. True, there was no price sheet to consult, but it seemed impossible that a hundred-foot walk—camel or no camel—could cost that much. Then again, Farah was Egyptian, so wouldn't she know if this guy was swindling us? And if fifty dollars *was* the going rate, then I didn't want to seem cheap by haggling over it. I pushed past my doubt and pulled out my wallet, depositing a ten and two twenties into the old man's hand. He made a fist around the bills and smiled. "*Salaam alaikum.*" Peace be with you.

Later that night my mother and I had dinner at a seafood restaurant along the Nile. Ferry boats drifted by, blaring Arab music and casting bright lights onto the water. Despite the unseasonably cool temperature and jovial atmosphere, my mother could tell I was distraught. "*Shoo?*" she asked. What's up?

"How much does a camel ride around the pyramids normally cost?"

She reached for a pumpkin seed and cracked it open with her teeth. "Two, three guinea." Approximately eighteen cents. "Why?" she asked, spitting out the shell. "How much did you pay?"

I passed my napkin in front of my mouth as I answered. "Fifty dollars."

"Fifty *U.S.* dollars? Was it a turbo-powered camel?"

"No, but the guy said—"

"Of course the guy said! Do you believe everything everyone tells you?"

I'd been swindled, of course. Why hadn't Farah said anything? Unless she'd been in on the deal, I saw no excuse for her ignorance. She was Egyptian—shouldn't she know better?

Of course the problem was that *I* should've known better. Though I'd been enjoying the role, I wasn't actually a tourist. The fact that I grew up outside the Middle East doesn't make me feel less Arab. I speak the language, albeit cautiously and brokenly, often failing to get the correct pronunciation and inflection. Fairuz, Oum Kalthoum, Abdel Halim Hafez—classic Arab singers, as important to the musical landscape in the Middle East as the Beatles are in the West—I can sing their songs by heart. I've spent long, seemingly endless nights in Nablus, in un-air-conditioned homes in dry August heat, sleeping on feather-stuffed mattresses and pillows as rough as the hair on a camel's back. I've marched and protested on the Washington Mall in support of ending government funding for foreign occupations in the Middle East.

Yet it's the idiosyncrasies of culture that keep me an outsider, and leave me with a persistent and pervasive sense of otherness, of non-belonging. Basic but nuanced knowledge; the stuff that no one really teaches you. That an invitation for eight o'clock really means nine thirty. In Beirut, I once arrived at a rehearsal dinner on time, and the restaurant's staff was still cleaning up from the night before. That no one wears flip-flops outside the house except to the pool. That noting one's weight gain is an expression of love, and that every price, rule, and border can and must be negotiated.

And yet, in the U.S. I'm just as much of an outsider. Even though America is built upon the idea of assimilation, a so-called melting pot, we Arabs stand out. As a child I was made starkly aware of our nonconformity when my friends would come over and ask why my parents were going out to dinner at nine p.m.— on a Tuesday. Why wasn't my mother wearing mom jeans, but rather, formfitting leather Moschinos? Why did my father call me "daddy" and speak to me half in English, half in Arabic? At the time, they found it funny and harmless to tease me about my otherness; they'd even call me "the terrorist," which I laughed along with, not fully processing nor having the courage to resist the insidious danger of such "jokes," ones that just a few years later would be deemed microaggressions or else blatant hate speech. Back then, to be different was simply a bad thing; diversity wasn't yet something to celebrated, and being white was necessary if not sufficient for coolness. The white girls basked in the light while the rest of us suffered quietly in the lunchroom corners and bore our lot. The best we could hope to achieve was camaraderie among ourselves, united in our outcast status. It is a bizarre and unsettling feeling, to exist in a liminal state between two realms, unable to attain full access to one or the other.

"Fifty dollars is the price of the camel itself," my mother said.

"So, technically, I own the camel."

"Technically, yes," she said. "Make sure you declare it at customs!"

•

I felt flustered by the group's accusation. I told them that I wasn't trying to be condescending, that I didn't think I was better than anyone. "Besides, why do you care what I think?" I asked.

"Great question!" Richard said, and winked at me. "Why do *you* care? Do you always need everyone's approval?"

Sometimes his explicit assessments were annoyingly astute.

IN COLLEGE, AFTER THINGS ENDED WITH KATE, I couldn't make myself straight no matter how hard I tried. And I *tried*. I slept with as many Lambda Chis as possible, and as they drilled away on top of me, my boredom ever-increasing, I'd close my eyes and picture Kate.

I eventually gave up, and in resignation I spent the summer between my second junior year and my senior year of college in Boston, attending outpatient eating-disorder treatment and attempting to come out. At the end of each day I would leave the treatment center in Cambridge and head directly to a gay dive bar in Jamaica Plain. I'd walk in alone with my iPod blaring courage into my ears, choose a stool toward the end of the bar, and hover over a vodka soda. After being force-fed three balanced meals at the center, I had already reached my daily calorie allotment. If a woman approached and tried to flirt with me, my heart would jump and I would waver. "I'm straight," I would protest, too ashamed of myself to accept the advance. I would watch her order a drink, then clench my eyes shut and wince at my own cowardice, hoping she would see my desire through my stated opposition and do the work of pushing past it. As she'd walk away, I would hesitate and call out, "Wait, actually, I'm not!" But by that point it was usually too late. The pattern persisted until I finally learned to take several shots of tequila upon sitting down. Once I started getting too drunk to worry about everyone's judgment, especially my own, I slept with New England dykes to my queer heart's content. Each time, I refused to ask for their names or offer mine. I would always accompany them to their places, never to my shared sublet, to guarantee that I could leave before dawn, with no risk of intimacy or even sober interaction.

About a month into treatment, amid these anonymous evening interactions, Anna and I met. She was in for bulimia, an equal but opposite force to my anorexia. Our first coffee date led to drinks, which led to dinner at an actual restaurant rather than the center's cafeteria, which led to sex.

After we started sleeping together, we would periodically smile at each other across the therapy group; rolling our eyes at the counselors' false enthusiasm. We were careful to never leave at the same time—dating among patients was frowned upon, it could lead to co-conspiracy against the daily regimen and the recovery process.

When I left Boston and returned to school for my final year, Anna and I would text occasionally, usually about posts on the counselor's Myspace or things that happened during group, as she was still a patient there for the next three months. By the time I graduated we had fallen out of touch. We didn't reconnect until we both ended up in New York two years later, me in Harlem and her in Staten Island. We met up at a trailer-park-themed bar in Chelsea, and when I walked in and saw her, I sensed that we would resume right where we left off. She was wearing a checkered button-down and flat-front pastel shorts. I was glad to see that she had come into her own; until then she'd always seemed torn between chunky costume necklaces and full-on preppy boy. She was soothingly easy to be with, and it felt good to spend time with someone familiar in a city that still felt foreign to me. This time we attempted an actual relationship. On one of our first proper dates in the city, she took me to a sports bar in Murray Hill to watch a boxing match: Manny Pacquiao versus Miguel Cotto. We sat at the bar and drank domestic beers while she explained the rules to me. Before the final round, she leaned over and whispered in my ear, "I want to come in your mouth." I shivered at the thought of it, and smiled.

The second time we had sex, she fucked me with a strap on. It was my first experience with dildos, and they became a regular feature of our relationship as she veered increasingly masculine. She'd wrap her towel around just her waist when getting out of the shower, slap Old Spice onto her smooth never-shaved cheeks, pack her jeans when we'd go out at night. I understood these behaviors—I had often fantasized that I had a dick, but I couldn't imagine trading in my God-given breasts, not even for a straight married woman.

Anna and I quickly fell into a pattern of her giving and me taking, and for a long while, she appeared to enjoy it. In bed, I didn't do much besides lie there and enact dramatic orgasms. She was working at a women's health clinic, barely making a livable salary for New York—hence Staten Island—yet she often invited me for long weekends at the Standard, the London, the Bowery, shelling out hundreds of dollars for each stay. She helped me move apartments three times, from East Harlem to Alphabet

City to South Park Slope. She gave in other ways, too; she sent me literature about cycles of abuse and internalized homophobia, documentary films about being queer and Arab, queer and Muslim. I read and watched none of it, and I now realize these weren't intended for my benefit only.

Early on in our relationship, Anna had said that her attraction to me made her so nervous that all her spit dried up. It was a mistake to let me know how much she liked me. I couldn't handle the responsibility—Anna's feelings for me were things I would always hold against her. Every gesture of love I found fault with. When she tended to me when I was sick, I berated her for buying generic medicine instead of name brand. I constantly accused her of being sheltered. In truth, she was; she'd been raised in an upper-class family, her father an intellectual property lawyer, her mother an art history professor at Brown with inherited wealth. But her privilege ended there. She'd suffered abuse herself, which I only knew about because she'd once broken down and told the group during treatment. She never discussed it with me, and I never asked.

The day she called to tell me she'd gotten into law school at Columbia, I panicked. The Upper West Side was where the professor and I would meet for our coffee dates and lunches—activities that I thought might lead to her Riverside Drive apartment. The right response to Anna's news was to jump up and down and squeal, take her out to a celebratory dinner, offer congratulations, at the very least. Instead, I breathed audibly into the phone and asked, "Does this mean you're going to start hanging out at the Hungarian Pastry Shop, too?"

Anna hung up and avoided me for a week. I went crazy, calling dozens of times, leaving desperate, incomprehensible messages that I wept my way through. I was terrified at the thought of not having her, and I mistook the pain of losing control for love and compassion. I finally rode the ferry across the harbor to Staten Island, where I had never once visited. At her doorstep I held her for as long as I could. I invited her to live with me in Brooklyn, knowing it was a bad idea. What we needed was to break up. But I just couldn't stand to be without her, entirely alone without the possibility of anyone else.

On her doorstep, Anna nodded through tears. "I'll move in," she said, then smiled and kissed me on the cheek. "Someone needs to tame you." I felt my heart sink at the fatalism of her reasoning. Yet we laughed and kept holding on to each other. Besides, we both knew it was too late: we had already started to shatter.

•

Maybe I didn't want the professor to end up like the real people in my life. The people I kept things from because I couldn't face them myself. Maybe she offered the possibility of escape.

11

IT WAS OUR FOURTEENTH DAY, AND THE START OF A NEW two-week cycle. A fresh group arrived that morning—and they happened to all be women. The five of them banded together, eating their meals outside on the picnic tables where no one ever ate, waking up a five forty-five to go on pre-coffee walks, sitting in the porch rocking chairs during the morning meditation instead of on the couches with everyone else. "Who do they think they are?" I said to Molly. "Showing up to yoga in sports bras and little-ass shorts. Poor Greg was snapping away all morning!"

In addition to heroin addict, alcoholic, and weekend cokehead, Greg was a sex addict. Not only was he having an affair, he was also obsessed with porn and couldn't stop watching it. After group the day before, Richard had given him a rubber bracelet to wear around his wrist, and whenever he was lusting he was supposed to snap it against his skin to remind himself to stop. I heard the incoming women talking about Charlotte, how great they thought she seemed based on what I assumed was her appearance and her adorable intro. "I often wish I could be a horse," she'd said to the group after morning meditation, "and just trot in a field all day."

Everyone laughed. "Oh my God, totally" sounded throughout the room. "I really want to work with her as much as possible," said Nina, an alcoholic-turned-love-addict. "I feel like we'd really connect."

I glared at her while forking lima beans into my mouth. Did Charlotte just make *everyone* feel special? I resented that. I also hated the idea of Nina getting close to Charlotte, working with her one-on-one. What if Charlotte liked her better than me? "Honestly," I said to Molly as she paged through a contraband issue of *Us Weekly*, "someone needs to put them in their place."

Molly looked at me blankly. "Well, I'm not gonna do it. I think they seem really nice!"

I decided I would confront Nina myself, after I walked into the bathroom the next day and noticed that my towel was covered in mascara and foundation. "What the fuck!" I yelled so loud that the mirror above the sink vibrated. I ripped the towel off the rack and marched over to the main lodge, bursting into the living room and interrupting every conversation. "Who did this?" I held the towel in the air as if it were a manifesto.

"Sorry," Nina called out. "I thought that was the house towel."

"And if it were, you'd smear makeup all over it and make it yours?"

She said she'd wash the towel for me. I told her not to bother, throwing it in the trash on my way out for added impact.

Unsurprisingly, all the new women hated Greg. Anytime he spoke they'd shoot one another looks, roll their eyes, exhale dramatically. During coffee one morning, while Nina was stretching, lifting her leg over her head in a way that felt obviously suggestive, his chastity bracelet snapped in half and shot across the room like a rubber band. "Oops," he said, snickering, as Nina pretended to ignore him. Later that day, she was eating a bag of peanut M&Ms, and Greg called out, "Melts in your mouth, not in your hands!"

"What the fuck is wrong with you?" she yelled. "Why does everything have to be a sexual innuendo?"

He scratched his head, appearing genuinely confused. "Wait a minute, how was that sexual? It's the slogan!"

She threw down her leg and looked at me over on the opposite couch. "How can you stand him?"

Greg sat down beside me and peeled open a banana. "He's pretty harmless," I said as he chomped into it. "Really."

Molly tried to make friends with the incoming women. She'd sit outside with them at the picnic tables and they'd toss her scraps of attention, smiling tight-lipped at her comments before changing the subject. They didn't invite her on their post-lunch or pre-coffee walks. They'd give her questions one-word responses without asking any in return. And they'd talk about her when she wasn't around.

"Why does she pick at herself so much?" I overheard Nina say to the other women in the cafeteria one day. "I just want to tape oven mitts to her hands or something!"

As I eavesdropped on their conversation, I found myself wincing. I recognized her arbitrary, superficial judgments; they were just like the ones I came in with and applied to everyone there. I too had always felt repulsed whenever anyone tried to get close to me. But who was it I actually loathed? Who was I really judging?

"You know," I said to Nina as we walked outside with our

trays. "The picking is annoying. But maybe you shouldn't hold it against her. She really hasn't done anything to you except try to be your friend."

Nina said nothing. And as my hypocrisy shined, it began to cast a light on other areas of my life.

"I think I know who you remind me of," I said to Molly that afternoon. I so very much didn't want to admit it. "You remind me of me. Or the me that I might've been, if my mom didn't insist on whipping me into who she wanted me to be. I guess I miss that other version of myself, even though it sort of terrifies me.

A memory of standing barefoot on the cement balcony of my mother's apartment in mid-December pops into my head. She had banished me from her living room for coming home from school for winter break with unpedicured feet. "I'd rather you bring home F's than feet looking like that!" she called out as I stood hugging myself to keep warm, protesting that at least I'd gotten A's. "What man's going to look at you, with such feet?"

Later that same day we were shopping for formal dresses. I tried on a long Dolce & Gabbana gown that she'd chosen and that neither of us could afford. It was silk and beaded and hung from me in a way that made me feel sexy and stupid, like I was playing the role of a girl who could wear a silk and beaded designer dress that delicately draped her body. I stepped awkwardly out of the dressing room to show my mom, feeling completely foreign to myself. She stood up and walked over to me, then put her hand on my back and turned me around.

"*Beyakhud el a'el*," she said, stepping back and smiling. Her words reverberated through my mind. In that moment, the morning's pedicure incident no longer mattered—I'd gotten it right this time. The desire to hear her say that motivated me to get from moment to moment, day to day.

I continued as Molly stared at me. "And in a way, I'm glad she *did*, and I hate that." I shrugged. "I guess I want to do the same to you, sometimes. You know," I said, making air quotes, "for your own good."

Molly said nothing, she just kept staring at me wide-eyed, until Greg called out from the landing above, "The upstairs rooms are unlocked!"

We ran upstairs to the group room, and I shuffled through the stack of CDs. They were mostly just affirmations and nature sounds, but there were a couple of normal ones in the bunch. We found a Billy Joel album, not exactly dance music, but it would do. I put in the CD and turned the volume all the way up on "A Matter of Trust." On the platform above the living room, we danced and sang along. *Some love is just a lie of the mind, it's make-believe until it's only a matter of time.*

Greg took me in his arms and dipped me. *I know you're an emotional girl,* he mouthed. Soon everyone below was dancing. The women formed a circle around Alex while he did the running man in the middle. At the end of the song the lights in the room flashed; I looked over and saw the security guard. "Time to lock up in here," he said. "And you know you're not supposed to play with the stereo."

"Don't tell Richard!" I said.

"I won't tell," he assured me. "Ain't nobody watching."

•

On Day 19 we wrote "goodbye" letters. I was advised to write two: one to love addiction, and another to my toxic relationship with my mother. When it was time to read them out loud, I volunteered to go first. Once again, Charlotte and Richard were sitting beside me, the empty chair facing me.

Still unable to visualize her, I spoke directly to the chair. "I'll always remember the way you mix up your words, and ask me 'what's the count' when we're playing a board game, or for 'IB-buffin' when you have a headache." I tried to keep it light this time, especially after the H.I.T. list. I looked up between sentences, expecting people to laugh, or to at least smile, but no one did. "I think I'll stop here," I said, folding up the letter and tucking it into my pocket.

"How do you feel?" Charlotte asked.

I shrugged. I felt nothing. "I feel nothing," I said. I got up and returned to my seat in the circle. Greg read his letter to heroin, Molly to her meth-addicted and manipulative boyfriend, and Alex to his martyr habit, of which we'd managed to convince him. The three of them wept while reading their letters. Once we were done, Richard and Charlotte suggested that we give one another hugs. They both joined in and made their way around the room. I stood with my arms crossed, finding this all somewhat sentimental and unnecessary. By the time Richard pulled out the stereo and put on R.E.M.'s "Everybody Hurts," I felt entirely embarrassed by the gratuitousness of this spectacle. I watched Alex sob into Charlotte's arms as Michael Stipe whined in the background. Greg cried into her, too, though I figured he just wanted her boobs pressed against him. When he finally let go, Charlotte started walking toward me. I sat down as she approached, and she veered off to hug someone else.

As I watched the others, I felt something swirling around inside me, like leaves before a storm. I was breathing heavily and starting to shiver again. Bubbles were once again popping in my throat.

"Why don't we take a twenty-minute break," Richard said.

I exploded out of the room with my notebook. I ran down to the basement, found an isolated corner, and scribbled out another letter. I wrote with fury and without punctuation until I heard the bell ring: break was over.

Back in the group room Charlotte started explaining another activity. I interrupted her.

"Charlotte," I called out, "I'm not feeling well."

"Do you want to lie down?"

"I wrote another letter to my mother," I said. "Can I read it?" I didn't wait for her to answer. "I can't believe I'm still trying to protect my image of you." My voice was an octave higher and quivering like a frightened bunny. "You have taken my weaknesses, insecurities, and confessions and used them all against me." My hands were shaking, I could barely read what I had written. "I won't ever let you near my heart again," I said, and I threw my notebook across the floor as if it were on fire.

"Good work," I heard Richard say.

I felt completely exposed, as though my clothes had been suddenly stripped away. "Do you want to take the bat and beat the cushion?" Charlotte asked.

"No," I said. "I'm okay."

"Do you want to squeeze my hands and scream?"

I did want to. "I don't," I said a little too loudly. Then, softer, "I just don't. I'm sorry."

When it was time to break for dinner I called my father from the client phone. It was the first time I'd called since getting to the Ledge. "I need to talk to you about something," I said after he answered. "Do you have a minute?"

There was silence on the other end. "Dad?"

He coughed, then cleared his throat. "Ash just put dinner on the table."

I could sense he didn't know what to do, that he was afraid of upsetting me, but more concerned about upsetting Ash. His uncertainty made me want to scream. "Fine," I said, "so, we'll talk next week, then?"

"Yeah," he stammered. "Okay."

I hung up and stepped out of the booth. Molly, Alex, and Greg were all huddled around the ping-pong table. They immediately stopped talking when they noticed me. "What's going on?" I asked.

"Oh, nothing really," Greg stammered. "We were just saying how pissed you got, reading that letter. It was pretty shocking!"

"So you were talking about me behind my back?"

"No," Molly chimed in. "We just—"

"You know, I really don't need this right now." I turned around, opened the door that led outside, and slammed it behind me. As I trudged into the woods, I could hear Molly calling out my name. I kept going. Everything inside me was beating: my heart, my chest, my throat. This wasn't normal: I shouldn't have gotten so upset, I shouldn't have lost control the way I did. I needed help, I thought to myself, and then remembered that I *was* getting help. But it just didn't feel like I was getting any better. I thought of that slogan: *Insanity is doing the same thing over and over and expecting different results.* I never confessed; I just hoped the feelings would go away. But instead they spread like a disease, rushing through my veins and lining my stomach until I felt nauseated. I then stopped and stood still as another slogan seeped into my head: *Secrets keep us sick.*

12

"TELL HER." RICHARD NODDED IN CHARLOTTE'S DIREC-
tion. He sat with his legs crossed, shoes off, holding a socked foot
in his hand. "Tell her, 'Charlotte, I'm struggling with an attraction to you.'"

I looked around at the others, at the poster-board signs taped
to the walls listing in crayon the different ways a person could feel:
Sad, Bad, Mad, Afraid. I looked out the window onto the woods,
and then at the sloped ceiling. My ponytail reached farther down
my back as I tilted my head. I would need to cut my hair when I
got home. I shifted my eyes to the Sanskrit character tattooed on
Charlotte's ankle peeking out from underneath her pant leg. Her
dark hair was pulled back that day, making her cheekbones more
pronounced, her round hazel eyes even rounder. I fixed my gaze
just below them as I spoke. "Charlotte"—my voice sounded like
it belonged to someone else—"I'm struggling with an attraction
to you."

A gong sounded inside my chest and vibrated through my
fingertips out into the room. I regretted bringing it up. I continued, "When I told you I was falling for someone, it shouldn't have

been you that I went to for help." I glared at the floor, unable to look at her anymore. "I'm so sorry if I violated your boundaries."

After confessing I felt hollow. Deflated, like someone had popped a balloon that had filled up inside me. I could feel my shame morphing into anger, and suddenly I was furious. It didn't seem fair that I longed for this woman I hardly knew. It didn't seem fair that I was there at all.

As first ranked in her class, a distinction that still exists at the Quaker Friends School in Ramallah, Alia Abu Sa'ab's firstborn daughter, Minister of Finance Khaled Abu Sa'ab's first granddaughter, the owner of two highly pronounced cheekbones and the first girl in 1960s Nablus to wear a London-imported miniskirt, Laila Abu Sa'ab was certain to have a great life. She was born in between two catastrophic years in Palestine's history: '48 and '67. The Six-Day War broke out when she was eight years old. In less than a week, Jordan, Egypt, and Syria lost control of the West Bank, East Jerusalem, the Gaza Strip, the Golan Heights, and the Sinai Peninsula. Another wave of Palestinian displacement ensued. The possibility of a state called Palestine receded even further into the distance, becoming nearly unattainable.

The extent to which violence affected her childhood is unclear; she rarely speaks of her youth, and never relates much information when asked. She recalls that on weekends, she and her four siblings would travel through three checkpoints from Nablus to Ramallah, for two scoops each of pistachio ice cream at Rookab. She remembers that her youngest brother was sent to an Israeli prison eight times when they were teenagers, the stays ranging from nineteen to forty-five days, for joining the resistance. After throwing stones at an IDF Humvee convoy that blocked a mother from taking her seizing child to a hospital in Jerusalem, he was placed in a solitary cell so small that he couldn't stand upright and had to remain hunched for an entire three weeks.

After college, Laila turned down a slew of suitors: rich ones, handsome ones, good-familied ones. Though everyone expected her to, she knew she wouldn't marry for a while. What was the rush? Things were changing. Women no longer had to go straight from their parents' home to their husband's anymore. In the late 1970s, the waves made by the sexual revolution in the States were just washing up on Middle Eastern shores. Against the return of the ayatollah in Iran and the rise of the mujahideen in Afghanistan, the U.S. seemed like a bastion of freedom and liberalism. In America, she would be able to date whomever she wanted and not worry about her reputation. "Play the field," her Harvard Med School–educated father told her. "Go places. And never settle."

Besides, she'd spent the last twenty-one years watching her parents, her mother constantly screaming at her father, him trying to drown her out with his cardiology work, fellowships, books. He loved his wife, but he certainly couldn't connect with her, not with a mind like his. Laila wouldn't let that happen, she would never be like her mother, cleaning and cooking and using her kids as leverage against her husband, forcing them to take her side, a decision they would regret once they were older and able to think for themselves. No, she would never repeat her mother's mistakes, and she certainly wouldn't let herself be beholden to a man. She planned to get a master's degree, and eventually a PhD. "The thing about education," her father told her the day of her college graduation, which coincided with a sharp increase in Israeli settlement construction on confiscated land in the West Bank, "is that no one can take it away from you. Everything else can be stolen. Everything else can be lost."

When her parents moved to Chicago, where her father had just accepted a position as head cardiologist at Northwestern Memorial Hospital, Laila decided she would stay with them and apply to master's programs in the States. At her goodbye party before leaving, she met Talal.

Talal was also from Nablus. He'd grown up poor, one of nine brothers and sisters. At the time that he met Laila, he was also on his way to the States: to California, where he would attend business school. He wasn't suave or especially handsome, but he was determined, and he pursued her relentlessly. Every week he sent a letter to Chicago from L.A., and he eventually traveled to Illinois to visit her, flying into O'Hare and renting a flashy red Mustang that he hoped would impress her. Laila's three brothers all made fun of him for it. Her father had been skeptical of the match from the beginning and saw the car as further evidence of how ill-suited the man was for his daughter. "Anyone who rents a red convertible must have an inferiority complex!" he said, and told Laila not to date him because of it.

Laila and Talal spent most of their time together in the red car, since it was one of the few places where they could be alone. Before he left Chicago, he proposed to her in it, and a few months later they were married in Bridgeview. Grad school applications had been replaced by wedding plans. After a brief honeymoon on Lake Superior, the only destination Talal could afford, she returned with him to California.

Laila hated Los Angeles. It was too spread out, too detached, and even farther from the West Bank than Illinois. And the anonymity of the place was entirely unfamiliar. She would walk around their neighborhood and not recognize a soul. Back in Nablus, she'd once left her passport at a café, and by the time she got home someone had already dropped it off. Even the telephone operator knew her life story.

Talal taught her how to drive on the way to the DMV for her Behind the Wheel test, on Interstate 405. After that things felt a little better; she could explore the city and make it feel less foreign. It helped that she was fascinated by all things American. She developed an appetite for In-N-Out cheeseburgers and Neapolitan shakes. She watched *The Young and the Restless* and *The Price Is Right* daily. In home videos, she uses the phrase "Come on down!" at least a dozen times—when it's time to blow out the candles at my birthday party; at the beach, encouraging us to get in the water; on the first day of school as we make our way to the bus stop. Infomercials captivated her as well; she'd sit in front of the TV mesmerized by the promise of cleaning products that could get out any stain imaginable, vitamins that could provide unlimited energy. Usually she'd pick up the phone and place an order, consulting Talal after the fact, though he didn't mind. He found her enthusiasm charming. She'd hold on to the goods until losing interest and getting rid of them; at their one garage sale she tried to sell a Be-Dazzler that she'd ordered off the television in 1982. And whenever any mail would arrive from Ed McMahon, she'd call Talal at work, screaming that they'd just won a million dollars.

Seat belts, speed limits, and fire drills were novelties as well. Once, while she was six months pregnant, Laila was in the middle of a seminar on interior decorating when the building's fire alarm went off. Everyone else groaned and got up, slowly filing toward the door. Laila jumped out of her seat and ran, pushing people out of her way and screaming, "Let me out, I have a baby inside me! I have a *baby* inside!"

By then she still knew no one in California, except for Talal, and the baby growing inside her. But he was in class most of the day, business school at USC, forty-five minutes from the apartment, an hour and a half with traffic. When they did have time together they spent it either watching TV or at a local Italian restaurant, then getting ice cream cones and driving to the beach to catch the sunset. Most days she spent sitting by the window looking out onto the ocean, touching her hand to her ever-expanding belly and trying to enjoy the view. But beautiful scenery could never make her feel less lonely. "Who cares about the view?" She would say whenever Talal would remark on it. "I've seen it, it's beautiful, now what?"

Her water broke one summer night, while they were both asleep. After frantically pulling a robe over his pajamas and grabbing the bag they'd prepared, Talal sped along the freeway to the hospital in downtown L.A. For once there was no traffic.

It turns out that they didn't need to speed; it took another day for the baby to arrive. Talal was back in class when it was time to start pushing, her mother on a plane, hoping to make it in time. The day Laila became a mother, and me, a daughter, we were the only ones there to greet each other.

On the fifteen-year anniversary of the war that had ravaged

her hometown, Laila gave birth to me, her first child, a daughter. On that ominous day the doctor who performed the delivery forgot to remove the placenta. It rotted in her womb, causing her to bleed internally, and then externally. She returned to the hospital for a month, leaving me in my grandmother's care. "There was so much blood," Teta would say. "She almost died."

Three months later, Laila and Talal moved to Washington. Talal bought a used Ford van, which had a built-in bed in the back and a carpet of sunflower seed shells. It looked like it should belong to either plumbers or kidnappers. They drove across the country with me in a basket between the driver's and passenger's seats. By the time they bought a house in the D.C. suburbs, Laila was better acquainted with America's nuances and idiosyncrasies. Her feelings of loneliness and alienation had somewhat subsided. Besides, Washington was more like Palestine: densely populated, noisy, and filled with more Arabs than Palos Verdes.

Talal and his brother built a deck in their backyard. Laila planted roses. In a home video from when I was a toddler, I inch my way toward the rose bed. "Don't touch the flowers!" Laila calls from behind the camera. As I get closer I call out to my father, "*Baba*, come sit with me! Sit with me—"

And I topple over, onto the ground and onto my head. He rushes over to where I'm sprawled, my leg bent backward behind my neck. Instead of lifting me up he simply readjusts my leg, then offers me his hand. "Do you know why you fell?" he asks.

"Why?"

"Because you were touching the flowers!"

A non sequitur, but I accept his logic as valid. In the video Laila laughs behind the camera. "Something to remember," she says.

•

When I was eight years old, they sent me to French sleepaway camp in Quebec for a month. My mother flew with me to Montreal and together we took a train to Saint-Alexis-des-Monts. "I don't need you to come along," I said as we boarded a pre-dawn train. "I'll be okay on my own."

She would return to Montreal that evening and travel to Amman the following morning for the rest of summer. I spent that first day of French camp reveling in my newfound independence, thrilled to be around teenage counselors and away from my parents. In class that afternoon we were instructed to draw a stick figure and label its body parts in French. Eager to impress the others, I drew a man dancing barefoot in the rain with an upturned umbrella. When the teacher came by to inspect my work he frowned at the sight of my drawing. He then glued the pages of my notebook together, as if to cancel out the incident.

Soon it was dark. No one in my dorm spoke English. I lay in bed listening to the unfamiliar French around me, trying unsuccessfully to stifle tears. The older girls in the room attempted to comfort me—one even offered her teddy bear—but I wouldn't stop crying. It wasn't them that I wanted. I felt abandoned—a whole month without my mother. In the morning, I begged the camp's dean to let me call her before she left for Jordan. They finally gave in, and when she answered I cried, "*Mama!* Don't leave me! I need you!"

And so my mother stayed in Canada. I spent the weekdays in Saint-Alexis-des-Monts, and on the weekends I took a bus to Montreal. I'd sob when I had to leave her on Sunday afternoons. The routine persisted for the entire month of July, until finally, we went home.

•

A few years after their house was built, when I was two and Karim a newborn, Laila got a license in real estate. She became a top agent almost instantly, taking on Arab families that relocated to D.C. as her primary clients. She worked practically non-stop for fifteen years, our basement filling up with little plaques and paperweights that said things like "Super Agents' Club" and "Number One in Sales," until she and my father separated. After that she'd take on the occasional client, but the economy was in recession, and fewer properties were being sold at the time. The constraints of financial necessity rendered her obsolete.

When my father moved out, my mother decided to downsize, renting out the house and moving to an apartment in D.C. proper. It wasn't long before she discovered Cafe Milano, a place where politicians, lobbyists, and the occasional Hollywood actor schmoozed. George Clooney once offered her a seat at his table. "Where are you going?" I would ask as headlights seared through my bedroom window, her friend honking from the driveway.

"*Yalla*, bye," she would say, spraying a spritz of perfume and rushing out to the car. I would watch her open the passenger door and climb in, kissing the friend hello as they backed away. She would stay out late, so late that I often thought there'd been an accident, that she'd died, she was dead, my mother was dead. I'd pace the hallway upstairs crying, until I'd finally break down and call the restaurant. The hostess would wander off to find Laila at her table and moments later she was on the line. "*Habibti*, everything's fine," she said soothingly, the hum of chatter and music in the background. "We're just ordering dessert now. Go to sleep."

One night, when I called Café Milano, the hostess told me that my mother refused to come to the phone. When I heard the rumble of the garage a few hours later, I came running down the stairs to embrace her, and she immediately smacked me across the face.

I never called the restaurant again, or worried about accidents.

•

One afternoon, just before I moved away from D.C. to New York, I came home and found her sitting at the kitchen counter, a full tray of cookies on the table beside her, the prepared kind from the grocery store. I pointed to the cookies. "What are those for?"

"They're from an open house for new clients I held this morning." The tray was full, not one cookie missing. "No one came," she said, looking up at me then quickly looking away, as though she was ashamed. "Have one, if you like."

I imagined her sitting at an empty table in a model home kitchen, her business cards beside her in an untouched stack, waiting for someone to show up. I thought about the other real estate agents at the firm with perfect English, who continued to secure clients despite the recession. I thought of the bills that arrived at her one-bedroom apartment, now solely her responsibility. She wasn't supposed to be paying bills alone. Things weren't supposed to turn out this way for Laila Abu Sa'ab, but she had chosen the wrong marriage and the wrong life. And though she resented me because of it—I was, by default, the wrong daughter—I also understood. I had come from my mother, I had lived inside her, but I was not *of* her. I was not an Abu Sa'ab, a wedge driven even deeper after she divorced my father and dropped her married name entirely.

After that I was a foreigner, an unfamiliar thing, other. I would never belong to her again, though I desperately wanted to. No matter how hard I tried I would never attain the status of being hers. It would always remain just beyond my reach.

•

My words hung in the air like laundry on a clothesline. *Charlotte, I'm struggling with an attraction to you.* They repeated themselves over and over again in my head. "Can I respond?" Charlotte asked. "Or would you rather I didn't?"

"No," I said. "I want you to."

Charlotte took a deep breath and let it out slowly. "I don't feel violated," she said. "I think it makes sense that you feel the way you do. I'm unattainable to you. I exist only in possibility. And that's intoxicating."

She looked nonplussed, unfazed by my confession. I suppose I wasn't the first. "Plus, I'm giving you all this positive attention, all this acknowledgment and approval." She said what didn't need to be said, because by then everyone in that room already knew it, everyone but me. Her response seemed somehow reductive, as if she'd taken everything and plugged it into a simple formula: Acknowledgment + Approval – Mother's Unconditional Love = Attraction. *Good luck finding someone to love you like I did.*

Finally, I was able to lift my head and look at Charlotte. My eyes pooled as I smiled stupidly and hoped no drops would escape.

•

170

In the remake of the Hepburn/Bogart classic *Sabrina*, the driver-father of the title-character glances disapprovingly as his daughter sits perched in a tree overlooking the object of her fantasy's dinner party. "There is so much more to you than this obsession," he says to her.

"There's more to *you* than these obsessions!" Each new therapist echoes the movie line back at me when I charmingly quote it to her, a signifier that I at least recognize the problem, so no need to waste time getting to it. Many moves to new cities equals many new therapists, and I am good at bringing them up to speed with matter-of-fact, clinical detachment—recovering anorexic, Borderline mother, love addict—one that almost makes me think we could treat me together. "You have so much going for you," each therapist says, resisting the impulse to touch me in a way that always feels intentional. I'm used to being touched, I *need* to be touched, I promise I won't fall in love with a touch. "There's so much in you to desire," each therapist says. "You're smart, you're funny, you're pretty—"

"I'm smart and funny. But, please, don't. Not that."

You don't know pretty. *I'm beautiful, and you're average.* I accepted her challenge that day. She might be beautiful, but my life would not be average. I would never be ordinary.

And yet what's more ordinary than an unattainable crush? Is there anything more familiar, anything less extraordinary? How pathetic is it that I still think of the professor? I want to stop. I think I want to stop. I think I'm afraid to stop.

Sabrina eventually moves to Paris and discovers all that is more to her. But I don't live in Paris, and I'm not sure how much there is to discover here.

13

I EVENTUALLY STOPPED GOING TO THE TWELVE STEP meetings. They had gotten redundant—same people, same obsessions, same neglectful spouses and reckless children—and had reached the point of diminishing returns. Instead I found a coffee shop that I liked near the clubhouse, and after the van would turn the corner and everyone had gone inside, I would linger behind. One day Greg lingered, too. He spotted me heading off in the opposite direction and called out, "Hey, lady, where ya goin'?"

I looked around to make sure no one was within earshot before telling him. "Can I play hooky with you?" he asked.

I was surprised to not cringe at the thought of Greg accompanying me to the coffee shop, or anywhere really. Throughout four weeks in a place where near-strangers were encouraged to describe their life experiences in excruciating detail, I frequently needed breathing room. These offshoot outings had become almost sacred, a time to connect with thoughts that risked being drowned out by the voices of others. But that day, I didn't mind surrendering my solitary hour. As I got closer to the end of my twenty-eight days, the prospect of being alone seemed somewhat terrifying. And though a few weeks earlier Greg would've been the last person I would have wanted to spend extra time with, I'd actually started to crave his company. I was beginning to think he got me better than anyone, and that the understanding went both ways. There was something about his perpetual inability to escape his self-destructiveness that made him both vulnerable and tender. I almost felt love for him, or at the very least, kinship.

We sat down in a window seat near the front. Greg pulled his laptop out of his bag. "What!" I said. "How come they let you keep that?"

"They didn't," he said, "I just chose not to hand it over when they asked if I'd brought a computer. It's pretty easy to get around most rules, you know, and half the time you don't even have to lie!"

We sat across from each other, Greg staring at his computer screen and me at a blank page in my journal, struggling to conjure up any thoughts or feelings that needed expressing. The more time I spent in treatment, the less I needed to process in that space. My thoughts felt much less fragmented. In truth, I was nervous about leaving. I'd come to enjoy knowing what I'd be doing every day, and having no choice in the matter. In fact, not having to choose was one of the best parts about being at the Ledge; the only decisions I made involved which salad dressing I was in the mood for, or what T-shirt to wear. Being limited was surprisingly nice. I took comfort in unambiguous priorities, in having no choice in the matter; certainty by default.

"You want to use my laptop?" Greg asked. "Check your email or something?"

"No," I said without hesitation. "No, thanks."

I'd checked my voice mail a few days earlier, from the client phone. I had a message from my mother, which I was too scared to listen to. I'd spoken to Karim when I first arrived, who informed me that she knew I was off somewhere doing some "American-style self-help" thing, but as for where, why, and for what exactly, she had no idea. I hadn't checked my email yet, and I was happy to ignore what was waiting in my inbox.

"You sure?" Greg asked. "It'll probably be your last chance until you leave."

"I'm sure. How about you—any exciting emails?"

"Jill wants me to meet her in Miami. After I'm done here."

"Your intern?" He nodded.

I took a big sip of iced tea, so big that my throat ached. "Are you going to?"

He looked down at his computer, avoiding eye contact. "I don't know."

"But what about your wife? And your daughter?"

He made a joke about how it might be awkward to bring them along. I didn't laugh. "They'll still be around after Miami," he said, reaching for my hand and squeezing it. "Don't worry, darling!"

I pulled my hand away. I immediately felt like punching him. What was all of this for, then, all the time we spent talking about his family, listening to him cry about how much he loved them, how much he regretted everything he'd put them through? How much he wanted to change for them. "Look, I'm not strong like you," he told me. "I just can't help myself. You said it yourself: I'm a fucking pussy."

"Yup." I shut my journal and looked him in the eye. "I guess you really are."

•

My fourth Friday in treatment was my last day with Charlotte. I wasn't flying home until Sunday but she didn't work weekends. I watched the clock hands move forward, wishing they would just stop, but soon it was four thirty. In half an hour I would never see her again, a prospect that saddened me deeply despite the confirmed asymmetry of my feelings. We'd been working with just Richard ever since the midafternoon break, and I was scared that she had left without saying goodbye. I couldn't stand to sit in group anymore, so I asked Richard, "Is Charlotte still here?"

He tilted his head in the direction of their office. "She's doing some paperwork."

"Can I go back there?" I asked. I knew he could see the panic on my face, maybe he even recognized it. Maybe he looked forward to spending time with her each day and understood my fear of never seeing her again. How was everyone not in love with her?

He nodded. "Go for it."

I jumped up, ran out of the room, and burst into her office. She was sitting at her desk, wearing faded jeans and a heather-gray T-shirt, her hair tied back in a long, thick braid. She turned to face me. "Oh, hey!" she said casually, ignoring my dramatic entrance.

"Can I talk to you?"

"Sure," she said. She pulled a chair out from the empty desk behind her. As I sat down, I stole a glance at the postcards taped beside her bookshelves. There was one of a cat doing yoga, another of her standing beside a horse, a kid on each side. "What's up?" she asked.

"Sunday's my last day," I told her, hurt that she didn't already know. "And I'm just, sad, because—" I covered my face with my hands. I couldn't stand for her to see me cry again. "I like having you in my life."

She touched the top of my head, which made me shiver. "Hold on," she said, "do you think that after you leave, I'll no longer be in your life?"

I sniffled. "Isn't that how it works?"

"Well, maybe at other treatment centers," she said, "but I like to keep in touch with my clients."

And just like that, my stash of hope was replenished. I didn't have to lose her. I started to breathe normally again. "Do you use Facebook?" she asked, and I nodded. She then took out a pad of Post-its. "Here's how to find me," she said, writing out her full name, the letters bubbly and distinct. She peeled off the note and handed it to me. "I'm leaving the ball in your court."

•

On my last Sunday in group, I read aloud my goodbye letter to love addiction. "What will I find to replace you?" I asked rhetorically. "Hopefully the real thing. And if I don't let you go, there won't be any room for that." Molly and Alex both asked for a copy of my letter, and I couldn't help but feel flattered. I gave the farewell speech that I'd been eager to deliver ever since I'd decided to incorporate the Proust quote from the poster in the basement. "It's true," I preached to the group from the front of the room, "the real voyage of discovery is about having new eyes. And I leave here today with a brand-new pair."

They flocked to my outstretched arms in the form of hugs and applause. "You set the bar for recovery," Richard told me. "Call anytime, we're always here for you." He patted me on the back as I leaned into the crook of his elbow.

As the shuttle bus carried me away from the Ledge and toward the Nashville airport, emails started popping up on my liberated cell phone. It took forty-five minutes for them all to appear. I checked my voice mail; I had three new messages, all from my mother. I hesitated before pressing play. My heart flapped like a bucketed fish as I listened to each of them. In her last voice mail her pleading turned angry. "You owe me a phone call," she rasped. "You *owe* me." She pronounced *owe* as "awe." You awe me.

"I owe you nothing," I said out loud, then tucked the phone away in the front pocket of my backpack. The driver looked up at me in the rearview mirror. My throat tickled from the quiver in my voice.

At the airport my flight was delayed, meaning I would miss my connection through Detroit. I was still in the mind-set of the Recently Converted, and I told myself it was just my Higher Power at work. I breezed over to the check-in counter. "Anything you guys can do?"

Somehow they managed to get me on a direct flight to New York. "Just give us a minute to get your bags off the delayed flight and onto this one!"

I landed at JFK and took the A train back to my apartment. I'd asked the subletter to leave the keys with the bartender at the restaurant below my building, and I stopped in to grab them before heading upstairs. I climbed the five flights two steps at a time and arrived at my doorstep. I gathered up the takeout menus and flyers that had been left there. I opened the door, flipped on the lights, and immediately felt the sting of Anna's absence. It was everywhere: in the missing fridge magnets, the half-full closets, the photo book she'd made of us, still sitting on the coffee table. Over my twenty-eight days, I'd managed to stop thinking about her, along with most everything else on the outside. But now I wondered what she'd been doing, where she was living. Was she already seeing someone? Just the thought made me ache.

As the sting subsided, anxiety came rushing in. I had two weeks to sell my furniture and pack up all my stuff before the lease ran out. I took stock of everything I needed to sell—a bed, a couch, coffee table, bookshelf, desk and chair—then plopped down on the couch and realized I was hungry. I decided to order takeout and reached for the stack of menus, fumbling through them before choosing an Indian restaurant. I looked at my phone; I'd have to wait another fifteen minutes before it opened. At exactly five o'clock I called and placed an order. I then unzipped my suitcase and attempted to unpack until the food arrived. After scarfing down chicken tikka masala, I passed out.

When I woke up the next morning, the room felt excruciatingly still. I felt no urgency to get up, no need to rush to catch the coffee before it was taken away. I could hear the sound of the neighbor's TV, the hum of my refrigerator, the din of collective conversation from passersby outside the bedroom window, the occasional word detectable. The living room walls blared with blankness, something I hadn't noticed before. Had Anna taken artwork with her? Had there been any up to begin with? She did leave the ticking cat clock, which felt intentional.

I eventually dragged myself to the kitchen and brewed a pot of coffee. I tried to re-create the same structure I'd had at the Ledge, but it felt different, doing so alone. I was no longer used to solitude. After breakfast I puttered around the apartment, brewed a second pot of coffee, alphabetized the books on the shelf, then rearranged them by genre, and then again by height. As I wandered aimlessly from room to room, I kept thinking about my mother. I was surprised, hurt, and relieved that she hadn't tried to get in touch, and I debated calling her myself. Had she thought of me at all? Did she worry about where I was or what I'd been doing since the last time I'd last seen her? I picked up my phone and scrolled to her number in my contacts—she was no longer in my recent call history. Her info was saved under "Laila Abu Sa'ab" rather than "Mom," which I hadn't noticed until then. I stared at her name for several minutes before deciding against calling. Instead, I scrubbed the inside of the oven and the kitchen counters, then sorted the desktop files on my computer. At noon, when I knew everyone back at the Ledge was milling around after morning group and waiting for the cafeteria doors to open for lunch, I called the reception. Nancy answered on the third ring. "Well, hey you!" she said, chipper as ever. "Didn't expect to hear from you so soon!"

"I think I need to come back," I told her. "Can you ask Richard to call me please, as soon as possible?"

She promised to pass along the message, but by five thirty Richard still hadn't called. To distract myself I went to Walgreens and bought cards for everyone who was still at the Ledge. I spent all evening writing out personalized messages to each person, following upon specific issues they'd raised in group. I wanted them to know I'd been listening, that I actually cared. I mailed off the cards the next morning. Over the next week I received just one response, from Nina, who told me her twenty-eight days were almost up. She asked if I'd made it to the Midwest yet, and if I could send my new address. I packed her letter in one of my boxes and never wrote her back. I eventually received a few more letters, a yellow forwarding label with my new address affixed to the bottom of the envelopes. But by the time they arrived I no longer needed them.

•

I waited until I got to the Midwest, exactly two weeks after leaving the Ledge, before adding Charlotte as a Facebook friend. The night before, I'd paid my new neighbor twenty bucks for her Wi-Fi password. So far, the internet was all that existed in my apartment besides my laptop, two suitcases, and a sleeping bag.

Charlotte accepted the request five minutes later, and with her acceptance came a wall post: "Peace and love to you!" I clicked on her page and could see that she'd written the same thing to about twelve other former clients, including Molly.

The corners of my eyes burned in shame and disappointment. What had I expected? And more important, why was I still hopeful?

I sat on the floor of my apartment feeling more alone than ever. I was completely single for the first time in years, with no relationship or obsession to cling to. I missed my mother more than ever. At the Ledge, detaching from her had kept her ironically close, especially when I summoned her into the group room.

Now that I was out, on my own, I found myself experiencing excruciating withdrawal, which I guess spoke to our codependency. At least once a day I stared at her name on my phone and debated calling. I wanted to talk to her desperately that night, but still I resisted, perhaps out of some instinct whispering in my ear, telling me it wasn't yet safe. Around midnight, I unrolled my sleeping bag and lay down on top of it. I felt a surge of despair well up inside me as I closed my eyes and willed sleep to come. In truth I was exhausted. I didn't know if I had the energy to start over again. To break in new streets, to familiarize myself with the supermarket aisles, to make friends. Maybe I wouldn't this time. Maybe I would remain a stranger.

The next morning, I woke up bathed in sunlight as rays poured in through the large uncurtained windows. The despair had faded, and in its place was a feeling of excitement. Possibility. I opened my laptop and glanced at Charlotte's profile picture one more time. I then took a deep breath. "Remember," I said aloud, and it echoed through the empty chamber of yet another new home. "You have to make room for the real thing."

WHENEVER WE WOULD VISIT AMMAN, MY MOTHER would take Karim and me to Nablus for at least ten days. I dreaded these trips to our Palestinian hometown; a trip within the trip that required yet another day of packing into a smaller suitcase, with a new set of considerations and increasingly conservative clothing as I got older. If there wasn't a lot to do in Amman, there was even less going on in Nablus. My days there were longer and less varied. Some afternoons, we would visit the old souk that courses through the center of town, women scooping up handfuls of cardamom and letting the spice sift through their fingers. I'd stand against a stone wall while a man carved up *knafeh* that steamed atop a large gold saucer of a tray, strands of cheese hanging down from the spatula as he plated slices and passed them around.

Other days, I never left my great-grandparents' high-ceilinged house, which was a relic of Ottoman decadence, with Rococo paintings and wall-to-wall Oriental rugs, the couches fluffed up and decorated with tiny pillows. The glass-topped coffee table held framed pictures of my great-grandfather with Gamal Abdel Nasser, Anwar Sadat, King Hussein. I would explore the house's

numerous underutilized spaces, and once spent a full day trying to open a heavy wooden door that turned out to be the front
door. It hadn't been used since 1948, the year they stopped host-
ing parties, the year of the Nakba, when nearly a million Palestinians were exiled from their land. My great-grandparents
had been heavily involved in the Arab Revolt in the late 1930s
against British colonial rule and the Haganah. They assembled
their own bands of men, ones with less-advanced weaponry but
equal ferocity. When paramilitary troops came to remove my
great-grandparents and their twelve children from their home,
they refused to leave. "My father cried so much when the soldiers
came," Teta would tell me again and again, "but he wouldn't leave
his house." Instead, the soldiers moved in and lived alongside the
entire family, including my grandmother and her siblings. "They
slept in the garden," Teta would say.

Teta had been attending Schmidt's Girls College in Jerusalem, and had just returned home to her parents' house after being expelled for hiding in the nuns' private quarters. She claimed
that she wanted to see what the nuns looked like underneath
their habits.

"How did the soldiers treat you?" I would ask her.

"Some of them were okay. They'd give us candy. They'd even
let us touch their guns."

During our visit to Nablus at the height of the intifada, the
Israeli military imposed a twenty-four-hour curfew. We had no
choice but to remain indoors. Still, I would sometimes sneak
outside and wander beyond the gates of my great-grandparents'
house to play in the neighbors' yard. One of my early memories in
Nablus is of gunshots. I was six years old, sitting on the neighbor's

swing set, when I heard the rapid-fire popping sounds. I jumped off the swing and began to run. Though I was only next door, in the moment I didn't know how to find my way back home. Seemingly out of nowhere a woman dressed in white appeared. I ran directly into her outstretched arms, crashing into her bosom. She held me tight. A dry breeze blew, a chicken clucked by. The woman held me, and pressed my head tightly against the whiteness of her gown.

Who knows if I invented her—the things I remember, no one believes. "You can't possibly remember telling your father that your mother was in labor!" people say. "Your brother is only two and a half years younger than you." They tell me I can't remember my mother hemorrhaging and returning to the hospital right after I was born.

But I remember. Perhaps because I want to. I can just as easily forget when I want.

14

MATÍAS IS A VISITING FELLOW AT MY MFA PROGRAM.
He's in town from Argentina for the fall semester to work on his
fourth novel. We meet the day he arrives, during the welcome
barbecue at the fellowship director's house. He approaches me
from across the backyard, as though in a movie. "Hi," he says.
"Can I offer you a university-subsidized beer?"

We make our way to the drinks table, where he pulls two
dripping IPAs out of a cooler. We wander to a swing on the front
porch. "So do you know anyone here yet?" I ask.

"Nope," he says. "Just you so far." The conversation quickly
moves from pleasantries to relationships to breakups. He's recently separated from his wife; they stayed together too long,
he tells me. He seems surprisingly eager to talk about her, and
he describes the boredom that crept in, her growing disinter-
est in sex, leaving him constantly wanting more love. I feel an
immediately closeness. I tell him that my relationship with
Anna ended in May, intentionally avoiding any details about
my summer.

That's how we begin.

The next afternoon I run into him outside the local bookstore.

Apparently it's the kind of town where this happens often enough. "What've you been up to?" he asks. I tell him I wrote a short story, did some reading. "A story about what?"

I wasn't expecting him to ask. "Sex, actually."

He smiles. "Is it possible to write something short on that topic?"

I laugh. The conversation feels scripted, like we are two leads in a screwball comedy. "Well, it's more about women having sex 'like men' and vice versa."

"Interesting," he says, taking a step closer to me. "I'm always the one who needs to be held afterward, and who needs to feel loved."

The thought of holding him makes me feel warm, and I start picturing the two of us in bed together before my mind wanders to Anna, to a condom wrapper that materialized from inside my purse one night. I managed to throw out the incriminating object before she could see it. I think about intimacy as I'd learned about it over the summer: "Into-me-you-see."

"Right," I say. "And I'm out the door before the sheets have cooled."

Before we part ways he asks me to have dinner with him the following night, and I accept. When I arrive at the restaurant he is sitting at an outdoor table in a sports coat, smoking a cigarette, his bangs resting just above his green eyes. He reminds me of the lead in a nineties rom-com. "Do you mind if I smoke one more before we go inside?" he asks.

We end up spending the evening on the balcony, smoking and drinking. He talks about his five years in Paris, meeting his wife during his first week there—they had each been at a surrealism exhibit at the Centre Pompidou, alone—the birth of his son two years later, who he describes as the true love of his life in a way that makes me feel both awed and prematurely disappointed, the plot of his novel, his open marriage and subsequent separation. I safely tuck away the Things to Be Wary Of. I ask follow-up questions, engaging in his stories. He doesn't ask much about me, he seems happy to keep talking, and I am content to just listen. When we finally decide to order, the kitchen has already closed. "It's so comfortable with you," he says. "It feels like we're talking in bed."

The presumption of his comment is both off-putting and impressive. Later, as we say goodbye, I give him my cheek but he kisses my lips. He invites me to his hotel room, and though I am tempted, I automatically decline. For one thing, I know better; you don't sleep with a seductive Latin writer on the first date, even if—*especially* if—you find yourself charmed by him. Plus I'm not supposed to be doing this so soon after my twenty-eight days. "Not for a year," the counselors instructed. "You'll be too vulnerable anytime before that."

Though a year seems excessive, I know that less than a month out is too early, and I don't want to be derailed just yet. Besides, if this is going to be anything at all, then there's no need to rush. He seems impressed with my decision. "Fair enough," he says. "I'd ask for your number but I don't have a U.S. cell phone." He kisses my cheek once more before walking toward his hotel.

By the time I arrive back at my apartment, I already have an email from him. "Before tonight I was attracted to you," he writes, "but in a speculative, abstract way. After we kissed, though, I walked home with my muscles in tension, imagining the unpublishable things I want to do to you."

I write back, "While in a way this excites me, it also makes me nervous."

He answers, "It's the same for me. We may never do anything but talk, and so what: some friendships are driven by attraction. The only certainty is that there's too much complicity between us to hurt each other, no?"

It's a line I might've used myself. I don't respond.

The following Saturday I'm walking through town and it starts to pour. I run into the nearest building, which happens to be the bookstore. He is standing near the register, paging through Borges. He's wearing the same outfit he wore the day I met him, a black T-shirt and faded jeans. His hair's a bit messy, cheeks dark and unshaven, and he's carrying a brown leather messenger bag. He seems to possess just the right amount of concern for his appearance—style-conscious but not overly focused on it. I am both excited and nervous to see him, and I consider leaving before he notices me. Instead I say hello. He tells me he enjoyed the other night, and asks if I'd like to go out again this weekend.

I tell him I can't, I'm not ready to get involved with anyone. No need to go into details, Richard advised, when we talked about how I would handle such a situation. Say what needs to be said, reveal nothing beyond what's necessary. "Then let's be friends," he answers.

For a minute I feel thwarted before deciding I can do it, I can be friends with someone I'm attracted to. Soon after we leave I write to him and ask if he wants to come over in the evening. "Just friends," I add.

He arrives with a movie, *Notes on a Scandal*. We talk throughout. "Do you think Cate Blanchett is hot?" I ask.

"Nah," he says, "but Judi Dench I'd totally fuck." I let him smoke on the couch since it's still raining.

"Can I have a drag?" I ask, and he holds the cigarette to my lips. When the movie ends he faces me. He inches forward, slow enough that I can stop him if I want to. But I don't.

Afterward, after he's pulled me onto his lap, carried me to bed, and made love to me, sweat drips off his nose and onto my chest. "Is it all right if I stay?" he asks.

I wince. The thought of spending the entire night together nauseates me. Then waking up and seeing each other's body in slivers of light through Venetian blinds, the smell of stale sex and sleep breath. "No," I say. "It's not all right."

"Why not?"

"Because I like incrementalism."

He smiles and gets up. "Just promise me you won't disappear."

We spend the next few evenings together. One night he makes me dinner, fried steak. He cuts up Gouda and feeds me pieces while he cooks. "Who are your favorite twentieth-century poets?" he asks, and I'm so nervous that I answer Keats. "That's eighteenth," he says, smiling, "but yes, he's all right." We eat in the living room, and I barely make a dent in my plate, my appetite overshadowed by my libido. We put on a movie and five minutes into it we're undressing each other on the couch. We try to watch the movie again the next night; this time we make it halfway through before I am straddling him as he clenches my shoulder blades, the flicker of the screen casting our shadows on the wall.

Some nights he wants to talk about our pasts. He tells me about his mother, how she used to sing to him before bed. "It's amazing," he says as I run my fingers through his hair, "the pull of a mother. I guess that's why everyone relates to Proust so much." He then asks if I'm close to my own mother.

"I am," I say. "We were closer before, though." He wants to see a picture of her, and I pull a photo album out from a desk drawer, one that I put together several years ago and carry with me from city to city. There are pictures of her on almost every spread in the album, and I feel pride when he tells me she's beautiful. "She is, isn't she," I say, running my fingers across the cellophaned ridges of the page.

He tells me about his wife, which she still is. They're only separated, I keep forgetting this, that he's married to a woman I've never met. He tells me that part of the reason they broke up was because she wanted to explore her sexuality. "She was very matter-of-fact about it," he tells me, "as though she was telling me she wanted to go back to school or something!" On the fourth consecutive night together, I let him sleep over. The next morning I turn within his arms to face him. "Hi," he says as he smiles and stretches. "Shall I make coffee?"

He goes to the kitchen, and as he carries two mugs back to bed he asks me why I never talk about my last relationship.

Until now I've managed to sidestep the subject of Anna whenever he brings it up, always turning the conversation back on him. "Because," I say. "I was pretty terrible."

"Did you cheat?"

I nod. "With men, and sometimes other women." I take a sip of coffee. "Worse than that, though, I lied to her." Matías gives me a confused look, so I continue, "I don't know that lying and cheating always go together."

"So have you dated women other than Anna?"

"Is that okay?" I ask, worried that I've revealed too much. Surprisingly, it often isn't, at least not for men. At first it's a turn-on; they ask many questions, have you ever done this, would you ever try that, would I be allowed to watch sometime, and could we ever do a threesome? Then it becomes a problem, as everyone starts to seem like a threat to him, both men and women. Soon insecurity consumes the relationship and it crumbles around me.

"You know," he says, "sometimes I wish I were bisexual. But unfortunately I just like women."

I smile. It's exactly the right thing to say.

•

He tells me stories. Tells me about Guy de Maupassant's insatiable sexual appetite, his mentor Flaubert's fear that his protégé's lust would deplete his creative energy. Joyce's urine fetish, Dalí being bedridden for seven years after the death of Gala, the competitive friendship between Picasso and Matisse. He reads me Neruda, Calvino, the prostitute scenes from *Tropic of Cancer*. Tells me tales of his own sexual conquests: the neighbor's wife in Paris, a forty-two-year-old German woman in Berlin when he was twenty-one, a Vanessa Paradis look-alike in Rio whose dress fell to the floor with a gentle lift of the straps. I tell him my stories, too, and they excite him, as his excite me. He knows more than I know, has done more than I have, and I like it.

Once, he asks, "Is it weird that I fantasize about you pregnant?"

His question sends a chill of unease through me, and makes me wonder if he's toying with me. He must sense that I'm thinking this. "I'm not saying right now, of course," he continues. "But someday, I'd love to make you pregnant. Can I say that?"

"It depends. Do you mean it in a macho, spread-your-seed sort of way?"

"Of course not!" He laughs. "In an 'I would love to have a baby with you' way. I keep imaging you with Simoné." His three-year-old son. "Seeing the way you are with me, I think you'd be such a great mother."

Part of the reason for treatment was fear that I was becoming like mine. It had already started happening, me using Anna's faults as ammunition. My mother had taught me that trick. Once, Anna dropped a wineglass on my kitchen floor and I lost control. I screamed at her, insulted her, and stopped myself just before calling her absentminded and unfocused, her weaknesses, and using them against her for extra impact. Afterward, I stood in front of her breathing heavily as she stared back at me, stunned and afraid of what I'd just done. I've always wanted kids, but the risk of becoming my mother was too high to ignore.

"It would be great to have a daughter," Matías says. "I'd want her to be just like you."

In bed that night, he places his hands on my cheeks, looks me in the eye, and tells me he loves me. I immediately push his hands away and turn my head. "Don't say that," I tell him.

"Why not?" he asks. "Don't you feel the same?"

"I mean, don't say it that way, right now." I know that I need this from him—love—but I also need it to be real this time, and not an outcome of passion, or jealousy, or control. I need it to just be.

•

A week later, Matías and I are asleep when the phone in his hotel room rings. We both jump up immediately. I look to the clock on the nightstand and see that it's three a.m.

He picks up the phone and hunches over it. I can hear the faint murmur of a voice on the other end. I caress his back, but he doesn't seem to notice. I draw my hand away, feeling strangely afraid.

"What?" he says, cupping the receiver. "Of course, I do."

He mutters a few more innocuous words before hanging up. He then lies back down and tosses his arm over me like nothing happened. I scoot out from underneath it and turn to face him. "Who the hell was that?" I ask.

"Oh," he says, as though he'd already forgotten about the call, "it was just Claire."

His translator. She and I met a week earlier; Matías invited me to her birthday party, told me he thought we would really get along. "So glad you could make it," she'd said when we arrived, offering a tight smile, then looking to him. The look she'd given him suggested that she didn't know he was bringing me, and was surprised that he had. When he excused himself to chat with another visiting writer, he pressed his hand to her shoulder, which wasn't particularly troubling—he was rather indiscriminately effusive. But still. I noticed it. When it was just the two of us left standing there, I asked her where she'd learned Spanish. "Oh, everywhere," she said. "I just got back from two years in Argentina, before that I was in Madrid." I felt slight envy at this, given that I was living in Iowa.

"Claire's traveling early tomorrow to Mexico City," he says to me now. "She needed to ask me a few questions about a translation."

"At three in the morning?"

"I know, it's weird," he says. "She works nonstop. She's very American in that way." He laughs a little, then pets the top of my head. "I'm so sorry it woke you, *mi amor*." He kisses my cheek and I lie back down. I still can't shake a feeling of fear. He touches his lips to my neck. He places his hand beneath my nightgown, and I pretend that I'm already asleep.

Several days later, we are on our way to catch a flight for an impromptu trip to New York that Matías suggested and bought tickets for, and that I've been hesitant about. It seems hasty and extreme, and the impulsivity of it makes me worry. "Why the sudden need to travel?" I ask.

"Because," he says, "why not? It'll be great to explore the city with you." I am not so sure I need spontaneity right now, and I certainly am not ready to visit New York yet—I only just left a month ago. But against my better judgment, I agree to go, not wanting to seem boring or uptight.

"I did something silly last night," he tells me in the car on the way to the airport. "I kissed someone."

"You *what*?" I press the break unintentionally and the car jolts to a stop on the empty highway. He throws his arm out across my chest. I look in the rearview mirror, then at him. "Who?"

"Claire," he says as the odometer creeps back up to seventy. "Does that bother you?"

I feel my chest heaving, like I've been punched in the stomach and can't breathe. "Of course it bothers me!"

"I just thought I was moving too fast for you," he says, peering down at his shoes, then dramatically back at me. "And that you didn't care about me as much as I care about you."

My entire body is about to revolt. I've already grown tired of his need for constant reassurance. He's always complaining that I'm distant, asking if his emotions scare me. Asking if I faked it, to which I always respond, "Why must you ruin the moment by asking that?"

"I panicked," he says. "I told you I love you, and you didn't say it back."

"Yes, and like I told you then, during sex doesn't count. Plus last I checked, feeling insecure doesn't justify kissing someone else."

"I never know with you," he says, looking down at his lap. "Trying to detect how you feel is nearly impossible. I just—"

"Damn it, Matías," I interrupt, and by now I am yelling, "I'm going to New York with you! I'm not an escort, I don't just let men I don't care about take me to random cities." My heart is throbbing. "I told you I was afraid you would hurt me, right? That I wasn't ready for this?" My voice cracks and my eyes begin to burn.

"In a way," he says, placing his hand on my thigh and squeezing gently, "it makes me happy that you're upset."

I squint at him. "You're happy that I'm crying?"

"It shows me that you actually care."

I'm tempted to turn the car around, but instead I reassure him. "Yes, I do care. And maybe it's not very postmodern of me," I say, thinking of his open marriage, "but I get jealous. I know we have no claim on each other—"

"We do, though," he says. "I want us to."

At this, I begin to soften. By the time we're on the plane he's calling me his girlfriend. We're kissing and drinking tomato juice and even the flight attendant indulges us with sugary smiles. Periodically an image of him kissing Claire flashes in my mind, and I wince. "I just pictured it," I tell him.

He scrunches his brow, gives me sad eyes. "Don't," he says. "It was stupid. It lasted for two seconds and never would've happened if I wasn't drunk."

"Are you sure you didn't *sleep* with her?" I ask. "Because the thing is, you didn't answer when I called this morning at ten, and I didn't hear back from you until twelve thirty."

"I was at breakfast!"

"For two and a half hours?"

"If I slept with her, why would I even mention that I kissed her?"

In our hotel room that evening, Matías is in the shower and I'm sitting on the bed with my computer, looking up flights to Buenos Aires. "It's amazing to be in a vibrant place together," Matías said that afternoon as we walked through Washington Square Park. "Now I can't wait to take you to Argentina. Choose the dates, I'll buy you a ticket."

I smiled. "I've never been."

"Believe me," he said, "Once you're there, you won't want to come back."

As I'm sorting through flights I decide to check my email. There's one from my mother, which makes me literally gasp. We haven't spoken in nearly six months. "*Habibti*," she's written, "I'm in Amman with Teta. We wish you were here with us."

I feel an ache of desperately wanting to be there with them before my mind begins conjuring up images of the last time we saw each other, on the Manhattan side of the Brooklyn Bridge after she'd left the restaurant mid-dinner. "I miss you so, *so* much."

Her words travel past my head, down my throat, and land on my stomach. They stay there, effortlessly imposing their weight.

I hear Matías push back the shower curtain and pull a towel off the rack. He steps out of the bathroom. "My mother emailed me," I tell him. He knows I don't speak with her, but nothing beyond that.

"Are you okay?" he asks.

"I'm fine," I answer, shutting my laptop and placing it on the nightstand. He climbs onto the bed and lets his towel fall to the floor. He grabs me by my shoulders and props me up against the headboard, pulling the rubber band out of my hair. He pushes himself inside me, and I yell, "Stop!"

He jumps back. "Was that too much?"

"No." I break down into tears and tell him about her. I tell him about the summer, about Healing Internal Trauma, about grief letters. "I didn't want you to know any of this," I say.

He wraps his arms around me. "I wish you'd told me about your mother sooner," he says as I press my body against him. "Maybe you can think of me as someone who can fill that role for you. I have this urge to protect you. You're my girlfriend, but I also think of you like a daughter."

We planned to go to dinner that night in Nolita, but he suggests we stay in and order takeout. We pick up sushi and eat in bed while watching *When Harry Met Sally* on TV. By the end I can barely keep my eyes open. He turns off the television, and half awake, we make love. "I love you," I whisper. "I really do."

He comes, collapses, and I fall asleep.

•

As soon as we get back from New York I call Renata, who's now in her first year of residency at Georgetown and just coming off an overnight rotation. I catch her while she's driving home. I tell her about his kiss with Claire, the talk of pregnancy, saying "I love you." He sounds like such a cliché, she says, he obviously just wants to mess around.

"I feel like I need him," I tell her. "I can't stand being away from him for even an hour."

"You don't need him," Renata says. She then yells "asshole," presumably at another driver who's cut her off. "Sorry, what were you saying?"

As a first-year dermatology resident and newly engaged—Thomas flew them both to his family's villa in Italy and proposed—Renata has notably less time and patience for anything that isn't work- or wedding-related. "Clearly you don't trust him," she tells me. Her response isn't harsh so much as efficient; our conversations are usually curtailed by her sleep deprivation and need to maximize time between shifts for rest. I've memorized the exact amount of time it takes her to drive home from the hospital, and I know that we now have only two minutes before she turns onto her street. "What you need is to break up."

I'm immediately annoyed—as if it were that easy. She of all people should know! "Okay," I say, to allow a tidy ending to the call.

Twenty-five seconds until she pulls into her driveway. "By the way," she says, and I brace myself, knowing she's about to segue into wedding logistics. We are operating in accordance with a universal law dictating that whoever marries first can permissibly subject the other to indentured servitude vis-à-vis maid of honor duties, and expect enthusiastic, unfaltering compliance in return. "Do you think you could take a look at the bridesmaid dress options I sent?"

"Of course," I say. I hear her car door open then shut. "Sleep well."

I rush to get dressed for Matías's reading. I arrive to find people clumped around the room, holding plastic cups of pale white wine. I feel a sudden social anxiety set in, not wanting to be seen as I scan the room for him. He spots me before I do, touching his hand to my arm and startling me. "Hey," he says, "is something wrong?" When I am upset it shows all over my face. I look at my watch; his reading starts in five minutes. I don't want to get into things until after, but he keeps insisting.

"Are you playing me?" I ask. "I mean, we both know you're leaving soon," I tell him. "Is this just *une affaire de cul*?" A French expression he taught me.

"If so, then I'd have to be the worst womanizer around." He laughs, pressing his hand into the dip of my back. "I mean, think about it, would I take you to New York? Would I invite you to Buenos Aires, where sex is plentiful? Would I tell you that I want to have a baby with you?"

I don't know. Would he? And why, when we're already sleeping together? Why bother with all the extra gestures?

After the reading I go backstage to congratulate him, and he is holding roses. "Who gave you those?" I ask. He seems uncomfortable, and he turns to greet someone without answering me. I try not to overspeculate. I assume the roses are normal protocol for all readers. "I need to go to the hotel to change," he says, "but how about we meet for dinner? Maybe that place with the martinis you've been talking about?"

We get drunk that night at the restaurant. He turns to the table next to ours and asks, "Isn't my girlfriend cute?" I tell him to do his François Mitterrand imitation—*"Oui, j'ai un enfant naturel, et alors?"* I laugh and he does it again. By the time we leave I'm so drunk that I can barely walk, so he carries me home on his back. We stay in bed until late the next day, getting up only to eat and pee.

At around five in the afternoon, we decide to go for a walk along the river that runs alongside campus. "I keep wondering what I'm doing with my life," he says. "What my purpose is. I guess it's to write, but that's hard to accept when I haven't published a book in years."

"You're also a father," I remind him. "Someone's life depends on you."

We stop to share a cigarette under a tree. We talk about our imagined life together in Argentina. "Would you be interested in teaching?" he asks. "Because I could get you a job lecturing at the American university. You could take the spring and try it. Try living with me?"

"Maybe," I say. "Too bad I've been studying French all these years." He smiles, then leans forward and kisses me. After a while he stands and helps me up off of the ground. As we continue walking, we sing. Joni Mitchell, Leonard Cohen, Joan Baez. It's getting dark and the university crew rows by. "What are you thinking about right now?" he asks.

"The little red lights on the boats," I answer.

"Me too!" he says. "They're like clown noses, Matisse red, alarming but familiar."

"I never come back this way," I tell him.

"Good to know. Then I can bring my other girlfriend here."

I nudge him playfully, and he takes my hand. "Would you think I was a jerk if I went back to my room tonight, to write?"

"Of course not," I say. "We don't have to spend *every* night together."

•

Several evenings later Matías comes over. He ties me to the fridge using my bra, arms behind my back, skin drawn tight across my chest. For weeks now, he's been saying that he wants to tie me up, "and have my way with you," he'd whisper in my ear while pressing himself against my hip bone.

The next morning I wake up to the sound of the toilet flushing; he comes out of the bathroom and slides back into bed, shivering. I wrap blanketed arms around him and pull him close, and I fall back asleep. The second time I wake up, he is gone—he's spending the weekend in Chicago with the other writers-in-residence—and I am hugging a pillow that smells like him.

I go to make coffee in the kitchen, where yesterday's clothes have been folded neatly and placed on a chair. I gather them and carry them to my room, along with my laptop. I'm planning to spend the weekend without Matías catching up on my own writing. As I'm sitting in bed checking email my phone buzzes with a text from a classmate who volunteered to show the visiting writers around Chicago. *Sorry to ask, but do you have any knowledge of Matías's whereabouts? He's not on the bus with everyone else.*

I feel my cheeks tingle with a flush of blood. I've been trying to keep our relationship a secret—unsurprisingly, dating the visiting writers is highly discouraged—and I clearly haven't succeeded. Next comes concern. I imagine him leaving my apartment and getting hit by a car. He still doesn't have a cell phone, just the phone in his hotel room, which he never answers. I think back to a recent conversation. "Claire will also be in Chicago this weekend," he told me, "and we'll all probably be spending time together. I wanted to let you know, and if it bothers you, I won't go."

"No, it doesn't bother me," I responded, which was true. I no longer felt threatened by their tequila-infused kiss. "I've decided to trust you, remember?"

"Good, because you have nothing to worry about. Though I'm beginning to suspect that Claire's interested in more than just my work."

"Well, kissing her might've led her on a bit, Matías."

Annoyed, I respond to my coworker's text, *Maybe he got a ride with Claire?*

In class that afternoon, my mind wanders to the night before. I took part in a reading, and afterward everyone went to a bar. I had eagerly signed up, knowing I've been far less focused on both writing and getting to know my cohort than I should be. So far, almost all my attention has been devoted to Matías, and to how to act around him whenever we were together in public. "Want to go for a walk first?" Matías asked. He led me away from downtown, in the direction of my apartment.

"Where are we going?" I asked.

"The Midwestern landscape is almost obscenely demure," he said, diverting the question. "But there's something oddly thrilling about it." Soon we were standing in front of my building. "Why don't we just stay in tonight?" he suggested.

I was disappointed. I wanted to go out with the others after the reading, my first in this town. But we were already back at my place. Besides, it was always awkward to be in a group setting together. I never knew how to interact with Matías around other people, how to pretend to be "just friends" without seeming unnaturally detached. "Okay," I said.

"Great, I'm going to the hotel to pack for Chicago. I'll be back in an hour."

My mind now crackles with questions. What did he do in that hour he was gone last night? Why didn't he want to go to the bar? Why hasn't he called since leaving? Why wasn't he on the train with everyone else?

By Saturday morning I still haven't heard from him. I call Renata and it goes straight to her voice mail, meaning she's either working a weekend shift or asleep. I then email Matías. "I need to talk to you. Call me as soon as you get this. I hate that you don't have a cell phone."

My head spins with images of him and Claire gallivanting around Chicago. Feeding each other bites off small plates in restaurants. Having hotel shower sex. Him inviting her to Buenos Aires, her tossing her head back in delight before accepting. Later they'll laugh at the thought of me, how cute I was to believe that I was anything more than a fling.

The spinning is out of control and I know it would help to get to the nearest Twelve Step meeting—any kind. "It's all the same," Richard said on my first day at the Ledge, and by now I understand what he meant. But instead of looking up meetings, I scroll through my phone to find the number of a Lebanese med student I met at a a coffee shop last week. I overheard him speaking in Arabic over the phone, which led to a conversation and him giving me his number. I send him a message: *Any plans tonight?*

•

That evening, Matías finally calls. "I got your email," he says. "What's wrong?"

"Where are you?"

"In Chicago, where do you think I am?"

I tell him about the text from my coworker.

"I missed the train and got a ride in Claire's car with three of her friends," he says. "You're not mad at me for that, are you?"

"I don't know, Matías. It seems like it's always something. Either you kissed her, or she's calling at midnight to ask a question, or, oops! You missed the train and got stuck together!"

"It's funny that you're mad at me," he says, "because I'm here wishing I hadn't come on this trip. I'm about to take a train home right now."

I roll my eyes. "You don't need to be dramatic. Just tell me, are you cheating on me?"

"Of course I'm not, are you being serious?!" he asks, sounding incredulous. "I can't wait to see you tomorrow."

"Who are you rooming with at the hotel?"

"Oh, the Swedish guy. I barely even notice him. He hasn't spent a single moment in the room. He's such a playboy."

No part of me likes his answer. "What are you doing tonight?" he asks.

A Lebanese doctor is taking me to the movies. "Writing," I tell him.

"Can I call you in the morning?"

"Yes," I say. "Please do."

The doctor picks me up at nine. He's wearing a tie and seems excited to see me. "I was hoping you'd call," he says, "I wasn't sure if you would." I sense I'm supposed to say something to confirm this, but instead I just smile and stare at the road ahead. All I can think about during the movie is Matías, how much I'd rather be anywhere with him. I almost yell his name in the theater. Afterward, the doctor drives me back home, and I practically jump out of the car and run inside. I flip open my laptop and sign into my email. "I just want to tell you," I write to Matías, furiously and guiltily, "that I love you."

By Sunday at noon he still hasn't called. At one thirty he responds to my email. "I love you, too. I question whether I was ever happy before we met, if I even knew what happiness was."

I don't want his overblown professions of undying love. I want a phone call. I write back, "When will you be home? I'd like to see you." And I wait for a response.

I try to find things to do. I rearrange my bookshelf. I rewash all the dishes in the cabinet, then go through my clothes and make piles for Goodwill. By the time I've moved from the closet to the dresser he's responded: "Me and some of the other writers decided to stay in Chicago until Monday to see *The Winter's Tale* at the Shakespeare Theater. It's supposed to be a fabulous production. I thought maybe you could catch a train up here to meet us. If not I'll come over the second I'm back. I'll call you as soon as I can."

Right then, I know. All the unnecessary exposition, the time between emails. As if to confirm my suspicions Matías calls seven times that night. I don't pick up his first call. He leaves two messages. The first is breezy; the second, panicked. "Is everything okay? Why aren't you answering? I'm starting to worry."

This is what fear of getting caught looks like. Fear of losing. I know. I've seen it before.

"Hopefully you'll learn you can't treat people with such disregard." My mind summons the words from Anna's email. "Even yourself."

I think back to those terrible days in the desert after she found out. All along I knew what I was doing was wrong, that I was dangerously close to a precipice. But still, I need to fall in order to stop. Beyond the shock of getting caught was the realization that I had hurt someone, and badly. I'd lied for so long, and not just to Anna. But the idea of losing her because of something I'd done, a series of mistakes, the thought of being alone, was all too much to bear.

Matías has checked his email on my laptop, and I try logging into his account. I type "M" into the user-name field. His handle pops up, but the password isn't saved. I make several incorrect guesses before closing the browser and forcefully shutting the screen.

On Monday morning, I answer a call from an unknown number. "What the hell is going on?" Matías asks frantically.

I hang up and he keeps calling back. He sends me a text message: *I bought a cell phone, call me. Please.* He calls eighteen times throughout the rest of the day. Each time I hit "ignore," I feel momentary doubt—what if I'm wrong, and punishing him unnecessarily? I put my phone away, unable to watch as the calls accrue.

That evening I'm leaving my apartment and I run into him right outside. He's walking fast, lighting a cigarette, eyes pregnant with fury. He stops when he sees me. "I was just on my way up to your place. Are you ignoring me?"

"Obviously. There's nothing to say, Matías, I know you're sleeping with Claire."

"I'm not!" he protests, grabbing my arm and squeezing it. "Call her now, she'll tell you."

"Don't be ridiculous."

"I was being evasive this weekend, yes. But Claire has nothing to do with it." He sighs, then stares at the ground before making eye contact again. "It's my wife. She wants to get back together, and I needed time to think about it, for my son's sake."

Now I feel embarrassed. I feel low. "If that's true," I say, "then of course you should save your marriage."

He shakes his head. "But I decided that what I want is you. Besides, I think my son would be better off with happy, divorced parents than with miserable married ones."

I think of my own parents, how relieved I was when the fighting stopped. Back in New York I'd often wake up in the middle of the night certain I could hear them yelling at each other, only to peer out my window onto a sidewalk quarrel.

I look at Matías. I fear I'm being paranoid, that I'm projecting my own insecurities onto him. He takes my hand—he must sense that I'm softening. "I was a jerk for being so distant," he says. "I should've called. But I'm not cheating. I promise you nothing like this will happen again."

"I need some time," I tell him.

"I'll give you ten years, *mi amor*, if that's what you need."

Two days later I'm still thinking about Chicago and that extra night. Finally I call someone, a mutual friend of mine and Claire's.

"Hold on," she says, "you're still dating him?"

"Yes," I say.

"I had no idea."

"So he was with Claire in Chicago?"

"Of course. They've been seeing each other for a while now."

"Are you sure?"

"I'm sure," she says. "I would've told you myself, but I had no idea you were still together."

In that moment, I am surprised that rather than feeling angry or sad, I feel relieved.

My phone beeps with a call from Matías, which I ignore. He calls back, again and again. In between comes a call from a familiar D.C. number. And that one I do answer.

"*Ahlan wa Sahlan!*" says my mother. I take a deep breath as the sound of her voice courses through my veins. "How are you, *mama*?" she asks.

Over the next hour I pour out everything, collapsing the distance between us that I've spent the last six months working to create. "*Habibti*," she says, and again I feel her voice run through me. I can tell she's relieved that it's a man I'm torn up over, not a woman. "*Yalla*, come home for a few days," she says. "I'll take care of you."

I hesitate. "I'll think about it," I say. I know that by letting her

in when I'm in need, I tie myself to her again, this gaping vulnerability nothing less than the rope.

At home later that evening I hear a knock on my back door. I lift
the shade and see Matías standing outside the window, sweating
and frowning. I point to the phone pressed to my ear. "I'm talking
to Claire," I tell him calmly, as though that's normal. I'd sent her
an email after finding out, along with my number. She called ten
minutes later, and right then we're running through our calen-
dars, each remembering nights we weren't with him, the lies he'd
told about staying in to work when in fact he was with one of us.

He puts his hands in the air like I'm about to arrest him. "I'm
crazy," he says. "I'm just . . . crazy. I only did this because I was
terrified you were going to leave me. I need to tell you—"

"Why don't you tell Claire as well," I say, placing the call on
speakerphone.

"It's you, not Claire. I'm in love with you."

My stomach twitches. He's desperately trying to salvage one
of us, and I am the most susceptible. "You are a sick fuck," I say.
"You have no conscience. You're a sociopath. A narcissist. You're
a sex addict!"

"I'm not! Sometimes, people recently out of marriages—"

"Shut up," I say. "Just stop talking."

"I think I'm gonna go," Claire interrupts.

"Do you want to come over and confront him yourself?" I
give her my address and she says she'll be over in ten minutes.
We hang up, and now I am alone with him. "You purposefully
led me away from the bar after my reading the other night, didn't
you? Because you thought Claire might be there?"

He nods, and I shudder. I take a deep breath and wait for the wave of fury to subside. "I'm actually afraid of you."

"Look, I may be pathetic," he says, "but I'm not dangerous."

"How do I know that? I don't even know who you really are."

"Did Claire tell you I ended things with her on the car ride back from Chicago?"

I feel my blood heating. "After fucking her all weekend? That's classy."

"I know I've lost you," he says. "I know you don't believe anything I say anymore. But when she gets here, I want to tell her—"

"Don't. Don't even dare."

After what feels like hours I hear a knock on the front door. "Follow me," I say. "I don't trust you alone in my living room." I open the door and find Claire standing there, her hands cupping the sides of her waist, her weight shifted to one side. Her hip juts out from a turtleneck dress, like a finger beckoning from her body. The two of us take a moment to examine each other. I can't reconcile how different we look—Claire is about a foot taller than me, blond, and very angular. It seems strange that the same man would be attracted to both of us. We exchange polite smiles. "Come in," I say. She follows me through the corridor, walking past Matías without glancing in his direction, and into the living room. She sits down on the couch, and suddenly I feel this may be the worst idea ever. Once we're all seated, she crosses her arms and looks up at him.

"You disgust me," she says.

He doesn't answer. Instead he turns toward me. "Can I please tell you something?"

"Get out," I say, with difficulty.

"No," he says. "I won't."

His defiance makes it less difficult to insist. "I will literally call the police right now," I tell him. At this, he nods solemnly, and leaves.

Claire and I sit silently as the air thickens and then thins. I'm the first to puncture the silence. "Want some tea?"

She nods, and I get up to boil water. "I have mint, chamomile, and—"

"I ended a three-year relationship for him," Claire interrupts. "He was making all kinds of promises. And the sex . . ."

"Yes," I say. "I know."

I had never been able to escape the hollowness. Always, in the moments immediately after coming, I felt a sharp and excruciating emptiness. Within moments it was gone, but for those first few seconds, as my muscles relaxed and my breathing slowed, I would experience a despair that I'd come to dread. With Matías, though, the emptiness was replaced by something. Not so much a significance, but a barrier that kept me from descending into unbearable sadness. I'd interpreted this as a sign that our relationship was somehow meaningful, that it might carry me away from my past and allow me to untether from it.

"Well," Claire says. "I'm glad we found out. At least we won't romanticize him anymore. And we certainly won't be sad when he's gone."

Before she leaves we agree to keep in close contact. "Call me whenever you're tempted to call him," she says, "and I'll do the same."

"Thanks," I say. "Though I'm sure it won't be long before one of us runs into him. Definitely at the visiting writers' farewell party."

Clare rolls her eyes. "I forgot about that." She shrugs. "Well, let's go together, then. That way neither of us has to go alone."

•

It's almost been a week since it ended, and I've been wondering how I could've actually believed that Matías was sincere, that he was in any way real. How did I not see through him?

I leave the café where I've been all afternoon, and as I'm walking across the pedestrian thoroughfare, I spot him. I try to keep walking, to look down at the to-go cup in my hand, but I can't stay focused. Without meaning to, I walk toward him, as if a rope is pulling me. I stand in front of him and say nothing.

"Give me five minutes," he pleads. I cross my arms and stay quiet. "Two minutes. Please."

"Speak."

"I keep remembering." He looks away. "The little red lights."

He goes on to say things that sound sincere but that I can't let myself believe, as much as I want to. They sounded sincere before, and I believed them before. To my frustration I understand his behavior: I've been that person, the one holding two people hostage in case I were to lose one.

"I wish you knew how much I love you," he says to me.

"Of course you love me," I snap back, if only to keep my ego intact. "I have no doubt that you love me." I begin to laugh crazily. "I gave you the most authentic parts of me," I tell him. At least this is what I want to believe, that I've practiced healthy intimacy with him, despite how much I've actually withheld. I want to him to think that I allowed him every point of access, every vulnerability, and that he'd allowed me his, too, that we had guns to each other's head and he just happened to shoot first. "You don't get to love me anymore." I push past him and walk home, alone as ever.

I arrive home to his name once again in my inbox. And, of course, I open the email. "The trip to New York was real. My concern when you were upset about your mother was real. My pride when you read on stage was real." The sentences come at me like knives, each one cleaving deeper and deeper into my chest. "You cannot fake the affinity we have, and I very much wanted us to last. I finally met a woman I loved, and who loved me, and who made me happy, and whom I made happy—and I hurt her beyond repair. I did the terrible things I did because I was a mess. If we had met six months from now, when I'd fully recovered from the hang-ups of my marriage, everything would've been different."

The cheating, the lies, all of it should hollow out every last word. And yet somehow, in a way that disturbs me, it doesn't.

I forward his email to Renata, who calls me moments later. "Love aside," she says, "what matters is how he treated you."

"I know," I say, but then I find myself telling her about the emptiness, the feeling I've always experienced afterward, how I didn't feel it with him, how with him, I felt fulfilled. I felt healthy.

"Then maybe it's time you find some healthy love."

•

He sends more emails. Several each day, and their heaviness drains me. "There may come a time when you want to see me again," he writes. "And then, if you allow me a chance, I'll show you that the guy you knew, the one who wanted to stand by you in your life and your career, is really me, this time without baggage."

Baggage. No one ever breaks free from it. Everyone has to figure out how to go on living, to be decent, in spite of it.

"Trust me," I write back, emboldened by hurt, "there will never be a time when I want to see you again."

He continues to write to me. He begs me to see him before he leaves, half an hour, just thirty minutes. "There are things I am aching to tell you," he writes, "and I can't help but feel that the clock is ticking."

It's true. He's leaving in a few days. And I feel it, too, the pressure of time running out, though at this point it shouldn't matter. I've lost all faith in him. But the danger exists, that I might still leap.

Finally, I concede. "I will meet you in a public place, for one drink."

I bury my face in my hands, wishing he were already gone.

•

We meet at a wine bar several blocks from my apartment. The things he is "aching to say" turn into four hours of conversation, two bottles of Malbec, and countless tears. "I was just using her," he says. "To protect myself from getting hurt. You were just so . . . distant, and I was falling deeper and deeper in love."

I internalize his implicit criticism, his blaming his cheating on me. "Well, I was scared too," I say. "And trust me, I'm more scared now."

"Don't be!" he says. "There are no more secrets now. I'm just so relieved to be through with Clare."

We say our goodbyes on the street outside the bar. Just as I'm about to turn away and walk back to my apartment a truck comes roaring down the street. Matías grabs me and pulls me out of the way as it speeds past, the two of us tumbling onto the sidewalk, his hand protecting the back of my head. As we lie side by side on the cement, both breathing heavily, he looks at me and says, "That would be the *worst* ending . . ."

"I was just going to say that!"

He caresses my cheek with the back of his finger. "So will I ever see you again?" he asks.

I close my eyes and shake my head. "I don't know. Maybe someday."

•

It's the night of the farewell party. In the morning the visiting writers are all leaving. As planned, I meet up with Claire beforehand. "Have you heard from him?" I ask, and immediately regret it.

"Not a word," Claire says. "You?"

I hesitate. When you don't want to lose someone, it's so tempting to deceive them.

AFTER THAT NIGHT AT THE WINE BAR WITH MATÍAS, IT'S as if Claire, the cheating, and the lies never happened. That next night he is back in my bed, which entails more crying, and the following evening we are having dinner at the fanciest restaurant in town—the only fancy restaurant in town—followed by Tanqueray and tonics at the bar next door. I cling to his arm the entire night, not wanting to let go, knowing he'll be leaving in the morning. At five a.m. he kisses me goodbye as he gets up and returns to his hotel, where a bus waits to take him to the airport.

When he arrives in Argentina the next afternoon, he calls me right away. "There's someone here who wants to say hello."

"*Ciaoooo bella*," Simoné, his three-year-old son squeaks into my ear, giggling before handing the phone back to his father.

I immediately melt into a puddle, picturing myself with him and his son, mothering them both. At that precise moment Matías sweeps in with his initial invitation to Buenos Aires. Three weeks, all expenses paid, guaranteed time of my life. "Think about it," he says. "We can spend Christmas Day at Iguazu Falls."

I find myself accepting the offer the next day, just before

heading home to D.C. for Thanksgiving. Since things with my mother are still fragile in the wake of our six-month hiatus, I decide to stay with Renata and Thomas in Cleveland Park. "I'm going to Buenos Aires for three weeks," I tell them. "I've already decided. I know you guys disapprove, but I just don't think he would hurt me a second time."

"Okayyyyy," Renata says as Thomas sits beside her nodding solemnly. Now that he's finally committed, Thomas has taken on the distinct responsibility and conviction of a former player, called upon to fight on behalf of all women who've suffered at the hands of his abandoned ilk.

Over drinks that night, they ask me to hash out the events of the past few months, how I came to find out that Matías had been cheating on me for the majority of our relationship. As I retell the story, I feel a renewed sense of shock, and I'm humiliated by the depth of his lies. I chew an ice cube from my vodka soda as the three of us go through his emails, the ones he sent begging me to see him one more time, emails with pictures of newborn babies attached.

"Since you're craving kids right now," Matías wrote, "here's a picture of me holding my son when he was only a month old."

"You fell for this?" Thomas asks, seeming genuinely disappointed, and possibly ashamed. Maybe it reminds of his own past tactics. By the end of the night I am intoxicated enough to see things clearly. And to realize that I'm not going anywhere.

I tell Matías this in an email, that I no longer want to go to Buenos Aires, that I don't want to continue on with him at all. "It's just too much," I write. "Too much to try and move past."

I wake up the next morning to a deluge of missed calls and

emails. "At least tell me this to my face, over Skype," he writes. "Breaking up over email is like spitting on everything we've had."

I want to point out that he already did that by sleeping with someone else the entire time we were together. Instead, I sign on to Skype and accept his call. He sits on the other end, a lit cigarette resting in the ashtray beside his computer, his lips contorted into a forced pout. "Baby, what's going on?" he asks, cocking his head to the side like a confused monkey. "Come on, talk to me."

As I try to explain myself, staring into his eyes encircled by dark planetary rings of sadness and experience, my resolve begins to weaken.

"I just think if this going to work, we need to move a little slower," I say, completely reneging on my stance from the night before.

He nods. "I see. Well, since you won't come here—he pauses, swallows audibly and takes a deep, dramatic breath—"I'll come to you. Once the academic quarter ends in late January. I have a month off, and we can spend it together."

"I need to move on, Matías. I can't keep—"

"Just think about it," he interrupts. "That's all I'm asking."

"GREG'S DEAD." IT'S THE FIRST LINE OF MOLLY'S EMAIL. Blunt, with nothing there to soften it. "He overdosed in a parking lot. I wanted to tell you over the phone but you never answer when I call."

I'm in the midst of debating Matías's proposition when I get Molly's email. The news launches me back to that day at the coffee shop in Bowling Green, when Greg told me that he was planning to meet up with his intern in Miami instead of going home and putting his life back together. I think about what he told us during the first week, how his father had left when he was a kid, how he'd never thought himself worth sticking around for. Never thought himself worthy of love.

While I was in treatment I heard about others who'd checked out and died soon afterward. They overdosed, drove drunk, committed suicide. It was hard to make sense of these incidents, especially since everyone I encountered left the Ledge seemed so determined to get clean and sober. At what point did that resolve fade? After a few months, a few weeks? On the car ride home?

It terrifies me to think about how close to danger I've often lived. "Better safe than sorry." Everyone at the Ledge echoed the adage whenever I vowed to distance myself from destructive behavior and people, and especially from my mother. For a long time, I've imagined telling her that I want everything she's wanted me to pursue—a marriage, children, a lucrative career. But growing up in her house, subjected to her erratic rages, I didn't have the energy. I was exhausted just trying to survive.

In high school I would skid down the driveway to get laundry detergent—her discovery that the bottle was empty would trigger a rageful episode—only to wish to casually drive into incoming traffic on the way there. I couldn't always distract myself with sex or a drink, or any other usual means of distraction. In the meantime nonexistence often seemed like a viable alternative.

By the time I would return from the store she'd have calmed down. "*Yalla*, let's go for breakfast," she might suggest. I was expected to have brushed off the rebukes and be ready for eggs Benedict.

"I'm leaving," I would say, a halfhearted effort to stand up for myself, swearing to sear the memory of the incident onto my consciousness. I knew better than to leave myself no out. But inevitably, the hurt would fade too quickly, and two hours later we'd be having lunch.

Other times her rage surfaced if I tried to set a boundary and assert some control. Suggesting we set a time to run errands or help with her résumé inevitably led to an explosion—how dare I not give in to whatever she wanted, the moment she wanted it, and have a life of my own that didn't directly involve serving her?

"Better safe than sorry," everyone says. But for a while I've been afraid I could never truly be either.

15

"YOU FUCK WELL," I SAY TO THE ARAB ENTHUSIAST AS he lies heavy on top of me, still inside me. He pulls out slowly and rolls the condom off, tying it in a knot and tossing it onto the nightstand. He then lies back against the pillow, his chest still heaving as I rest my head on it.

The Arab Enthusiast is a twenty-two-year-old Oriental Studies major—they still call it that out here. He's a native Midwesterner, a double black belt in jiujitsu, and the linchpin in my attempts to distract myself until Matías returns. So far it's working, despite the fact that I've almost called out Matías's name several times during sex.

I met the Enthusiast through a friend. He had just come back from the West Bank, so we had plenty to talk about on our first date. He'd been once before—with Birthright Unplugged in high school, the alternative to Birthright Israel, which involves touring the occupied West Bank.

"So you're Jewish, but Pro-Palestinian?" I asked as he chalked the tip of a pool cue. "Do you get a lot of heat for that?"

"Sure." He shot his stick and sank two balls. "But I'm not changing my beliefs because of it."

Over dinner a few nights later we discussed Egypt. There was unreported talk of protests brewing against unemployment and government corruption inspired by events in Tunisia, where a street vendor had lit himself on fire in frustration, spurring demonstrations that toppled their own fifty-year military dictatorship. The Enthusiast knew everything about what was going on in Cairo.

"Apparently more than ninety thousand people have signed up on Facebook for a 'Day of Revolution,'" he told me. "And it's supposed to happen in the next few days, in Tahrir Square."

Over dessert I noticed a thin scar just underneath his left eye. "I got knifed," he said when I asked about it, running my finger along the puffy skin. "By an Israeli soldier while I was protesting the wall."

The idea of him resisting on Palestine's behalf left me both thrilled and certain that I should invite him home with me. "So should we pay and get out of here?"

By the time we made it inside my apartment I was already halfway undressed. As he groped me against the wall before leading me to the bedroom, I felt an eerie familiarity, as though he were channeling Matías. For a moment I genuinely believed he was there in the room with us. I fought to the push the flashes of him from my mind.

I've seen the Enthusiast almost every evening since. Tonight he's over at my apartment. We watched a documentary about the Boycott, Divestment, and Sanctions movement before making our way to my bedroom. "I better get going," he says afterward. "I've got an early class tomorrow."

"No problem," I tell him. Perfect, in fact.

At eleven the next morning, I'm still in bed when my phone

rings. It's an international number—Matías. I haven't thought about him in almost three days.

"*Mi amor!*" he says when I answer, a frantic urgency attached to his voice. "I need to ask you something."

"What is it?"

"Do you still love me?"

I look at my nightstand and notice that the Enthusiast forgot to throw out his used condoms before leaving. "Yes, I do love you," I respond. "Why are you asking?"

"Because I just booked my plane ticket," he tells me, the urgency replaced by smug satisfaction. "I'm coming to see you, baby."

•

I know that I need to move on, I need to forget him. But in between nights with the Enthusiast, Matías becomes a character in every novel I read and reread. He is Swann. He is Heathcliff, Valmont, Rodolphe. He is Henry Miller, the one I know through Anaïs Nin's diaries. We Skype almost every day, him regularly appearing in boxer briefs if it's the end of the evening, or in a leather jacket and tight-fitting Diesel jeans if he is on his way out. We describe our airport reunion to each other dozens of times—twenty-first-century TSA security never factors in to our fantasies. All the while, I'm hoping that I'll wake up the next day and no longer want him.

"You're not sleeping with anyone there, are you?" he asks periodically. "Because I just think it will be so much better when we finally do see each other, if we both hold out. I know I'm planning to."

Renata and Thomas each remind me that Matías wasn't able to "hold out" from sleeping with someone else *while* he was sleeping with me, when we lived in the same zip code, let alone thousands of miles apart. "He loves himself too much to go without sex," Thomas tells me over FaceTime, Renata visible in the background, shaking her head while studying for her board exams. "He needs the constant validation that comes with boning a variety of random women."

I nod in fake agreement. I can't help but feel that Matías is sincere this time, that he wouldn't risk losing me twice. The reward for both parties is just too great: four weeks together in a freezing Midwest winter, the perfect measure of his determination and commitment, at the end of which I'll leave school and accompany him back to Buenos Aires, just in time for spring. Once there I'll write and teach at the American university.

"Chances are you'll be working the register at the neighborhood supermarket," Renata chimes in without looking up from her textbook. "Do *not* quit school, trust me, you'll regret it."

"I end up regretting most of my decisions," I respond. "So I guess I'm doomed either way."

Matías and I discuss the possibility that it might not work out, that our relationship might always be haunted by "the hell," as he's come to term the cheating months, as if he'd been assigned to his infidelity and had no control over it. He might never succeed in fully restoring my faith in him, and my resentment and mistrust might be too great to overcome. He assures me that doubt is an inevitable, even necessary, component of any relationship, and that any love worth pursuing entails risk—some more than others. Though we bicker over the specifics, we both agree that the wager is worth making. And so I spend my time counting down until his visit, running diagonal lines through the squares on my calendar as the months turn to weeks, and, eventually, days.

But as his arrival approaches, something unexpected takes hold. A phenomenon in which he begins to appear smaller. Less exciting. A little pathetic, even. Just like with others who came before, I've crystallized an illusion of Matías that's composed of an initial fantasy and the filter of distance. Yet this time, the illusion doesn't hold up. Ever so slowly, it begins to disintegrate.

As it does so, practical concerns began to seep in. I make an appointment at the local clinic to get tested for everything he might've given me, which in a turn of luck is nothing. I sit on the edge of the examination table, feet crossed at the ankles, feeling I might shatter if even the nurse touches me. I tell her about him. "Could you be pregnant?" she asks.

I shake my head and feel an ache in my chest. "I don't think so."

"Did he use protection?"

"Not always," I tell the nurse.

Finally, just two days before Matías is supposed to fly here, I muster up the strength to tell him that I've changed my mind about us, that I don't want him to return.

"I don't get it," he says. "You're saying you feel differently than you did just last week?"

"Yes. That's exactly what I'm saying."

But he refuses to accept this, he keeps insisting. "I'm coming there, even if it's just so you can break up with me in person. Then I'll leave the next day. That night, even."

"Matías—"

"If I don't come," he raises his voice, "then we'll both always wonder what seeing each other might've done for us."

As promised, he comes. In truth I'm happy to let him, rather than risk regret. And during his visit, I manage to resist him. Sex with the Enthusiast seems a harmless distraction compared to the potential destruction of Matías. We sleep together only once, on his first day, and I realize before we even make it to my bed that the spell is broken, the appeal of him no longer exists. I am amazed by how quickly and completely it's diminished when faced with his reality.

I see him only a few times after that, once for dinner, then again for coffee. We spend an afternoon writing together in his hotel room, with no sex, just feedback and a few laughs. Pavarotti sings on low volume in the background as we work. I ask Matías if he thinks we could transition into a friendship, supporting each other in our creative lives and in our future relationships. I could see him being an excellent confidant, which is ironic, I tell him, given that he broke the trust by conducting a parallel relationship the entire time we were dating. He seems hurt by the question. "I think it's a bit soon to think of us as just friends," he says, "but maybe one day we can braid each other's hair."

After ten days, he surrenders. He changes his flight to leave two and a half weeks earlier than planned. I drive him to the airport and drop him off outside the airport, underneath the departure sign, with no extended farewell. By the time he leaves he can no longer save me, even if either of us had still wanted him to.

16

TARA GREW UP IN SOME SORT OF COMMUNE THAT I CAN
never quite visualize when she mentions it. Her dad is a drum-
mer and a bit of a player, she tells me, her mother needy and
dependent—both drug addicts. A poetry MFA student, Tara
moved into the apartment next door to mine a few days ago.
Her divorce was finalized over the summer. "He stopped effing
me years ago," she tells me when I stop by to give her the Wi-Fi
password. She's just finished baking banana bread and offers me a
piece, along with a glass of lemonade. "I once mentioned that we
didn't have enough sex, and as punishment, he stopped sleeping
with me entirely."

It's been a year since things ended for good with Matías. I
quickly lost interest in the Enthusiast, mostly because I wasn't yet
over Matías. Even though I felt relieved when he flew home two
weeks early, I still find myself wondering what my life would've
been like had I gone to Buenos Aires. To quell these counterfactu-
als I started dating someone new, a visual art professor at another
university in-state. It's quasi-long-distance; he lives and teaches
an hour and half away. We see each other on weekends. It's cozy
between us, our relationship lukewarm, and for now that's okay.

Tara and I become fast friends based on shared daytime boredom and light evening alcoholism. *Wanna meet on the front porch?* she texts me a few nights after she moves in to the building. *I could use a glass of vino.*

I find her outside, sitting on the top stair in a pink chiffon dress, her legs stretched out across the next few steps. She wears rubber sandals and her toes are unpainted. She pours me a glass of red wine. Tara only drinks red, I quickly learn, no matter the season. We get intimate fast, exchanging stories of family trauma. She tells me she's of Syrian descent, that her grandmother was from Damascus. I tell her about Matías and Claire. I talk a little about Kate, and about Anna. I wouldn't have guessed you were bi, Tara tells me. I shrug. "Isn't everyone, these days?"

I run into her sober the next day. It's a little awkward, we maybe said too much last night. "Just so you know," she says, "anything you told me stays between us."

It's a nice assurance, but unnecessary—by now I've grown more comfortable telling these stories. Still, I feel shy, and I blush a little. Thanks, I say. Same for you.

Our drinking sessions become more frequent, and I look forward to them throughout the day. As the nights grow colder, we switch to drinking in my living room. She takes off her ankle boots and socks and lies barefoot across my green couch. She is small against it, like a child in a swimming pool. I sit in a blue armchair facing her, as though I'm a psychiatrist, though she asks most of the questions. She asks about my current relationship. "He's done teaching for the week by Wednesday but he never comes down until Saturday," I tell her. "I guess he's pretty clear about his priorities."

"He seems subdued," she says after meeting him, tapping her finger against her chin. "Not nearly as dynamic as you."

I've been feeling increasingly slighted by his work and self-absorption. The infrequency with which he throws me down to fuck me and how quickly he is up and out of bed on our Sunday mornings.

I admit to some mild dissatisfaction.

Her observations become increasingly suggestive, her questions more leading. Most of our conversations feel intentionally weighted, though maybe I'm imbuing them with intention. One night we arrive at the end of a bottle around midnight, at which point it's time for her to go back to her apartment. I walk her to my front door. She smiles and reaches forward to hug me. When she pulls away we make eye contact before saying good night. Her eyes are icy gray, almost blue. They seem to hold both intensity and surprising vulnerability. They seem to say what she doesn't want to.

•

Tara is a runner. She does it to relieve anxiety, she says, for peace of mind, and I assume to stay thin, as well. She stretches on the front porch, sweaty after her long runs. One afternoon, I step outside with a *New Yorker* and I sit down on the steps. I watch her stretch; her legs are tan and long and tight. She presses her heel into the cement and bends over to hold the toe of her sneaker at a forty-five-degree angle. I suddenly feel self-conscious. She asks if I'll wait for her to shower so we can walk to the reading together. Yes, I say, I'll wait for her.

She steps back out an hour later, freshly showered and wearing fishnet tights and a dress—always a skirt or a dress. She somehow looks even tanner now, glowing.

At the reading, we end up sitting a few seats apart. My eyes keep catching her legs, bound up in netting. Afterward we go to an imitation speakeasy with a few others poets in her cohort. We talk about dating other writers, about "MFA goggles," a phenomenon in which men who would be considered unattractive in any other setting became appealing here, due to the lack of options. "I slept with Jimmy again," Tara tells the group. Jimmy is our across-the-street neighbor and her intermittent hookup. "Case in point."

I feel slightly disappointed, momentarily forgetting that I sleep with my boyfriend every weekend. I'm also a little relieved. Tara and I can go back to just being friends, with no possibility of more, none of the efforts that come with attraction. I drink several cocktails, and at last call we order a martini to split. It's sufficient, we're drunk. We walk home together, and once we arrive at our building she invites me to her apartment for one more drink, though we both know we don't need any more.

She lies on her couch, which is a futon that the last tenant, a fellow poet, left behind. I sit on the edge of it. We make small talk. I start to shiver. "You're freezing," she says. "Let me get you a blanket."

She returns with a colorful knitted quilt and proceeds to drape it over me. We keep talking. I start touching her leg, cautiously at first, and then with increasing confidence. I move my hand up her thigh. I'm still shivering as I press my fingers against the holes in her fishnets. We keep talking as if nothing is happening. I inch my hand higher; her body feels warmer. I ask inane, mindless questions. She smiles and laughs a little, and asks, "Do you really care?"

I shake my head. "I don't."

I kiss her. At first it just feels like mouth on mouth, lips against lips. But I keep kissing her, and it starts to feel good. I run my fingers through her hair, I move my body on top of hers. She bends her knees and I am between her legs. I cup her hips with my palms as I kiss her. Her kisses are full, she flicks her tongue against mine, her body beneath me feels tiny and I like it. She says we should probably go to her room. I let her lead me through the dark and to her bed. She tells me this is new for her. I tell her I already know this.

I pull back the waistband of her fishnets and place my hand beneath them. I ask her if it's too much. No, she says, it's not. I slip my fingers inside her. After a few moments her body shudders. I roll off her and we lie beside each other. She takes my hand and kisses the top of it. Then she says she'd like to make something to eat. "You hungry?" she asks.

"I'm okay," I say, sensing I should leave. "I'm gonna go."

"Don't feel like I'm pushing you out," she says, which of course means "I'm pushing you out."

I return to the living room and get dressed. My clothes are embarrassingly strewn about, much less sexy in the aftermath. I call out good night and close the door behind me.

The next morning I leave the building through the back door, afraid of running into Tara in the hallway. I'm shaky and hungover and my heart is beating fast. I'm not yet sure how I feel about what happened, but I know she is now different to me. She's imbued with an electric charge. Around three in the afternoon I get a text from her: *No shame, friend. How's your hangover?*

Shame isn't what I feel. I tell her this, and I wait for a response, but she doesn't answer.

•

Tara and I continue, with inconsistency, despite some hesitation on her part, following a profession of desire on mine. "No feelings," I promise her before the second time. It's her only condition. That and drunkenness. So we drink a lot. Some nights nothing happens and I get in bed alone, drunk and disappointed.

I begin to dread my boyfriend's visits. One night the three of us go to a bar, and when he gets up from the table to buy us a round, she admits to feeling possessive of me whenever he's in town. She links her leg with mine under the table. She tells me she's going to head out soon, and when I ask about her plans for the rest of the evening, she smiles but doesn't answer. I can't tell if she's jealous or trying to make *me* jealous. After she leaves, he and I sit there with not much to say, or maybe he is saying something, but I am definitely not listening. We leave soon after she does. It's snowing out, and when we finally get in his car to leave, we search for her on the sidewalk. I twistedly accuse him of having feelings for her. "I just don't get why you care so much about how she gets home," I say as we peer through the windshield into powdery whiteness. "She probably went to see that guy across the street." I begin to burn inside.

"I *don't* care how she gets home," he says. "You're the one who wanted to look for her." I lower my head and close my eyes. Am I really doing this again?

More than occasionally, I sit on the floor and press my ear to our shared wall. She is in her kitchen, cooking for someone—I can never identify the other voice. I hear her laugh; hers is a laugh that I would like to bottle and drink. I hate whomever she is with. I panic, I pace. I call Renata, who's on her way back from meeting with the wedding caterers. Earlier in the day she'd sent me screenshots of different cakes she'd found online, as if any of this mattered to me right then. I didn't bother to pretend like it did, and I launched right into things. "I can't tell who she's with," I say. "All I hear is muffled sounds."

"Stop listening," Renata says. "Just stop."

•

By a weird and unexpected coincidence, Tara and I are both offered positions to teach at the same satellite campus of an American university in the UAE. At first I'm elated. I imagine us spending weekends together in Dubai, camping in Oman, hopping over to Turkey during school holidays, and of course, her eventually falling in love with me.

By now I know better, though a part of me wishes I didn't. A part of me would like to keep living inside this fantasy, and for a while I cling to it. I write a letter accepting the teaching offer, which I save in my drafts folder. When I can no longer put off responding I delete the draft and write a new letter to decline the position.

The faculty members who offered it to me are stunned. How

could I not want to do this? "Are you sure?" they ask, giving me one last chance to reconsider this huge mistake. Who in their right mind would pass this up?

"It would be a ten-year setback," says Renata. "It would be completely insane."

A week after I turn down the teaching offer, I rent a car to drive us to a writers' conference, where Tara meets someone new. He's a tenure-track poet with the air of a player who's ready to settle down for the right woman, and immediately I know that woman is her. She and I had planned to share a hotel room, but he stays over instead, and I sleep on the floor outside one of the conference center's ballrooms. A security guard wakes me up at around five a.m. and tells me to use my purse as a pillow.

When the conference ends we drive home together in silence. A few nights later, we sleep together for the last time. "I'm going to go down on you until you come," I tell her. I want nothing in return. Besides, she has nothing to give me, not even acknowledgment that any of this is happening. In fairness I can't give her that either, since I'm technically still attached elsewhere. After she comes I scoot up to face her. She kisses me on the cheek, and as she turns away I catch her mouth with mine, so that together we taste her. She presses her foot against my shin and lets me kiss her for what seems like a very long time. It feels like a goodbye and I treat it as one.

The next morning, I decide to move back to New York once the semester ends. It's a decision propelled by a barely audible survival instinct, a whisper—*Insanity is doing the same thing over and over, and expecting different results.*

During our last month as neighbors, Tara and I engage in

innocuous, friend-type activities. We get pedicures. We take our unwanted clothes to thrift stores. We organize a yard sale. We host a dinner for our neighbors. We caution the ones who plan to renew their leases against sleeping with the incoming tenants, never admitting to anyone what we've been doing. We avoid eye contact during these conversations; only once do we look at each other and wink. She wishes I were coming with her to the UAE. As our travel dates approach—hers to the Persian Gulf, and mine back to the East Coast—I find myself wishing the same. There is still a lingering hope, the possibility of something good, maybe even great. But I can no longer afford the cost of finding out.

I'm not sure what I'm expecting to happen at the LGBTQ center reading on Sunday night. That I'll meet someone who is neither straight nor married, that I'll find some sort of community, that I'll hear writing I can relate to. I arrive at the front desk and try to peer into the room behind it.

"Do you want a ticket?" the woman sitting at the desk says. But I hear, "Are you still a closeted dyke?"

I am certain she knows what I really want, that her eyes have seared through me, leaving me exposed. Appetite is embarrassing enough; visibly trying to satiate it, utterly mortifying.

"Yes," I say. "One, please."

17

I AM RUNNING LATE TO OUR FIRST DATE. I'M COMING
from a friend's apartment in Sunset Park. I've been back in New
York for six days, working an entry-level office job and crashing
on the couches of various friends until I can find my own place.
It's not exactly ideal, but at least I'm back in the city. The decision to come back to New York put a circumstantial and friendly
ending on my quasi-long-distance relationship with the visual
artist. He didn't appear to be terribly upset, and we agreed to stay
in touch. For once, friendship after a breakup seemed possible.

Until I can find a teaching gig, harder to come by in New York
than in the Midwest, an office job means regular hours and potential for a more "normal" life. I'm still readjusting to the crammed
subway ride, hovering beneath someone's armpit both to and from
work, arriving everywhere disheveled and sweaty. In this environ-
ment there isn't much to live for post-lunch, not until the stirrings
of pre-dinner hunger. But for now that isn't so bad, and I've discovered that having a job I dislike makes writing seem more appealing, an act of resisting against what I'm supposed be doing.

A, as I knew her through OKCupid, suggested two possible
meeting spots. "One is quieter," she wrote, "the other louder and

more lively." A quieter bar seemed like a more adult choice and therefore the right answer.

I push through the door and the heavy curtain and see her sitting at a small round table near the front. "Hey," I say, breezy, as though we know each other, as if this isn't our first encounter.

She plays along with the instant familiarity. "I almost just said hi to someone else," she tells me, smiling to break the awkwardness, "thinking it was you." I quickly glance from side to side, searching for someone who looks like me. She already has a drink in front of her. "There's no waiter," she says.

"Cool," I say. "Be right back then." I go to the bar to order. I'm a little hungry and afraid of getting too drunk, so I ask for a vodka cranberry, thinking it has more sustenance. When I return to the table with my drink she teases me playfully for the collegiate choice. She asks many questions in rapid succession; she seems simultaneously inquisitive and nervous. Where am I originally from? Nablus, I say. Her best friend spent a few years living there, she worked at the cultural affairs center. It's an uncanny coincidence, one that creates community.

Soon it's my turn to ask questions, and I find that I am genuinely curious to know everything about her. Her name is Anouk—I realize I didn't know this until now. She's half French, half American, and she grew up in Paris. She dropped out of her comparative lit PhD program to become a filmmaker. Her first feature premiered at the IFC.

She feels warm to me, as though we've always known each other, but the familiarity makes her exciting. There is a lull in conversation between drinks two and three, one that momentarily makes me panic and worry that we shouldn't have ordered a third round. I say something to fill the space. "You're fun to talk to." She half smiles and says nothing. It's an underwhelming compliment.

We talk about suffering from morning melancholy. I ask her if she thinks there's a solution. "I don't know," she says. "Probably a relationship?" I don't mention that I just ended one. That in each of my relationships I've woken up to despair. I do bring up Tara, though—I can't resist mentioning her. I still think of her more than I should, more than she likely thinks of me, but distance is helping. Quitting social media helps. And the possibility of someone else helps, too.

When we leave, Anouk walks me to the train. We continue talking but I'm already thinking about the goodbye. Will we kiss? Too soon. Hug? Too friendly. We arrive at the subway's entrance, and I am standing in front of her. "It was nice hanging out with you," I say. "We should hang out again." The words echo through my mind. *Hang out, hang out, hang out.*

"Yeah," she says. "We should."

No kiss, no hug, and I feel good as I descend underground.

The next morning she texts me: *I woke up today feeling less sad than usual.*

•

For our second date I suggest a Mexican restaurant in Crown Heights, one that I noticed while staying at a friend's place in the neighborhood. I arrive early and wait for Anouk on a bench outside.

"Hey," she says, stepping out from inside the restaurant. She is wearing a denim skirt and a loosely fitting pink-and-white striped top. "I just put our names on the wait list."

She sits down beside me, her side flush against mine, and I feel a surge of attraction run through me, the first time I've felt it with her. She scoots away a little, which makes me wonder if she felt it too. I ask about her day. I'm too close to face her, so I look straight ahead. She tells me she's coming from her building's co-op meeting. "So you own," I ask.

"Yeah," she answers quickly. "Well, my parents do. It's kind of a double-edged sword."

"How so?"

"I guess it ties me here. Or at least it feels that way." She seems uncomfortable. "I know. It's a bratty thing to complain about."

Before I can respond, the hostess steps outside and calls her name, a relief, because I'm not sure how to calibrate the depth of our conversation for the bench outside. "Should we sit at a table or the bar?" Anouk asks me. Since it's our first dinner date, a table seems right. We order margaritas, and when our drinks arrive I remember that I am still a little hungover after a night of doing shots with coworkers. I would've slept it off, but I had to move out of my friend's apartment in Sunset Park by noon, and spent the morning transferring between trains and buses to Bed-Stuy. I choose not to mention any of this to Anouk. I don't want her to know about my transient life. Usually, people arrive in a new city and get settled first. They sort out their jobs, find an apartment, and *then* start dating. For me, the latter took precedence. A relationship was the whole point.

We order nachos and combination chicken-and-steak fajitas, a decision we come to easily. "Good to know we like the same foods," she says. "That bodes well for us." She laughs, and I laugh too. I like that she's assessing this openly, as though we are two members of a committee evaluating the potential for our relationship from a detached vantage point. I nod in agreement. When we finish, the waitress asks if we want a box for the left-overs. Yes, but Anouk says no. The waitress clears away the food and brings us the bill, which we split.

Even though we are the last ones to leave the restaurant, it feels early enough that I don't want our night to end. "I'm not ready to leave you yet," she says as we walk to the subway.

"Do you want to come over?" I ask, then remember my current living situation: a pot-reeking, barely furnished studio on the border of Bushwick and Bed-Stuy. "Or maybe *I* could come over?"

We take the 4 train to Atlantic. I comment on there being more stairs from the train to the street than I remember, and she laughs, presumably at the filler-like quality of my comment. On the walk to her apartment, we talk about productivity. Sometimes she's like a squirrel with a nut, she tells me, other times she watches porn and masturbates all day. I blush at the word *masturbate*, our first overt reference to anything sexual. "I'm like that too," I tell her. "Always at the extremes."

She leads me to her building and up two flights of stairs. She unlocks the door and flips on the lights to reveal a beautiful apartment: spacious, wood-floored, huge windows, and minimally decorated with elegant furniture and equally tasteful, professionally framed art. I cringe thinking about my apartment in grad school, the walls bare aside from a few postcards and photographs. "Do you want something to drink?" she asks. "I have whiskey."

"Sure." I never drink whiskey—I'm not sure I've ever had a glass of it—and find it sexy that she does. She goes to the kitchen and returns with two tumblers, each filled a finger deep. We sit beside each other on the modern elegant couch. We make awk-ward, self-conscious conversation while sipping our whiskies. I am not mentally present, my teeth chattering a little. Finally we stop talking and I ask if I can kiss her. She says yes.

Our kiss is long but chaste. Closed-mouthed. When I pull away I look into her eyes.

"What?" she says.

"What what?"

"Why are you looking at me so dramatically?"

"I don't know," I say. "Isn't that what you do when you kiss someone?"

She smiles. "It's a little intense." We continue making out on the couch until she invites me to her room. I lead her to the bed, feeling oddly comfortable in her space. "You're pretty," she tells me, and I feel myself blush. I kiss her lips, her cheeks, her neck. Periodically she opens her mouth wide and breathes heavily into my ear, which I love. We keep our clothes on.

After a while we stop and lie beside each other. I look at my watch. "It's late," I say. "I should go."

"You're gonna leave now?"

She seems disappointed. I shrug. "Is that weird?"

She shrugs. "Has anyone ever left you in the middle of the night?"

Often, around four a.m., Anouk is up and anxious. I'm usu-ally roused by her wakefulness, and she asks me to run my fin-gers through her hair. I pet her head softly, falling back asleep mid-stroke.

Anouk and I joke that my heart is a fleshy, blubbery, trembling whale of a heart, one that lies bleeding on an unidentified beach somewhere. Hers is guarded, hidden inside a cage, at the bottom of a well, tucked away. "This doesn't bode well for us," she tells me. And at times, she's proven right. She rejects my sentimentality—when I buy her an iPod Shuffle and fill it with two hundred songs, she expunges the love ballads, keeping only the Cure. She's demanding and particular and forthright, and I love her for these things but I can't always live up to them. I've told her about my past relationships, and she's afraid that once my infatuation with her wears off, I'll lose interest. She keeps a distance to protect herself.

There is a constant fear inside me that any misstep could ruin everything. In my worst moments, I quell the anxiety of her leaving by preempting it. I threaten to end things. I hate myself for my immaturity, but old habits rarely go away entirely, and I can never fully escape myself. I relapse. I beg for her forgiveness, for her to be patient with me. Somehow, she is. She doesn't excuse the push-pull, but at the very least, she gets it.

Eventually she begins to open up and allow herself to trust me. And as she does, I find that I love this version of her, with all of its circumstance, even as the initial excitement gives way to cozy routine, with its own kind of intimacy. I find that I enjoy the stability even more than the highs, certainly more than the lows. And whenever she catches me projecting idealized versions of herself onto her, she calls me out for doing so. Throughout our relationship, she insists on remaining real.

I nod in response to Anouk's question. "People have left me," I say. "Though I guess it's usually me who leaves."

But this time, I don't want to. I want nothing more than to stay.

243

18

AT THE ALLENBY BRIDGE CROSSING, SUNLIGHT RICO-
chets off a white-painted archway and onto the mountains loom-
ing in the distance. I have already been in transit for eight hours
by the time I arrive there at noon. I left Paris at four that morning, after a weekend stopover to meet Anouk's family. "They're
like poodles," she told me on the flight over. "Uptight and yippy."
Though I immediately saw the poodle reference—her father big
and Flemish, his hair abundant like fur, her mother curly haired
and put together—they seemed neither yippy nor uptight; on the
contrary, they seemed incredibly laid-back, which didn't surprise
me, since they're retired and wealthy. Their apartment is a modest
one-bedroom, tasteful in its décor with big molten-glass windows
that open onto a leafy boulevard in Montparnasse, and that they
shutter each night before bed. Mornings were spent reading, her
mother painting in her studio loft just above the apartment. We
had lunch both days at one, fresh fish and salad from the *marché*,
followed by museums in the afternoon, and a light dinner out
on the promenade. Their routine, the calmness, was something
I had never known in my own family. Such structure! And they
guarded it, they protected it from any outside disruption.

I landed in Amman at ten thirty and went straight from the airport to the Allenby Bridge. Everyone else is already in Palestine, where the last four days of Teta's week-long funeral will take place. All of Teta's grandchildren will be there, as well as her children, including, of course, my mother. Anouk wanted to come to the funeral. But the idea of introducing her to my family, especially in that setting, seemed too stressful, so I suggested she come another time. She agreed that it made sense to wait.

It's a Thursday, so the border crossing is crowded with commuters trying to return home to the West Bank before Friday, the Muslim holy day. The room is stale with the smell of smoke. Everywhere I look children run around chasing one another, their mothers yelling at them to sit still. I stand in line at the Jordanian-run security counter behind packs of men in wrinkled suits, some carrying briefcases, all of them smoking. When I get to the front, I hand my luggage and passport to the official at the desk. "Wait for the bus out there," he says, pointing at the door. "It will take you across."

Outside, there are at least two dozen people waiting on the tiled platform. I see a bus parked on the other side of the bridge. I drop my bag on the dry earth and sit under a barren fig tree, rolling a fallen branch between my palms as I wait.

Forty-five minutes later, the driver finally appears and walks onto the bus. The engine rumbles as it chugs over to us. I rush to get on before anyone else and choose a seat near the front. A man walks down the aisle and collects our passports. Even though we'll get back once we cross, parting with my passport makes me anxious. It's another thirty minutes before we actually start moving. The moment we do, warm orange liquid pours onto my head and down my back. I look up—an open can of Mirinda that someone left on the luggage rack has toppled over. I breathe deeply and gaze out the window at the Jordan River passing beneath the bridge, which serves as the demarcation line between Jordan, to the east, and Israel and Palestine, to the west. It's really just an idyllic stream running over stones and between muddy banks. But the word *river* makes arbitrary borders seem inevitable.

Less than two minutes later we are on the other side. The driver pulls in front of the Israeli customs office, turns off the ignition, and steps off the bus, shutting its door behind him. We wait. I'm hungry, thirsty, tired, and covered in sticky orange soda. The bus door opens and a new official steps onto the bus. He walks up and down the aisle calling out names and handing back our passports. By the time he's done we are all standing, eager to exit. When the doors open once again, I push my way past the others and rush inside to customs.

A large Israeli flag hangs over the officials' booths, along with Hebrew letters. A line has somehow already formed. I eventually get up to the counter and again hand over my passport. As I've come to expect, the official holds on to it, and I am told to return to the waiting area. "For how long?" I ask.

"Someone will come for you," he says. "For questioning."

I sit in a plastic chair and wait. A box of tissues sits on the table in front of me, a plastic waste bin beside it. I look around at pictures of President Clinton seeming pleased with himself as he presides over Yasser Arafat and Yitzhak Rabin shaking hands on the White House lawn. I glance past the customs desk and out the window at the giant banner that reads, "Welcome to Israel," knowing I may not make it in. I try to sign on to the complimentary Wi-Fi but can't connect to the network. I give up trying and take out a book instead.

Almost two hours later a soldier approaches me, casually slapping against her leg a passport that I assume is mine. She is tall and thick, and the scars around her mouth signal that she once had a cleft palate. I also can't help but notice that she is beautiful. The sight of an attractive woman in a military uniform and combat boots is somewhat jarring. She stands over me, unsmiling. She offers no greeting. Instead she asks, "You've been to Lebanon?"

"Yes," I respond.

"Why were you there?"

"For a wedding," I say.

"Where in Lebanon?"

"Beirut." Beirut is the right answer. If I said anywhere south of the city—the south is Hezbollah territory—I likely wouldn't be allowed in.

She flips through my passport. "Wait here," she says, then rushes off. I wait, again, as instructed. I have little choice anyway. I watch groups of soldiers chatting, drinking Cokes, eating Magnum candy bars, and laughing while guns hang lazily from their chests. They all look very young. They're mostly brunettes, like me, with the occasional blond. One soldier catches me staring and I quickly avert my eyes.

The day passes by slowly. With little to focus my attention on, I enter the cycle of hope followed by disappointment, thinking that each person I hear coming around the corner is her. It isn't—not until late afternoon. By that point I am numb, and the excitement that I anticipated feeling at the sight of her doesn't come. She is carrying a bottle of water and wiping crumbs off her chin. "Follow me." She leads me to a white table with soldiers seated around it. One of them is shuffling a deck of cards. He deals them two at a time. Behind them are piles of suitcases, some held together with string or duct tape. "Find yours."

I frantically search, feeling the pressure of the other soldiers watching me, of the clock ticking. I don't want to take too long. Finally, I find my suitcase. I bring it to the table, where the soldiers are now all smoking. My soldier looks up at me from her cigarette and the hand she's been dealt. She puts down the cards and leans her cigarette against the side of a dirty tin ashtray, then gets up and plops my suitcase onto the middle of the table. The other soldiers boo her for interrupting the game, but she ignores them and proceeds to open it.

First she takes out my camera, a brand-new point-and-shoot Canon that I bought specifically for the trip, knowing my entire family would be together for the first time in years. She points it up toward the unfinished ceiling and snaps a picture, making sure it doesn't explode when she presses the shutter button, the camera shattering into tiny pieces, along with the rest of us. She snaps another shot, this time of the wall. She then points the camera at herself and takes a picture, a sober expression on her face. I hear the film rewinding as she puts it down.

Next, she searches through my clothes. She unfolds them, holds them up to the light, shakes them as though something incriminating might fall from the fabric. She crumples them into little balls before tossing them aside. Then she looks through my toiletries bag. She pulls out tampons and toothpaste before shoving them back into the pouch and dropping it next to my suitcase. She gets to my shoes at the bottom. She picks up a boot and examines it. "Why do you carry men's shoes?" she asks. "You are lesbian?"

The soldiers all laugh, but she doesn't laugh along. She keeps her eyes fixed on me.

"They're mine," I say. "They're not men's shoes."

"You can put your things away," she says, dropping my boot onto the table. I do as instructed and zip up my suitcase. I look to her for more directions, but she says nothing. Finally I ask her where I should go next.

"Wait here," she says. It's growing darker now, and I am getting anxious. My mind starts to wander. Is she planning to keep me until after the border crossing closes? Until no one else is around? I feel an unexpected wave in my stomach at the thought of being alone with her.

"I need to leave now," I say. "I need to get across before it's too late."

"You want to go?" she asks. "You can."

What was all this for, then? To make me panic? To make me never attempt to come back?

The customs official is about to stamp my passport and let me through when I stop him. "Can I ask you to not stamp it, please?"

"Why not?"

"Because I plan to go back to Lebanon. To Beirut," I emphasize. Mine is a common request, and depending on the particular official, it is either honored or it isn't. I hold my breath. The official keeps his eyes on me while he opens the desk drawer. He then takes out a square of paper and hurls the stamp down onto it. He tucks the square between the pages of my passport and hands it back to me. I thank him and continue past customs, past the currency exchange, until I am outside.

The sun is now just barely visible behind the mountains. A few taxis idle in the parking lot. I get into one and head toward Jerusalem, where I'll catch a bus with specially designated license plates that will take me to the West Bank.

•

I see everyone during the four days of Azza. On the final day, we pile into cars and drive from Ramallah to Nablus. As we sit in mourning and receive guests who've traveled through numerous checkpoints to pay their respects to my grandmother, laughter fills the air. We tell stories about the time she thought she'd gone blind while driving, only to realize she'd entered a tunnel with her sunglasses on; the time she stayed up all night playing the slots in Atlantic City, then slept on the floor of our shared hotel room to avoid waking us; the time she bought six-inch patent leather heels at age seventy-three. My mother and I grow close again, we fall into old patterns, we choose to momentarily forget the tensions between us. What does any of it matter in the face of nonexistence? Both Karim and I have come from New York to be with her, and it feels good to reestablish intimacy. It feels good to be a family.

Two months later, I take a bus from New York to Washington to see my mother, who's just returned from overseas after settling all of Teta's affairs. Anouk and I plan to move in together soon, and it's time to tell my mother about her, as much as I've resisted doing so.

I pick up the photos from the trip, and as I look through

them later that afternoon, it takes me a moment to remember how shots of ceiling pipes and cinder block have ended up among them. Then I come to her photo. I can only discern a vague figure and the outline of sunglasses resting atop her head. But her face has been obscured by the flash, rendering her indistinguishable from any other.

My mother runs out of the living room of her apartment and returns with a Qur'an. She sits down beside me on the couch and holds the book close to her face, almost touching her cheekbone. Her mid-calf-length nightgown is bunched up around her thighs, unintentionally tucked into her underwear. She breathes deeply. Sweat drips from her temples.

"I am a conservative, religious woman," she says. She has never shown signs of being one.

I've just told her the truth about Anouk. Until now, I've called her Adam.

"How many people know?" My mother's voice gets increasingly louder and more adamant, her body quivering. "How many people are laughing at me right now?"

Everyone knows. "Mom, I—"

"Shut up!" she shouts. "I talk, you don't. I would feel sorry for you if you were *really* a gay." She gets closer to me; I feel heat emanate from her chest. "I'd feel sorry for myself, most of all. But you just want to play games with people. Why did you cry about that guy from Argentina? You were either lying then, or you're lying now."

"I wasn't playing games," I say in a matter-of-fact tone, determined to maintain a composed, calm distance. She wants me to react emotionally, like a child, and that's when I get into trouble. I look at her and try to respond flatly. "I loved him, too."

"When you decide to fall in love with someone else, this woman will be just another one of your victims. And I'm sure you'll come to me for sympathy."

We are running late to dinner. I am fumbling through an attempt to tidy up the apartment. It's the only thing I can think to do in this moment that might please her, though I know it will do nothing at all toward that end. "We should get going," she says. "Does your cousin know where the restaurant is?"

My cousin is visiting D.C. for the week, and she's the reason, the excuse, that I've chosen to stay with my mother this time instead of with Renata, or at my dad's, or anywhere else.

"I don't know," I say. "Should we call her?"

My mother asks me to help with the zipper of her dress, and I do. I rub her neck gently when I get to the top, very gently. I want to soothe her, but I know she'll push me away if she senses this.

"How many times my father told me to watch out and be careful of you," she says as she puts on a string of pearls. Her father passed away when I was twelve. "He warned me that you were manipulative. He told me not to marry your father. Why, God, why didn't I listen?"

My chest begins to ache. Again I try to block her voice. It's increasingly difficult to do, but I keep trying.

I unplug my phone from its charger, and the screen lights up as I touch it. There's a text from Anouk: *Everything all right?* She knows that home is hard.

When we leave the apartment my mother runs ahead of me in the corridor. I struggle to catch up. In the elevator she asks me again who knows, and I tell her that my aunt does—her younger sister. I told her about Anouk while we were in Nablus for Teta's funeral.

"Great," my mother says. "So everyone knows."

At the restaurant, my mother and I sit beside each other, my cousin and her husband across from us. We all share pasta, rosé, and finally, crème brûlée. My mother and I dip our spoons into the bowl at the same time, shattering opposite ends of the crisp burnt surface and arriving at the soft custard underneath. Our silverware clinks. We look at each other, and I smile. She smiles back.

The next morning I find her asleep on the couch. I slept in her bed, which we normally share when I visit. I wake up disappointed that her side is empty.

19

NEAR THE END OF A TOO-LONG WINTER, SNOW GIVING way to sleet and finally to rain, the professor and I arrange to meet for coffee. We've kept in touch over the years, at varying degrees of distance. We meet on the Upper West Side. It's pouring when I arrive. I shake droplets off my umbrella and spot her waving at me from a table inside. She wears jogging clothes, New Balance sneakers, no nail polish. Though she hasn't visibly aged, she looks different.

I tell her about Anouk over cappuccinos. I wonder if having a French girlfriend makes her suspect a fetish, before realizing she has no idea how I once felt about her. She talks about her children, now both in school. She asks if I plan to have any. "I'd like to," I say. "But I'm nervous."

"Parenting is like piano lessons," she tells me. "It's not always something you know you want, but no one ever regrets it."

"Some people regret it," I say, thinking back to my most traumatic childhood memory, of participating in a recital at the home of my piano teacher, waiting for my name to be called as twenty-nine other kids stood to receive their awards while I remained seated alone on stage, smiling in shame and feeling the entire audience's eyes on me. "You'd be surprised."

It's stopped raining by the time we leave, and we walk together for a few blocks. We're both headed in the same direction; she to pick up her daughter from school, I to a dentist appointment. I like walking beside her. I am taller and it makes me feel somewhat authoritative. We get to the crosswalk where we will part ways. We turn to face each other and I find myself anxious, still hoping that something might happen. It doesn't. I lean forward and hug goodbye, possibly holding on for a little too long. Keep in touch, she says as always, though now I'm not sure she means it.

Back home at the end of the day, I'm still thinking of her. I search through our email correspondence. Some of my letters make me blush; effortful pontifications on Proust and Baudelaire, confessions about wanting to succeed as a writer so I could quit spinning records, reminders to send the essays she'd mentioned over that first coffee at the Nespresso café. My efforts were palpable and teeming with subdued flirtation—is there any way she couldn't have known?

I come across one particular chain from six years earlier. Not long after our lunchless lunch date, I'd sent a first draft of a piece about my relationship with Kate. "I notice that sex is missing," she'd written in response. "Also, you mention her orientation, but what about yours?"

"Sex is hard to write about," I'd responded, ignoring the question of my sexuality. "I don't want to be vulgar—is there anything worse?"

I sent her another essay a month later, about unattainable love as a quest for the familiar, a quest for home, for a homeland that may not exist. A quest for a mother. I wrote the second one, like the first, in the hopes that She would read it and that She would approve, that she would deem me interesting or worthwhile if not both. How many stories have been penned for unrequited love? How many must I write to earn my existence? *There's more to you than these obsessions.* "I'm sending you this piece because you're a writer and I value your aesthetic opinion," I asserted in my email. I had built a barrier around my true feelings, one even I couldn't break through, my love for her impervious to us both, my resistance impenetrable.

She did not care for the piece.

"From you, I expect more out of a story about love," she'd written in response. "Tell us about something that left you shattered."

SOON AFTER I MOVE INTO HER APARTMENT, ANOUK AND I watch a home video of my family from 1990. In a scene marked "Sunday Morning," my father films us in the master bedroom of our house in the D.C. suburbs. Periodically, he points the camera at the full-length mirror and catches shots of himself. My mother lies in bed propped up against the headboard, a pot of coffee and two empty mugs on the nightstand. I sit in front of her, wearing a new vest and leggings that she bought for me from Limited Too, the tags still intact. Karim runs in circles wearing his pajama bottoms and a pillowcase around his neck like a cape, lisping, "I'm Thuperman!" A brand-new boxy Macintosh glows on a desk in the corner.

I stand up and face the camera, posing for it, then walk to the mirror to admire my new outfit. I look to my mother for approval, but she is looking elsewhere. My father captures a few moments of my catwalk before losing interest in me and returning to her. He zooms in as she removes a stray hair from her nightgown sleeve. In that moment, she is unaware that he is filming, that anyone is watching, that this simple gesture is being recorded and will exist in perpetuity. Her face is movie-star gorgeous; her eyes piercing, her nose and cheekbones sharp, her top lip resting on her lower lip in that casual non-smile.

Yet despite her striking appearance, she seems absent. While watching the scene, I feel a tremendous sadness at her beauty. I feel despair for her misspent youth. In the video I am seven years old, Karim is five, and she is twenty-eight.

Until now, it's never occurred to me that my mother was—my mother is—a child, forever stunted by her own traumas. I reconsider everything that was inflicted upon her. That she grew up under military occupation, that she was married by twenty and pregnant the following year, that her husband's ambitions undermined her own and further displaced her, casting her into exile with a fragmented sense of home. All of her present power—her fearful rage, her enviable status, her unrelenting beauty—fades against this reality.

In this Sunday-morning scene, there is no sign of cruelty. My mother smiles shyly when she realizes that my father is filming her. She asks him to stop recording, and he does. The screen cuts to snowy static before giving way to blackness.

I sit staring at the screen, feeling ashamed. While my mother is the one who is beautiful, she doesn't feel the need to be seen.

Anouk touches my arm and asks if I'm okay. "You seem elsewhere," she says, and I am. I am lost in my mother's possibility, in what could've been, caught between her frustrated potential and a desire to fulfill my own. I lament the disappointments that have come from surrendering her approval to pursue my own desires. I lament what she's given up for me. Our mutual sacrifice creates wounds that may never heal. I will carry sadness for her pain, and also for mine. In receiving love from others, it will always be hers I crave most.

I look to Anouk, and I kiss her. She kisses me back. There is something to protect here, something else to long for. I then look to the screen and catch our reflection before turning it off, making room for the two of us.

Acknowledgments

For so long I have used the fantasy of writing these acknowledgments as a reward for finishing this book. Now that the time has come, I find myself daunted by the amount of gratitude I feel.

Thank you to my agent, Michelle Brower, who saw this book in exactly the way I hoped it would be seen, even beyond what was initially present on the page, and who championed it wholeheartedly. Thank you also to Danya Kukafka, Chelsey Heller, and everyone else at Aevitas Creative Management who has helped bring this book into the world.

Thank you to Jonathan Lee, whose incredibly perceptive, smart, and thorough edits elevated this novel beyond measure. To Carla Bruce-Eddings, for being such a fierce and genuine advocate. To Nicole Caputo, for designing the absolute perfect cover. To Yuka Igarashi, for editing an excerpt of what became this book for Granta. To Katie Boland, Wah-Ming Chang, and the entire Catapult team, thank you.

To the NWP at Iowa, thank you for the time and space and support to write, and for giving me a teaching fellowship so that I remained at least somewhat social and sane in the process. Thank you to my advisers and teachers, Robin Hemley, Patricia Foster,

Honor Moore, and Geoff Dyer. Thank you also to Christopher Merrill, Natasa Durovicova, and Hugh Ferrer at the International Writing Program for their support, and to Daniel Khalastchi at the Magid Center for Undergraduate Writing. Thank you to my teachers at Columbia as well, Anya Schiffrin, Claudia Dreifus, Peter Godwin, and to Susie Lebryk-Chao.

Thank you to Kima Jones and Jack Jones Literary Arts for those precious two weeks surrounded by inspiring women and peaceful mountains. I am awed by what you've created and so grateful that it exists.

Thank you to my NWP classmates, my people: Jen Percy, Rachel Yoder, Ariel Lewiton, Inara Verzemnieks, Laurel Fantauzzo, Mieke Eerkens, Deborah Taffa, Matt Siegel, Kristen Radtke, Lucas Mann, Lina Maria Ferreira Cabena-Vanegas, Alea Adigweme, Sandy Allen, Olivia Dunn, Amy Bernhard, Catina Bacote, Blair Braverman, Quince Mountain, Helen Rubinstein, and Gemma de Choisy. To Gallywagon Leach, for, among other things, providing me a safe and loving home in Iowa. And to my NYC writing group: Meredith Talusan, Lilly Dancyger, Nina St. Pierre, and the rest of Ronny's Children—thank you.

To the friends who have read drafts and who provided the support I needed to make it to the finish line, especially on dark days, thank you: Natalie Moon Brown (for your ongoing love, humor ,and patience with my equine nature), Jen (for all the rotisserie chicken days), Tony Tulathimutte, David Busis, Ariel (who has been there through both weeps and laughs, and always keeps me from becoming boring), Kristen (I am forever obsessed with Scarsdale), Caitlin Roach Orduña (especially for the Megabus moments), Lisa Wells, Catherine Blauvelt, Callie Garnett,

Amber Fares, Mallika Rao, Bilal Qureshi, Hope McClure Sypert, Farah Hussein, Sandra Reishus, Jake Rollow, and Alyse Burnside. To Eve-Alice Roustang-Stoller. To Libby Flores, for providing me with a stable home in which to finish this thing, as well as a new friendship. To Ani Lhamo. To Chantal, for lifelong friendship, love, and compassion in the face of all this, and for gently but humorously knocking reason into me whenever I needed it ("Why would she?!"). To Nate Nash. To Anne, also for lifelong friendship. I don't know how to convey my love and appreciation for you, it'll certainly take more than a bottle of Josh wine. I hope we can sing to Captain together forever.

To Gabrielle, for whom I will always hold a very special place in my heart. Though our story did not turn out the way I'd imagined and hoped, I am grateful for your faith in this book, and in me as a writer. I hope you know how much I believe in you, too.

Most of all, to my family. To my brother, Zaid, who called me every day over the last year, the hardest year of this marathon, just to check on me. To my father, Fawaz, a.k.a. Winnie. And of course, always, to my mother, Randa Masri.

© Carleen Coulter

ZAINA ARAFAT is a Palestinian American
writer. Her stories and essays have appeared in pub-
lications including *The New York Times*, *Granta*, *The
Believer*, *The Virginia Quarterly Review*, *The Washington Post*, *The Atlantic*, *BuzzFeed*, *VICE*, and NPR. She
holds an MA in international affairs from Columbia
University and an MFA from the University of Iowa
and is a recipient of the Arab Women/Migrants from
the Middle East Fellowship at Jack Jones Literary Arts.
She grew up between the United States and the Middle
East and currently lives in Brooklyn.